THEODORA'S BABY

400
cl
9/12

D1318093

Also by Penny Culliford

Theodora's Diary
Theodora's Wedding

THEODORA'S BABY

Penny Culliford

faith,
joy &
chocolate

ZONDERVAN™

GRAND RAPIDS, MICHIGAN 49530 USA

ZONDERVAN.COM/
AUTHOR**TRACKER**

ZONDERVAN™

Theodora's Baby
Copyright © 2006 by Penny Culliford

Requests for information should be addressed to:

Zondervan, *Grand Rapids, Michigan 49530*

Library of Congress Cataloging-in-Publication Data

Culliford, Penny.
    Theodora's baby : faith, joy and chocolate / Penny Culliford.
        p. cm.
    ISBN-13: 978-0-310-26558-0
    ISBN-10: 0-310-26558-4
    1. Pregnant women—Fiction. 2. Married women—Fiction.
    3. Motherhood—Fiction. 4. England—Fiction. I. Title.
PR6103.U46T467 2005
823'.92—dc22
                                                              2005020439

Penny Culliford asserts the moral right to be considered the author of this work.

All Scripture quotations, unless otherwise indicated, are taken from the *Holy Bible: New International Version®*. NIV®. Copyright © 1973, 1978, 1984 by International Bible Society. Used by permission of Zondervan. All rights reserved.

The website addresses recommended throughout this book are offered as a resource to you. These websites are not intended in any way to be or imply an endorsement on the part of Zondervan, nor do we vouch for their content for the life of this book.

All rights reserved. No part of this publication may be reproduced, stored in a retrieval system, or transmitted in any form or by any means—electronic, mechanical, photocopy, recording, or any other—except for brief quotations in printed reviews, without the prior permission of the publisher.

Interior design by Michelle Espinoza

Printed in the United States of America

06 07 08 09 10 11 • 17 16 15 14 13 12 11 10 9 8 7 6 5 4 3 2

Contents

July

Sunday 2 July

11:45 p.m.

Shhh! I'm writing this really quietly by torchlight so that
Kevin doesn't know I'm doing it. It feels a bit dishonest, but
after two years of jotting down my thoughts in a diary, I feel
as if I can't think properly without it. He's not at all happy
about me keeping the diary. I'm not actually banned from
writing in it; he just makes little whimpering noises and looks
pathetic when he sees me scribbling away. He even tore out the
pages describing our Greek honeymoon on the grounds that if
Diana's grandma found them, she'd have a heart attack. I tried
to explain that (a) Yaya doesn't read English and (b) if she
could read it, it would probably brighten her day considerably.
Kevin would have none of it, though.

'I just don't like it. It's like you're keeping things from me,
Theo,' he whined.

'They're nothing, just thoughts.'

'If they're just thoughts, why don't they stay in your head?
Mine do.'

'I don't know. It's as if I can sort things out better if I see them written on the page.'

'You could talk to me.' He pouted. I couldn't deny it, he had a point. And I did talk to him; of course I did.

'It's just that ...' I hesitated, trying to think of a reason. 'Most of it's boring stuff like ... what colour nail polish should I wear today, or do I need to order an extra pint of milk? What was the name of the guy with the spiky hair in the Bay City Rollers? Stuff like that.'

'Then why don't you like me reading it?'

'Because you laugh at me.' Now it was my turn to pout. He went to the table and picked up the diary. He held it closed as if the pages were fastened with an invisible padlock.

'Sometimes it's like you're ... shutting me out. Theo, please don't write in the diary any more.'

I took the diary from him and put it in a drawer.

'I'll think about it.'

He looked at me for a long time as if he was weighing me up. I thought he was going to say something else, but he didn't.

I love him, and I don't want to keep things from him; on the other hand, he doesn't have a right to know all my thoughts, everything that is going on in my head. Does he?

Monday 3 July

Didn't sleep well last night. Dreamed that God was reading my diary. God didn't say anything, but I watched his expression, which passed from puzzled, to amused, to irritated, to completely perplexed. If I asked Charity Hubble about my dream, she'd pray for my deliverance; if I told my sister, Ariadne, she'd blame it on the blue-cheese dressing I had on my salad last night. The irony is, if I wasn't so worried about whether to keep a diary or not, I wouldn't have to keep a diary! What is a girl to do?

One thing this girl must do is to go job-hunting. Despite Kevin's pseudo-chivalrous offer to be the sole provider, I'll go mad with boredom and drive Kevin mad, moaning about it. The job as church secretary occupies less than one day a week, and the only intellectual challenge is how to change the photocopier's toner cartridge without looking as if I'd just swept a chimney. I can't deny it's kind of Chrissie to keep the job for me, but I prefer her being my friend and my vicar to being my boss. I've never met anyone so disorganized. I discovered that she'd mixed up the burials register with the register of marriages. Poor Darren Clooney nearly got booked in for a full service at the local crematorium, and goodness knows what would have happened if his fiancée, Janice, had turned up at the church and found the mortal remains of ninety-seven-year-old Mr Gainsborough waiting for her in his wooden box.

11:30 a.m.

Just flicked through the small ads in the local paper. Unless I have a burning ambition to be a barmaid or an office cleaner, options are limited. I have no burning ambition to be either.

I got rather distracted by the 'pets for sale' and was very tempted to 'provide a loving home' for a pair of unwanted ginger kittens. I decided against it on the grounds that I preferred Kevin the budgie without a feline overcoat.

Needless to say, the budgie's name was my mother's choice. She cared for 'Kevin' while we were on honeymoon.

'But, Mum,' I protested, 'you can't call it Kevin. Half the time I won't know if I'm talking to my husband or the budgie.'

'If he turns out anything like your father, you'll get more sense out of the bird.'

Tuesday 4 July

Woke up early, made Kevin a cup of tea and brought him breakfast in bed. As we snuggled up, a picture of contentment, Kevin asked me if I was happy.

'Of course,' I replied.

'You're not worried about anything?'

'No.'

'Are you sure?'

'Positive. Now would you mind telling me what this is all about?'

He opened my underwear drawer.

I was starting to get worried.

'If everything in your life is so hunky-dory, then why are you still writing in that blasted diary?'

He rummaged through the bras and pants and pulled out my diary.

Discovered. What could I do now? I looked away and pretended to brush some toast crumbs onto the floor.

I'd managed to keep away from the diary for nearly a fortnight after we got back from honeymoon, but I'm like an addict. I just can't stop. The compulsion is even worse than the worst kind of chocolate craving – and I should know. The only solution would be to agree to let him read it. I was just about to make my magnanimous offer when I discovered a large blob of marmalade in my hair. By the time I'd scraped it off, the moment had passed. He gave me a peck on the cheek and a hug.

'You smell of oranges. Do you know what you remind me of?'

I shook my head, expecting him to say, 'An orange grove in springtime,' or something equally romantic.

He grinned and gave me another squeeze. 'You're just like a big cuddly Paddington Bear.'

8 p.m., the toilet

Have taken to hiding in here to write my diary. Kevin looks even grumpier this evening. What was intended to be rice pudding turned out more like rubber.

'Theo, for goodness' sake!' He tapped it with his spoon. 'Rice pudding is not supposed to bounce!'

He didn't even cheer up when I nipped out and returned with a large packet of indigestion tablets and a copy of *Goal* magazine.

Wednesday 5 July

The Situations Vacant section of this morning's paper contained one ad for a security guard, several for shelf-stackers at the local supermarket and one for a cook at the Red Lion. I quite fancied working in the oak-beamed coaching inn.

'Great!' muttered Kevin. 'Then you could poison the whole village rather than just making me suffer.'

'Funny, you never complained about my cooking before we were married.'

'That was when it wasn't my only source of nourishment. Once or twice a week I could cope, but every day ...' He groaned, picked up his toolbox, pecked me on the cheek and went out of the door. I must do something about this culinary crisis. I wonder if Ariadne's at home. My sister is always good for a bite of something that doesn't result in terminal dyspepsia.

4:30 p.m.

Ariadne, of course, was at work, but Tom invited me to call in for a coffee before he took Phoebe to Little Luminaries, a group 'to nurture cosmic promise for the generation of the future'.

'What is it, a playgroup?' I inquired.

Tom looked horrified. 'It's an interactive theatrical, musical and gestalt experience designed to enhance creativity, boost confidence and ameliorate the influence of our indolent culture.'

'Oh,' I said. 'So what's the difference between that and a playgroup?'

'About seventy quid a week,' replied Tom.

'Ariadne's idea,' we said in unison.

We sipped our coffee in companionable silence while I stuffed away as many of Tom's chocolate brownies as I could without appearing uncouth.

'Is this just a social visit, or is there anything I can help you with?' asked Tom as he removed the brownie plate from my reach.

'Well ... you know I've never been what you'd call the world's greatest cook ...'

'You can say that again,' Tom said with a little too much enthusiasm.

'Well, it's all getting on top of Kevin. He's moaning about having indigestion all the time. Mealtimes in our house are just ... horrible, and I don't only mean the food. What can I do, Tom?'

'You survived for over thirty years before you married. What did you do then?'

'Ate out a lot, relied on relatives ... and had frozen dinners.'

'Couldn't you do the same now?'

'It's just that now I'm married I sort of feel, well, obliged. It's conventional.'

'Who makes the rules, Theodora? Look at Ariadne and me. We're not conventional.'

You can say that again, I thought.

'She does the nine to five, and I get to spend time with the most gorgeous little lady in the whole universe.' He swept up Phoebe, who had been playing on the floor with some stack-and-sort rainforest creatures, and blew a raspberry on her tummy. 'There's no commandment that says, "Thou shalt provide a hot three-course meal every evening or thou shalt be struck down by a lightning bolt from on high!"'

We both laughed. Phoebe joined in.

'You're making it too difficult for yourself.' Tom peered at me over his glasses. 'Why don't you find something you *can* cook and learn to do it well? We'd be delighted to have you both round occasionally. So would your parents, and I heard that mother-in-law of yours does fried chicken and rice and peas to die for ... and what about Kevin? He has a reputation, you know.'

'He does?'

'Kevin cooks a wicked Prawn Vindaloo. I should know. You must get him to make it sometime. Just ensure there's a big jug of water available.'

Kevin accuses *me* of keeping secrets. I didn't know he could cook.

'Tell you what,' said Tom, glancing at his watch, 'I'll lend you a recipe book – it's here somewhere.' He rifled through a bookcase in the hall, returned with a ragged, stained thing and handed it to me.

'*Cookery for Complete Morons*. Thanks!'

'No, it just goes through the basics. You can't go wrong. It was the first cookery book I ever owned, and you wouldn't say that I cook like a moron now.'

I shook my head.

'The best thing,' he continued, 'is that I seem to have spilled some on the pages, so you not only have the ingredients and method; you have a sort of scratch-and-sniff sample as well.'

9:30 p.m.

Chickened out (literally) on the cooking tonight, bought frozen chicken kievs and oven chips.

Kevin is becoming suspicious about the amount of time I am spending in the toilet. I shall have to find another secret hideout to write my diary, either that or develop some fictitious bowel disease.

Thursday 6 July

Sits Vac – crossing-patrol person or slaughterman in an abattoir. No thanks!

Decided it was time that I got round to writing the thank-you letters for our wedding presents. Toyed with the idea of using the church photocopier to duplicate 'Thank you very much for the beautiful bread-maker you gave us as a wedding gift; it will be so useful' for the eight bread-making machines we received. I think bread-makers are the new toasters. In view of the fact that I had a flatful of kitchen equipment and soft furnishings and Kevin, in spite of living with his mother, owned enough clutter to supply a small market-stall, it would have been far more useful if each wedding guest had taken something away.

I flicked through the wedding album. Was it really only three weeks ago? It feels like a lifetime. My memories of the wedding day happen in snatches, like snapshots in my mind.

Flash! Walking out of my parents' front door, arm in arm with my father. I'm not sure who was steadying who.

Flash! Seeing the ivory Bentley, driven by Vague Dave who was dressed in a navy blue chauffeur's uniform. Arriving at St Norbert's overwhelmed by the flowers, the smiling faces of my friends and relatives.

Flash! Kevin, grinning nervously from the front pew, looking so gorgeous and handsome that I kept looking round for the beautiful girl who must be there to marry him instead of me.

Flash! Chrissie in her robes with her white stole and bright scarlet lipstick, inviting us to make our promises.

Flash! The thundering organ fanfare, showers of confetti and barrage of good wishes as we left the gloom of St Norbert's and stepped into the dazzling sunshine.

Flash! The whole village had turned out to wish us well as we crossed the road to the village green for photographs.

Flash! The reception in the lounge bar of the Rose and Crown, with Mum's wonderful spread of Greek delicacies. Couples dancing – Ag and Cordelia, Ariadne and Tom, Auntie Mildred and Gregory Pasternak! Vague Dave changed out of his chauffeur's uniform into a suit so white that it made it look as if John Travolta's mum hadn't used new white-brite Bizz. Me holding Kevin close as we smooched to 'Three Times a Lady'.

Flash! Cuddled up to Kevin in bed in our cottage. We had waited so long for this moment. Not only were we *allowed* to make love; it was practically obligatory. All I can say about our wedding night is ...

Oh blast! Kevin's knocking on the door. I've been discovered.

Friday 7 July

That was close! I had to stuff my diary up my jumper and pretend to flush. Kevin looked highly suspicious when I came out, but he didn't say anything.

Off to work in the church office. I wonder what treats parish life has in store for me today. Perhaps there's been a punch-up at the Allotment Society's Annual General Meeting over the size of Mr Wilberforce's marrow and allegations that artificial performance enhancers have been employed. Maybe one of the mini-Hubbles has bitten the postman again. I can hardly wait!

5:30 p.m.

Well, that's blown it! I really must try hard to find a new job now. When I got to the office, Chrissie, who was wearing a police uniform, handed me some sermon notes to type. I stood with my mouth open as she put on a slick of her trademark red lipstick, adjusted her police hat and headed for the door.

'Close your mouth; there's a bus coming.'

'Why on earth are you dressed like that?' I blurted.

'I'm on duty. Special Constable. I'll pop back in before you go. Oh, and if the bishop rings, chat him up. I need a favour.'

And she was gone.

I glanced at the sermon notes: shepherds, angels, magi. Had Chrissie completely lost the plot? What was the favour she wanted to ask the bishop? Did she intend to ask his permission to completely reorganize the Church's calendar?

The title of the sermon was 'Not Just for Christmas', and this Sunday she proposed to preach on the birth of Christ. I shook my head and began to type. My mind wandered to all those things I could – no, *should* – be doing with my spare time. I could live the life of luxury for a while, spend my days at the gym, getting perfectly toned; I could wile away hours with a beauty therapist, getting my nails painted or my eyelashes tinted. Ah, bliss! One thing was certain; I had no regrets about resigning from my job. When we returned from our honeymoon, there was a letter from my boss, Myrna, asking if I'd reconsider my resignation. My colleague Covenant Blake, a kind of blend of Billy Graham, Bill Gates and David Beckham, had suddenly felt a calling to Outer Mongolia (seriously) and was threatening to leave her in the lurch. I'd written back politely, declining her offer, saying that I wouldn't be requiring the job as I now had a life instead.

I tucked Chrissie's notes back into her folder and turned on the tape machine, ready to type her letters. The first letter was one of condolence to a woman who had just lost her nine-year-old son in a road accident. Her husband had died the year before, and she was obviously demolished by grief.

'... words cannot begin to express the sorrow your news brings to myself and St Norbert's congregation. I will not attempt to offer platitudes, just to say that I, and anyone on the pastoral team, will be available at any time. Are you still happy for me to visit on Sunday afternoon ...'

The next letter was addressed to a parish in Uganda where Chrissie had spent six months helping to construct a new church building and community centre.

'... delighted that you are now able to host a community clinic and that Wemusa and Samuel were able to get the old Land Rover fixed to pick people up from the villages. I hope Joseph will soon recover, and our prayers are for Kissa and her son in prison. Was a lawyer found? Send our greetings to ...'

Suddenly the world felt so big and I felt so small. Here I was, healthy, affluent, moderately talented and wondering how to fill my time. If I hadn't just managed to stop the ancient office chair from tilting precariously to the left, I would have got down on my knees. I thought of all the need in the world and of how small my problems were in comparison. I prayed for the people in Chrissie's letters. Then I prayed that God would show me how I could become less self-centred and obsessed with my own little universe. My mind flicked back to last Sunday's reading from Matthew 25, 'Whatever you did for one of the least of these brothers of mine, you did for me.'

I had never fed the hungry or given water to the thirsty. I had never invited a stranger in. Taking last year's sale 'bargains' to the Oxfam shop felt a poor substitute for clothing the naked, and I rarely set foot inside a hospital and never a prison. Standing before my maker and telling him that I'd bought a copy of the *Big Issue* once hardly put me in the same league as Mother Teresa. I prayed that God would show me a way that I could do more for others. I was about to do that praying thing where you totally give God control of every part of your life and he sends you off to convert the entire population of some remote tribe on a Pacific island that only eat fish in spite of the fact that you are allergic to fish and come out in heat rash if the temperature goes above fifteen degrees. Everyone knows that's the way God works, isn't it?

At that moment Mr Wilberforce and his dog, Rex, who was on his way to the vet for his annual de-worming, had come in and interrupted my train of thought.

Chrissie, still in her police uniform, came back at about half past four and gave a cursory glance at my day's labours. She swooshed her signature on the letters and cast her eye over the sermon notes, then she pursed her bright red lips and wrinkled her brow.

'Did you notice anything strange about this sermon?'

I snorted a laugh. 'Did I? You're preaching about Christmas halfway through July!' I cast my eyes towards the ceiling and laughed again. Chrissie wasn't laughing. She looked distinctly irked.

'The reason I'm preaching about Christ's birth in July is to try to stop people putting him into little boxes – born at Christmas, died and resurrected at Easter – Holy Spirit – oh yes, tucked neatly into one Sunday at the end of May! Jesus' birth is relevant all year round. That was what I was driving at. Glad it made such an impression on you.'

I glanced at the floor. 'I see your point. Sorry.'

Now it was Chrissie's turn to laugh. 'Theo, are you bored with this job?'

'Well, er … of course I'm very grateful that you gave me work when I left the office …'

Chrissie looked as if she was going to burst. 'What on earth were you thinking about when you typed this?'

'What's wrong with it?' My mind flicked back. My thoughts had been fairly innocuous, as I recall – beauty salons and how glad I was to have left the 'job from hell'. That's all.

Chrissie was studying the sermon intently. 'Firstly, Theo, Herod massacred the innocents; he didn't mascara them. Secondly, nowhere in the Bible does it say that God sent an angel to give the shepherds a massage. And finally, when there was no room in the inn, the Virgin Mary "laid him in a manger": she did not "lay into the manager".'

'Oh dear!'

'Oh dear indeed! What's the matter, Theo?'

I bit my lip. 'Well ...'

Chrissie tilted her head to one side. 'I know this job isn't challenging you. Have you thought about the big picture? Have you asked God about his plans for your life yet?'

I shook my head, thinking how much I didn't want to join those Pacific fish-eaters.

'Then do it and do it quickly before you trash any more of my sermons.'

Saturday 8 July

Kevin has just discovered me sitting in the garden shed writing this. We had yet another row which played like a looped tape. He feels left out; I need to write down my thoughts; he worries that I'm not talking to him; I worry that he's worried; the more worried I am, the more I need to write. On top of that, I know Christians aren't supposed to worry, and that makes me even more worried. I know I love Jesus more than ever. In fact, since I've been writing it, I've become even more aware of my shortcomings and how I need to rely on God's grace and mercy every day. My only recourse was to agree to let Kevin read it, with the proviso that he is only allowed to read from now onwards. He agreed reluctantly, then stomped off to mow the lawn. I love being married, and I love Kevin, but I am beginning to miss my own space.

Sunday 9 July

Got up, went to church. Had lunch – spag bol. Recipe from Tom's book. Read the papers after lunch. Did some ironing, went to bed.

Monday 10 July

Went shopping, read a book. This evening we watched a film on television, and Kevin put up a shelf – it was just the right height and beautifully straight!

Tuesday 11 July

Put things on Kevin's wonderful shelf, did some washing. Had tea with Mum and Dad – moussaka again! What would be really nice now is if Kevin would put together that self-assembly wardrobe for the spare room. That would be lovely.

Kevin is beginning to need a haircut. Should I book an appointment, or will he?

Wednesday 12 July

I wonder if Kevin will be coming to church with me on Sunday. I do hope so. The problem is that he tends to stay out rather late on a Saturday night. I know a married man should still be allowed some time with his friends (male bonding), but he hasn't been getting back much before midnight and consequently finds himself a little tired the next morning.

Thursday 13 July

Things came to a head this evening. Kevin accused me of not writing in my diary properly. I retorted that I was letting him read it, wasn't I, and he muttered something about 'nagging on paper as well as in my ear-hole'. When I protested, he just asked me what kind of an idiot I took him for and stormed off to see Jez. I phoned Ariadne in tears.

'You mean you've lasted this long before having your first row! Tom and I didn't even get to our honeymoon hotel before our first bust-up, did we, Tom? Platform One of Gare du Nord at six o'clock in the morning.'

I heard a muffled grunt of assent in the background.

'Come round, you silly thing, and let big sis sort it all out.'

Taking advantage of what passes for sympathy from Ariadne, I drove to their house and poured out the saga of the diary before Tom, who was nodding sympathetically, and Ariadne, who was stifling her giggles.

'Why is it that important to you?' she said. 'Why don't you just think things? Why do you have to write them down?'

'I don't know,' I said, exasperated. 'It's just that most people's thoughts are internal. Mine are sort of ... external.'

'Visible thought bubbles,' suggested Tom. 'Fascinating.'

'Hey, Mr Amateur Psychologist, after all the hassles we had getting these two together, the last thing we want is to assist their divorce.'

'True. So you feel you have to keep your diary, but you don't want him to read it.'

'It sort of cramps my style. I couldn't bear anyone seeing what I write in there; I feel like an idiot half the time. There's personal stuff, things between me and God. I couldn't have got through last year without writing things down and getting them clear in my mind.'

The doorbell rang; it was Kevin. He ambled in, looking around suspiciously.

'Thought I'd find you here. What is this, some kind of Llewellyn conspiracy?'

'Precisely that, dear brother-in-law,' replied Ariadne. 'Now let's see if we can't thrash this thing out. Gloves on, to your corners, ding-ding, round one!'

Kevin and I both smiled in spite of ourselves.

Kevin's main objection to the diary was that I was using it as a substitute for talking to him. I promised to discuss my hopes, plans, fears and worries with him as well as writing them down, and that seemed to satisfy him. I also promised not to write anything personal about our love life. Rather bizarrely, his reason for this is in case it is published after our deaths. As if! He's the first man I've heard of who has been anxious not to gain a reputation, posthumous or otherwise, for being a super-stud. In turn, he has promised not to read my diary unless I ask him to.

We had a cuddle and a cup of coffee, then Kevin bored Tom with news of his team's latest signings whilst Ariadne bored me with reports of the current fluctuations in the stock market.

Friday 14 July

According to my diary, today is Bastille Day in France. Ate a croissant to celebrate. Unfortunately, I'm not feeling quite so liberated. The only guillotine I'm likely to come across today is the one used to cut the paper for *The Church Organ*, St Norbert's church magazine.

5:30 p.m.

Now swamped with job offers! Doris Johnson asked me if I wanted to work as a cleaner for her kindergarten. Alfreda Polanski from the Post Office needs someone for a paper-round, and Mum wants me to type up the recipes for her now-famous range of Greek cuisine. Had to say I'd think about it. Didn't want any of those jobs but didn't want to sound ungrateful. To cap it all, Chrissie suggested that I could do worse than becoming a Special Constable too. I can't see it, myself. Reminds me too much of Dad's terrible old police jokes.

Q. What does a copper have in his sandwich?

A. Truncheon meat!

Saturday 15 July

Kevin has gone into a sort of decline; he blames it on the absence of football in the summer. Tried to make helpful suggestions, even proposing that he watch some obscure European semi-final on the Sportsview channel, despite the lawn needing mowing. He demurred. I suggested that he call Maurice Johnson to arrange a round of golf. He gave me a withering look. Finally he asked if he could ring Kev 2 and meet up at the park for a kick around. How old is he?

I pretended to sulk. Now it was my turn to feel left out. 'We're married now; we should be doing things together.'

'Great! You can come too.'

'But ... I don't play football ... and –' I looked down at my white suede sling-backs – 'I'm wearing the wrong shoes.'

Drat! The last thing I wanted was to stand there and hold their jumpers while Kevin and his mates played 'David Beckham'.

'You don't have to play.' A wicked grin slid across Kevin's face. 'You could always be a goalpost.'

He narrowly managed to dodge the cushion I threw at him.

While the 'boys' were out playing, I decided to investigate Tom's cookery book again. I couldn't believe it. *Cookery for*

Complete Morons even tells you how to boil a kettle. I skimmed past the chapter on how to butter bread and went on to the advanced stuff – Beans on Toast. 'Do not attempt to put the beans on before putting the bread in the toaster,' it warned. I felt quite smug. After my first two weeks of living alone, even *I'd* discovered that.

I selected a recipe for Shepherd's Pie, which the book helpfully informed me isn't made with real shepherds, and started writing my shopping list.

9:30 p.m.

Success! I have just cooked a meal which didn't send Kevin straight to the bathroom cabinet for indigestion tablets. It really did taste like proper food. I even finished with dessert – Banane au Crème Anglaise, or Bananas and Custard to the likes of me.

Sunday 16 July

Chrissie has concluded her unseasonal sermon series on Christmas and has moved on to Easter. Nigel, who was assisting with Communion, announced the sermon.

'Today, Reverend Monroe is going to be speaking about Christ's passion. She will acquaint us with his torture at the hands of the Romans and describe his crucifixion. By the end of the sermon, I'm sure we'll all have experienced what suffering really is.'

Monday 17 July

Went to London to meet Ariadne for lunch today. It made me realize how much I don't miss the commuting. I caught the 9:30 train, anticipating a comfortable seat and a chance to read the paper. Unfortunately, the rest of Sidcup seemed to have had the same idea. I'd wedged myself into a space between the luggage racks and had done the necessary origami to fold the newspaper into a square only slightly larger than a postage stamp to read it. An elderly gentleman waved to catch my eye.

'Have a seat, love.' He hoisted himself painfully to his feet.

How kind, I thought. He looked rather more in need of the seat than I did.

'Thank you very much for the offer, but I really don't mind standing.'

'Suit yerself.' He shrugged and lowered himself just as painfully back into his seat.

I didn't want to appear the raving feminist and snub his kind offer, but I was clearly fitter to stand up for the journey than he was. I glanced at the sign in block letters above his head. 'THIS SEAT IS INTENDED FOR USE BY ELDERLY OR DISABLED PERSONS OR THOSE WITH CHILDREN.'

I began to wonder which he thought I was. I pulled in my stomach muscles in case he thought I was pregnant. How could he possibly think I merited that seat? I scrutinized his face. He was well over sixty, possibly nearer seventy. By the way he moved, I would think he had arthritis. I was patently fit and healthy. How dare he offer me his seat? By the end of the journey, I despised the man.

The tube journey was only marginally less fraught. I managed to get a seat, but there were delays, waiting in tunnels and sitting in stations for what seemed like days on end. An underground employee attempted to reassure passengers with his announcement, which began, 'Due to signalling problems at Pimlico, this train will only be stopping at one station at a time.'

So now I know.

Tuesday 18 July

Going to London again yesterday stirred up a real mix of feelings. Ariadne had regained her driven, determined businesswoman look. She has lost the weight she put on having Phoebe and no longer has that crushed appearance the postnatal depression had assigned her. However, her pale complexion and dark circles betray her tiredness.

'Phoebe still wakes a couple of times a night,' she explained in a matter-of-fact way. 'And if Tom's had her all day, it only seems fair that I see to her. And I'm still breast-feeding.'

I plucked up courage and asked. 'Why do you do this?'

'What?'

'Work in this demanding job with a baby that needs so much attention. I'm not saying don't do both, but do you need to do both at the same time?'

'I think that one of the things that made the depression worse was the feeling that I'd be condemned to spend the next five years "doing the mother thing" – you know, mum and baby groups, mum and toddler groups, nappies, potty training, Teletubbies and Fimbles. It just makes me shudder. Don't get me wrong, I love Phoebe to bits, but I know I'm good at my job. It's where I belong. I'm so blessed to have Tom, who delights in every gurgle and squeak she makes and who knows the difference between colds and colic. Of course I feel guilty. If you're ever lucky enough to become a mum, you'll know that whatever you do, if you stay at home full time, if you're part time, if you work full time like me, you'll always feel guilty. That's just the way it is.'

Wednesday 19 July

I can't imagine myself ever being a mum. I just don't think I'm cut out for it. When I look around at the mums I know,

Ariadne, our mum, the women who bring their toddlers to the church playgroup, none of them look really happy. It is as if the responsibility for another person has changed their character. The little person not only invades their body for nine months but also invades their life for the next ... ooh, scores of years. Mum still worries about Ariadne, Ag and me, and we are all in our thirties and married. 'Supermother' Charity Hubble is the only exception. The more the merrier for her. But even she seems tired lately. The triplets perhaps have tipped the balance. Mind you, the single, childless people I know don't seem any happier. They may have more money and a better lifestyle, but they seem haunted by *not* having any children. I just don't understand it.

Friday 21 July

Church office again today. Oh joy! Chrissie came back after Special Constabling to check I'd typed her sermon properly.

'Tough day?' I enquired.

'Oh, the usual – crime prevention, sorting out a couple of shoplifting truants ... And we had one really extraordinary case. A box of expensive wigs were stolen from Prime Cuts in the High Street ... The police were instructed to comb the area!'

Chrissie then fell off her chair laughing. I don't see why that's funny. Wigs can cost a fortune.

Sunday 23 July

Snuggled up in bed with Kevin and the papers and a jug of coffee this morning. I felt guilty about missing church but would have felt even guiltier about leaving Kevin. Never mind. I'll go this evening instead. I still haven't managed to get him to drag his spiritually degenerate carcass along to St Norbert's. Kevin, as they say, is still a 'work in progress'. I wish he'd talk to me about his faith. I know he believes and calls himself a Christian, but he's so furtive about it all. Sometimes I walk in on him reading the Bible or just sitting with his eyes closed, as if he was napping, or praying. He still refuses point-blank to come with me to St Norbert's. So I sit alone in the pew, fending off questions which at first sight appear to be about Kevin's physical health and well-being but I suspect are a veiled cross-examination of his spiritual state. I just smile and nod and say that he's busy.

I sneered at the front pages of the Sunday tabloids with their celebrity tattle and unfeasibly breasted women. I slung them onto Kevin's side of the bed and picked up our local newspaper as an antidote to the sleaze.

My eye was drawn to a headline – 'Man Escapes Death-Crash'. It was a report of how a motorist, Mr Clive Bunyan (67), swerved when a lorry burst a tyre whilst travelling along the local stretch of motorway. 'I was fortunate the lorry didn't hit me,' reported Mr Bunyan. There was a photograph of the gentleman himself, pointing to the stretch of road where the catastrophe didn't take place.

So basically, some local journalist, appalled by the complete lack of anything interesting happening, decided to employ his skills writing about a crash that never happened. Of course, I was very glad for Mr Bunyan and the lorry driver, but Sidcup had never felt farther from the streets of New York.

Kevin leaned over to refill his coffee cup, pausing to read the paper over my shoulder on the pretext of nuzzling my neck.

'Look at that!'

'What?'

'Two houses in the village have had break-ins in the past week.'

'So …?'

'One was in the next street.'

'And?'

'We could be next!'

'I know … but … these things happen. Why are we more likely to have anything stolen this week than we were last week? Anyway, it's not really as if we've got much worth taking.'

'That's not the point. We ought to get some kind of security system installed. I hate to think of what might happen to you here all day alone.'

I nodded slowly, not wanting to discourage him. I appreciated Kevin's protectiveness, but I imagined I'd end up sitting here in our secure cottage with burglars consistently not breaking in.

St Norbert's evensong had an air of tranquillity that was a far cry from the typical hectic morning service with gaggles of Hubbles running here and there and the rush to get back to the Sunday roast before it shrivelled to a husk. After an unseasonably drizzly day, the sun started streaming through the stained-glass window at the end of the nave. I had arrived early, intending to just sit quietly for a while. I closed my eyes and breathed in the flowers-and-furniture-polish smell and wondered if heaven would smell like that. Gregory Pasternak swept his way majestically through a classical anthem – there would be no 'I'm gonna yodel, prance, skip, shout, wave my arms and bounce about for Jeeeeeeesus!' in the musical repertoire this evening. I heard a little cough and opened my eyes to see slimy, oily Roger Lamarck perched on the edge of the pew behind me. He had his arms stretched across the back of my pew, and the stench of his aftershave threatened to overwhelm the scent of the lilies.

'Well, well,' he oozed. 'Theodora ... It isn't Miss Llewellyn any more, is it?'

'No, Roger. It isn't.' I wanted to add, 'And well you know!' but didn't want to sound like a bad adaptation of a Jane Austen novel.

'So to what do we owe this pleasure? I expected you and hubby would be going to the cosy, cuddly, family-friendly morning service. Unless, of course, you've found other things to do on a Sunday morning.' He gave a little snorting laugh that made my flesh crawl.

'No!' I lied. 'I just enjoy the peacefulness of evensong, and Kevin is ... well ... busy.' I slid a little along the pew. Experience told me that if I didn't extract myself from his tentacles now, I'd be in for a warm damp handshake or, worse still, a slobbery embrace during the Peace. 'Now if you'll excuse me, I was praying.'

Roger raised his eyebrows and slithered back down the pew. Bother! Now I would have to spend the next fifteen minutes on my knees with my eyes closed and my forehead pressed against the pew in front.

When the service finally started, I creaked back onto the pew and tried to ease the kink out of my spine. Chrissie strode up the aisle, bowed slightly then turned to face the congregation. Her smile turned to a look of puzzlement as she saw me. I lifted my hand and felt a long dent in my forehead from where it had rested on the pew-back. I tugged at my hair to try to cover it and spent the majority of the service with my hand to my forehead, trying to look as if I was deep in thought. Chrissie told me later it looked as if I was saluting badly.

After the service Chrissie whizzed round giving out little slips of paper. She handed one to Alfreda Polanski from the Post Office, Gregory Pasternak and Roger Lamarck. I instinctively put my hand out to take one, but to my chagrin, Chrissie whisked them away, out of my reach.

'I'm sorry, Theo. It's just an invite for a walk and picnic lunch next Saturday ... for singles.'

And now I didn't qualify.

'That's all right; I'm busy Saturday.' I forced a smile.

She didn't need to say anything else. She was obviously embarrassed, but there was more than that. It was almost as if I had betrayed the status of singledom, as if I'd defected, renounced my nationality and broken faith with the members of the Sisterhood of Spinsters.

I walked home, deep in thought. It felt as if I'd been a member of the club for years without realizing I'd belonged to it. And now I'd had my membership abruptly withdrawn for breaking a rule I didn't know existed. I felt as if someone had sneaked in on my wedding day and built a brick wall between Chrissie and me. Does gaining a husband really mean losing your friends?

Monday 24 July

Spent the day sorting out the spare room. When we moved in, anything that didn't have a home ended up dumped in there. In addition, while we were on honeymoon, Kevin's mum and his brother-in-law Floyd had taken the opportunity to deposit what seems like the entire contents of Kevin's bedroom and their shed in our box room. I'm sure half of it never belonged to Kevin. There was even a shoebox labelled 'Pieces of string too short to be of any use'. As the Americans say, go figure!

Four trips to the dump later, I sat down, exhausted, with a mug of coffee which for some reason tasted disgusting. I ended up pouring it down the sink and made another one, which was also disgusting. Must be the water around here or something. Put my feet up on the sofa for five minutes. Three hours later, I woke up to find Kevin shaking me.

'Now I know what you do all day!' he grumbled.

Tuesday 25 July

Went into the local employment agency. The nice lady behind the desk offered, for a small fee, to test me to see what kind of career would be most suitable. Sounded right up my street. After half an hour of me sitting in front of a screen and answering questions on just about everything except my inside leg measurement, the computer came up with the results. Apparently I'm most suited to clerical work, the catering industry or nursing. By a huge coincidence, all the jobs they had on their boards were for clerical workers, caterers and nurses. I thanked them for their time and beat a hasty retreat. As the door swung shut, the lady called out that they were expecting a job for an office cleaner to come in next Tuesday and they would hold it for me if I was interested. I informed them as politely as possible under the circumstances that I was not.

Sunday 30 July

Held two of Charity's triplets in church today. Would have held all three, but I ran out of arms. Unlike the other Hubbles, who are built like mini sumo wrestlers, these babies are thin and pale and fractious. With a stroppy three-year-old, a just-walking baby and Neb with his facial hair and raging hormones, not to mention all the in-between Hubbles, poor Charity looked all done in. I was on the point of offering to take some of them out for an afternoon so that she could get some rest. Then I realized that if I took out all the ones that weren't at school, I would need at least a quintuple buggy. Unless I planned on taking a stroll around the M25, no pavement would be wide enough. Instead I said I'd call in for a cup of tea later in the week and keep the little ones entertained while Charity put her feet up.

Now have sore ankles from kicking myself. The Hubbles and I just don't mix. Why did I offer to go?

AUGUST

Tuesday 1 August

When I made my magnanimous offer to call round to the Hubbles, I hadn't realized that it was school holidays and all twelve children would be home. In fact, I heard the Hubbles before I saw them. As I walked round the corner of their road, such a din poured from their ramshackle Victorian villa that I felt I had run into a wall of noise. The children weren't being deliberately rowdy; there are just so many of them. I peered through the fence. They all seemed to be playing among the overgrown apple trees in the back garden. Their high-pitched squeals went right through me, and I instinctively covered my ears. I checked in my handbag. Yes, I had a packet of paracetamol. I took a deep breath, said a little prayer and opened the gate.

I battled my way up the red and black tiled pathway, pushing the drooping hollyhocks out of the way. A sea of plump little hamster-faces immediately surrounded me. My instinct was to turn and run, but a twitching net curtain indicated that Charity was aware of my presence. I ignored the barrage of questions and pressed the doorbell. The blue-painted oak door immediately swung open, and Charity, with a grizzling Methuselah on her hip, invited me in. I washed inside on a sea of little Hubbles.

In contrast to the outside of the house, the hall and living room were meticulously tidy and sparklingly clean.

'Come in; make yourself at home,' breezed Charity. 'Chicory coffee or a cup of herbal tea?'

I couldn't decide which would taste worse, so I decided to play it safe. 'Mmmm, just a glass of water would be great.'

Charity led me through to the lounge with its pine cabinets, stripped pine floors and home-made rugs and curtains. I thought I'd slipped into a cross between a Scandinavian sauna and *Little House on the Prairie*. There were examples of the children's artwork (framed) on the walls, a vase of flowers (fresh) on the table and a set of floral china (hideous) in the pine dresser.

By contrast, Neb lay sprawled on the sofa, a slab of human untidiness cluttering up the order of the room. He was wearing headphones and had his feet on the furniture. Ezekiel sat on the floor on a blanket, holding a little wooden hammer and peg set, determined to prove that a square peg *will* fit in a round hole if you hit it hard enough.

Charity bustled out to the kitchen, and eleven-year-old Zilpah drifted in. She sat in the chair opposite and studied me intently. Unsure of what to say and uncertain I would be heard over Ezekiel's enthusiastic hammering, I just smiled and studied her back. She did not return my smile. She has long hair, darker than the rest of the Hubbles, and the characteristic hamster-face with its rounded cheeks and protruding teeth had surrendered to gaunter cheekbones. She looked like one of the Addams Family, sitting there with her mournful expression and her hands folded primly in her lap. Finally she spoke.

'I've taken the pledge, you know.'

'Oh, what pledge is that?'

'The pledge to remain chaste until my wedding night.'

'Good for you!' I stopped myself just in time from adding, 'That shouldn't be difficult.'

'What are you talking about?' Priscilla flounced into the room and perched on the edge of the sofa. Neb grunted and kicked her. Priscilla ignored him.

'Zilpah and I were just having a little chat about grown-up girl things,' I replied hastily.

'We're talking about sex,' said Zilpah bluntly.

'Oh, I know all about thex,' lisped Priscilla, flicking back her long plaits. '"Don't have thex until you're married. Wait until after the wedding."' She wagged her finger to emphasize the words.

'Er ... that's right,' I agreed. Zilpah nodded darkly.

'Jutht one thing puzzleth me,' said Priscilla. 'If you have thex after the wedding, don't the people in the congregation mind?'

Fortunately, Charity came in carrying a tray with my glass of water, a cup of coffee-substitute that smelled better than it sounded and some delicious flapjack.

The rest of the afternoon passed in a blur. Bathsheba went to play with the little girl next door. Charity put the triplets and Methuselah down for a nap and took herself off to bed. I played Scrabble with Naphthali, Priscilla and Aquilla, then I dug in the sandpit with Ahimelech and helped Ezekiel fit the right shapes in the right holes. He kept hitting them before I could move my hand away and laughing as the wooden mallet cracked down on my knuckles. I listened to Zilpah playing the violin and had a sort of conversation with Neb about hip-hop music; that is, I talked and he grunted in reply. I glanced at my watch; two hours had flown by. My brain was befuddled, my back ached and I felt exhausted, but I couldn't say that any of the children had been difficult or unruly. I went into the immaculate kitchen to make Charity a cup of pseudo-coffee. There was a notice board and several colour-coded charts with titles like 'Washing-Up Rota', 'Bed-Making Schedule' and 'Laundry Register'. So that's how she does it, I thought. The whole household runs like a military operation! I made a mental note of a few ideas to introduce into our household. Just then a sleepy-looking Charity shuffled in carrying an equally sleepy triplet.

'Thanks for that, Theodora. I had a lovely sleep. I hope the children weren't any bother.'

'Good as gold.'

'You know, Theodora, I've misjudged you. If you ever did become a mother, you probably wouldn't even need a social worker.'

Friday 4 August

Went to tea with Mum and Dad as Kevin was out with his friends. It would make a change to sample more of Aphrodite's Greek Delicacies, à la Sidcup. When I got there, Mum was in a mood because Dad had covered the dining-room table with pieces of paper, old newspaper cuttings, books about genealogy and photocopied certificates of births, marriages and deaths.

'He's tracing his ancestry. Trying to draw up his family tree. I just wish it didn't have to happen all over our family table.'

Helped clear up to make room for the *Melitzanes, Tiganites me Saltsa Domada* and *Souvlakia*.

'So, Dad, what have you found lurking in our ancestry? Were we royalty or paupers, criminals or priests?'

'Nothing that glamorous, really, but it does appear we could be distantly related to Tom Jones.'

'Really?' I said, trying to sound impressed.

'There are druid and mystic connections to the Knights Templar ...'

I wondered if I should go and get my ancestors exorcised.

'Of course, the Llewellyn name dates back to the thirteenth century. Prince Llewellyn chased all the English out of Wales – so watch out.' He pretended to attack me with a rolled-up genealogy magazine. I picked up another, and we parried and lunged, and Dad kept jabbing me in the ribs. My screams brought Mum into the dining room. She raised her eyes heavenward, muttered something about 'barbarous Celts' and went to carry on with the cooking.

Over dinner, Dad told us some of the information he had managed to find out about our less distinguished and more recent forbears.

'Course, the Llewellyns have for a long time been involved in travel and transportation.'

That was a laugh. Dad has a pathological fear of flying and foreign places. The nearest he has ever come to the travel industry is when he worked as a ticket office clerk.

'When the railways first came to Wales, Great-great-grandpa Llewellyn was at the forefront. Before that, the family was sheep farmers and factory workers. One of his brothers even went down the mine, but Owen Llewellyn saw where the future lay. He worked as a labourer when they upgraded the service – it was originally freight only, see, serving the quarries – then when the station opened and the line started to take passengers, he worked as a porter. As time went on, he got promoted to stationmaster and fell in love with the steam trains *Mountaineer* and *The Princess*. Great engines designed by a great man.'

He paused to take a mouthful of his aubergines in tomato sauce, chewing thoughtfully.

'He also fell in love with the design engineer's daughter, but her father would have none of it. She lived up in the big house above the railway line at Porthmadog, and her pa did not approve of her courting a lowly railway employee. Eventually, to spite her father, they eloped.'

'How romantic!' I could imagine poor but honest Owen carrying his bride-to-be off into the night so that they could follow their hearts in spite of their differences in social class.

'Of course, you know what they used to say about Owen Llewellyn?'

'No, what?'

'That he married above his station!'

At that point my father started laughing so hard that he almost fell off his chair, and we had to pat him on the back to stop him choking on his aubergine.

Sunday 6 August

Today's sermon was about the kingdom of heaven. Chrissie very eloquently drew on Jesus' parables and gave us a kind of rough guide. Unfortunately, it failed to shed any light on the subject. I now know what the kingdom is *like*, but I still don't know what it *is*. It's like a mustard seed, a farmer sowing seeds, yeast, hidden treasure, a pearl merchant, a net, a man with a storeroom, a king, a landowner, the groom's father, ten virgins … I'm sorry, Jesus, but it really doesn't help!

Chrissie said that we need to accept it like little children, and I guess that means not worrying too much about the detail. I still felt confused. What if I didn't know it when I saw it? What if I was digging in the wrong field or if I ran out of lamp oil at a crucial moment? I sat at the back and prayed for a while. Wondered if I ought to kneel down. It might help. Someone had piled up the kneelers so they looked like a vertical library of tapestry books. I chose a red one with a white dove on it. After ten minutes on my knees, I was still none the wiser. I stood up to return the hassock to its place when I noticed two kneelers in the pile. The top one was blue, with the word 'Fishwick' stitched into it. The one under it read '... of such is the kingdom of heaven'. So now I know. I've just got to visit Fishwick and all will be revealed.

Monday 7 August

Paid a visit to the Employment Office today. Tried to sign on for unemployment benefit, now called 'Jobseeker's Allowance'. If I fill in all the forms to their satisfaction and I'm available for work, they may just give me fifty quid a week.

'Of course,' said Sandra (or so her badge informed me) behind the desk, 'you should have made your claim when you became unemployed back in April.'

'But I didn't,' I said through gritted teeth.

'But you should have,' she chided, smiling sweetly.

'What's the point in telling me what I should have done when I haven't done it?'

'If you'd come in straight away, we'd have told you what you should have done.'

'But I didn't come in straight away, so you couldn't tell me, so I didn't know, and I didn't make the claim.'

'I know,' she said calmly.

'I know too.'

'If you knew, why didn't you come in?'

'Because ... I didn't know then, but I do now.'

'Well, if it happens again ...'

'It won't happen again.' I rose to my feet.

'It might.'

'No, it won't.'

'But if it does, you know what to do.'

At that point, I gave up. I could see myself having the same conversation for the next five years.

'Thanks anyway,' I said, ending the cycle. 'You'll let me know when the claim comes through?' I picked up my bag and turned to leave.

'Wait! I'll have a look through the jobs for you now, then you might not have to claim.'

I felt as if I'd earned my fifty pounds already, but I agreed as Sandra obligingly flicked through a series of jobs on her computer screen. The Employment Office's selection seemed to be about as comprehensive and exciting as it was in the agency. Finally she looked up and said, 'Of course, we have got vacancies working here ...'

Friday 11 August

Chrissie had changed shifts for her Special Constable duties, so I had her company in the office as I tried to assemble the local news and gossip into a presentable form for *The Church Organ*. Nigel Hubble had written a commendable article on giving money to the less fortunate. The article eloquently explained that if we give out of compassion and from our Christian duty, we too will be blessed. My only quibble was with his last sentence, which confidently proclaimed, 'When it comes to giving generously to the poor, some people will stop at nothing.'

I tweaked the notices and corrected the grammar and spelling and finally ran the magazine through the photocopier. After that, Chrissie wanted to sort out some old files. She found a stepladder, hitched up her cassock and started to pass me down some ledgers and record books from the top shelf.

'We have to keep these,' she said, nodding at the baptismal, marriage and burial registers. 'But these can go.' There were some parish magazines covering almost half a century.

'We can't throw them away ... They're history!' I exclaimed, flicking through the yellowish pages.

'Well, I'm not having them in here cluttering the place up. You take them.'

I gathered up the papers and dumped them in the boot of my car, intending to go through them tonight when Kevin is out with his mates. I returned to the office as Chrissie was dusting off the last few box files.

'That's much better,' she said.

It was my turn to go up the ladder to replace the files, and I tucked a duster into my pocket to spruce up the shelves while I was there. The dark oak shelving was thick with dust, and by the time I'd finished, so were the desk below and the computers. Chrissie was coughing and spluttering, and her black cassock was sprinkled with grey. She handed the files to me, and I put them on the top shelf.

The next thing I knew, I was flat on my back on the office floor with a rather blurred Chrissie looking down at me. I could see her bright red lips moving, but I couldn't hear the words. Next, I felt my feet being thrust in the air and Doris Johnson trying to force-feed me digestive biscuits. I fought her off and tried to sit up, which wasn't easy with my feet on the office chair. My left knee was throbbing.

'I thought she was a goner,' giggled Doris.

Chrissie had turned pale. 'Theodora, are you all right?'

'Yes, yes, I'm fine.' I tried to get up. I felt a bit woozy, and my knee refused to take my weight. Chrissie and Doris helped me into the chair.

'Would you like a brandy?' Doris removed a small flask from her handbag.

'No, thank you.' I said. Now I knew the source of her per-petual cheerfulness.

'You don't mind if I do. You gave me a nasty shock.' She unscrewed the lid, took a generous swig and replaced the lid, tucking the flask back in her bag.

'What happened?' asked Chrissie, the colour beginning to return to her cheeks.

'I ... I'm not really sure. I felt a bit light-headed, started to climb down and ... I don't remember. I must have fainted.'

'You bashed your knee on the desk when you fell.'

'Yes, I'd noticed.' I rubbed the rapidly swelling joint.

'We'd better get that looked at,' announced Chrissie. 'I'll bring the car round.'

'Don't worry, I'll be fine. It's only bruised,' I called to her back as she disappeared out of the door.

'Best to be on the safe side, love.' Doris scurried off to get a cold compress.

I half hobbled, half walked to Chrissie's Mini and eased myself into the passenger seat. She was strangely silent as she drove me, much too fast, to the hospital.

'Shall I ring Kevin?' she asked when we'd settled ourselves in the waiting room.

'Of course not,' I protested. 'Honestly, I'm fine. You can go back to the office if you like. I can call a taxi when I'm ready to go home. No point in wasting your afternoon.'

Chrissie's brow wrinkled. 'I'd rather stay.'

'It's all right. I'm not going to sue you. Your employer's liability insurance premium isn't going to get a bashing.' She didn't smile. It occurred to me that she was actually worried about me.

'Don't look like that. Really, I'm fine, but thanks. Thanks for driving me here ... and,' I added, 'thanks for being my friend.'

Chrissie looked as if she was about to cry.

Remarkably, the casualty department of St Philibert's wasn't all that busy, and within half an hour I'd given them my name and address, had a brief chat with a nurse and found myself sitting on a bed in a cubicle being examined by a very preoccupied doctor. I explained what happened as he squeezed and prodded my knee and flexed and extended my leg.

'I think it's only bruised, but we'd better be on the safe side. You say you fainted. Has this happened before?'

'Um ...' I stretched my thoughts back. 'Once when I was at school. I was standing for too long in the sun. Most recently when I hadn't eaten enough and fainted at work, but that's got to be over a year ago.'

'Have you eaten enough today?'

'Yes.' I thought of the three rounds of tuna and cucumber sandwiches I'd put away at lunchtime, not to mention the crisps, apple, doughnut, banana ... no, two bananas. 'Yes, I've had enough to eat,' I said with confidence.

'Have you been feeling well recently?'

'Come to think of it, I've been a bit tired. You know, falling asleep in the evenings.' I'd put it down to Kevin's scintillating football discussions. 'But I've been busy. Just got married.' I flashed him my wedding ring.

'I think it might be wise to take a blood test. Just a precaution.' He smiled at me reassuringly. I didn't feel reassured. I felt far from reassured; in fact, I felt very worried. What if there really was something wrong with me? What if I had some dreadful disease? Newly married and just starting life and I'd contracted something that was going to finish me off. I was glad Chrissie waited, and I guessed she'd be praying for me.

'I'm sure it's nothing. I'll ask a nurse to come in to take the blood sample; we should get the results in a few days. Meanwhile, there's no sign of a fracture, but it's best to X-ray that knee anyway. I'll just go and get the form.'

Sitting alone on the bed, I started to pray. I felt lonelier, more vulnerable and more frightened than I'd ever felt before. I didn't want to die. 'Dear God, please help me to be brave. Help Kevin to cope … and my family and friends. I know you can turn things around so that what seems to be bad can be good. Thank you that you love me, and I trust you whatever happens. Amen.'

The doctor returned with a form and started to take my details. We skimmed through name, age and address.

'Can you tell me the date of your last period?'

'Err …' I blew out my cheeks and wrinkled my brow. I looked up at the ceiling and tried to count on my fingers. What was the date? Second week of August … should be due about now … what happened to July?

'The last one I remember, for definite, was just before the wedding … must be mid-June.'

'And you're newly married. What precautions are you taking?'

'Ah!'

I knew there was something we'd forgotten to organize. With the haste of the wedding and the relief that it had all gone so smoothly, the job-hunting and the stress over the diary and my cooking, it had been overlooked. How could we have been so remiss?

'I think we may have found the cause of your symptoms.' He got up and turned to the trolley behind him. He handed me a little pot. 'If you'd like to go and fill that, we'll do a test for you right now.'

Saturday 12 August

I am pregnant, with child, expecting a happy event, enceinte, gestating, in an interesting condition, in the family way, I'm up the duff, I've got a bun in the oven … I'm having a baby!

Sunday 13 August

I lay awake for what seemed like most of the night, thinking. I started off thanking God that I wasn't suffering from any dreadful disease. Then I started thinking about the implications of this pregnancy. What is God playing at? I haven't even found my 'ministry' yet, and it's looking rapidly like I'm never going to find it now. I've had a traumatic year, just got settled; now this happens! I'm not sure I'm cut out for parenthood. It's not in my plan. All right, I haven't actually got a plan, but if I had one, this wouldn't be in it. I don't even like babies – nasty small noisy smelly things that take over your life. Why have you let this happen, God?

But this is a different baby. This is not just *a* baby; this is *our* baby. This is something that Kevin and I made together.

We made a person! Now we have to care for it and love it and nurture it until it can look after itself. That could mean the next twenty years, or more. Look at my parents; my sister, my brother and I have all moved out, yet our parents can hardly say they're free of us and we're all well over twenty. Still, I promised I would trust God whatever happens, and I do. I'll just have to become interested in ironing, wear a smock and learn to talk about the merits of breast-feeding!

Kevin is fast asleep, breathing quietly with a smile on his face. He'll make a great dad. I know he will.

Monday 14 August

To say that Kevin was over the moon when I told him we were going to have a baby would be an understatement. He virtually went into orbit.

Chrissie drove me back from hospital, but I was too stunned to say anything about the pregnancy. I arrived home about four o'clock, supported on one side by Chrissie and on the other by Doris. As I fumbled for my key, the front door suddenly opened. Kevin had decided to leave work early and had providentially just put the kettle on. He clucked and fussed over me when I told him of my tumble, plumping up pillows and bringing me a stool to rest my foot. How wonderful, I thought: if he behaves like this over a bruised knee, what kind of red-carpet treatment will I get when I tell him I'm pregnant?

Chrissie and Doris retreated unobtrusively, and I took a deep breath and started to break the news to Kevin.

Tuesday 15 August

Went to see Dr Edison today, who insisted on doing another pregnancy test, took my blood pressure, prescribed folic acid, arranged an appointment with the midwife, booked my scan at twelve weeks and examined my purple knee. She also calculated when the baby is due – 17 March next year. It seems a long way away, but I've got so much to do. We've got to decorate the nursery, buy a cot, pram and all the other things a baby needs. I have to learn to talk in that funny way people speak to babies – you know, 'Do dum baby wan some milkies?' I wonder if one can take evening classes.

We've agreed not to tell anyone about the baby yet, just in case.

Wednesday 16 August

Keep looking for signs of pregnancy – morning sickness, cravings, increase in weight, frequent trips to the loo – but nothing. Feel like going back to Dr Edison to ask if she is really sure I really am pregnant.

Thursday 17 August

Desperate to tell someone, Chrissie, or Ariadne, or Mum, or Charity – or the postman, anyone!

Friday 18 August

Kevin took me out for a meal this evening. I put on my slinky black dress – who knows how much longer it will fit me? Kevin nuzzled my neck and offered to open the car door for me. One spin-off of my 'condition' is that Kevin has become very attentive, almost gallant. To my surprise, he held open the driver's door.

'Oh,' I said. 'I imagined I'd be chauffeur driven.'

'Well ...' He shuffled his feet uncomfortably. 'I thought as you weren't drinking, because of the baby, you might like to drive so I can have a pint.'

Who says chivalry is dead!

All through the meal, Kevin kept looking at me in a funny way. Started to get all self-conscious.

'What is it? Why do you keep looking at me like that?'

'You look ... sort of ... different.'

'Pregnant, you mean?' I couldn't have started getting big already.

'Not exactly ...'

'Glowing?'

'That too.'

'Well, what?'

'Your chest. What have you done to it? It's enormous.'

I looked down. I certainly seemed to have a bit more cleavage than usual, and they did feel rather odd and uncomfortable at night. Was it possible that the bust I'd always dreamed of was only a few hormones away?

'Must be a side effect,' I said.

'In that case –' Kevin rubbed his hands together with glee – 'we'll have to get you pregnant more often!'

Saturday 19 August

First football match of the season, so Kevin was out of my hair for most of the day. I had just put my feet up for a little doze after lunch when the doorbell rang. It was Chrissie with a big bunch of roses and a box of chocolates.

'I don't normally do visiting the sick,' she explained, 'but in your case I'm willing to make an exception. Not catching, is it?'

'I sincerely hope not,' I said with a laugh.

'Seriously, how are you?'

'I'm fine, honestly,' I said.

'How's the knee? And the blood test, nothing nasty?'

'All fine.'

'Good. Do you think you'd be able to do a couple of extra days this week? I want to get the cupboards in the vestry cleared. We need to box up the old hymnbooks and get the choir robes up into the storage space above the organ. The two of us could do it in ...'

My face fell.

'What ...? You're not all right, are you? What did the blood test show? Tell me, Theo.'

'I can't, not yet. It's just ... complicated. Look, as soon as everything's definite, you'll be the first to know. Promise.'

She looked doubtful.

'Tea?' I said breezily and bustled off to make some, leaving Chrissie looking pensive. When I returned with the tray, Chrissie had opened my box of chocolates. She looked up, guilty as Eve with a mouthful of apple.

'Ummm, just thought I'd get started before they go out of date,' she muttered through a Praline Delight.

She held the open box up to me, and suddenly a tide of nausea overwhelmed me. I put the tray down quickly on the table and sat heavily in the nearest armchair.

'I think I'll save it until later,' I said hastily.

'Go on, one won't spoil your tea. I saved you the ones with the gooey chocolatey centres.'

That did it. I ran to the bathroom just in time. I may not have morning sickness, but I certainly had something. Just the smell of the chocolate wafting up from the box made me heave – no, even the thought of the smell.

'Sorry about that,' I said meekly when I returned. 'I just seem to have gone off chocolate.'

She frowned. 'Now I know you really must be unwell.'

Sunday 20 August

Failed to get Kevin to go to church again this morning. He had to stay and 'do' his books. I don't see why that should take all day. I left him with a large pot of coffee and a big smoochy kiss and scooted off to St Norbert's morning service.

Sat down next to a rather flustered-looking Doris Johnson, who was fussing over Maurice and making him turn out his pockets. I was rather concerned that she was going to start strip-searching him.

'I don't know whether I'm coming or going this morning! He's forgotten his glasses and his hearing aid, and I've forgotten my mobile phone.'

Oh well, I thought. See no evil, hear no evil, speak no evil.

Chrissie came and fussed over me, even bringing me a cup of tea. I shall have to tell her about the baby; it's not fair that she thinks I'm seriously ill.

Came back to find Kevin still doing the books, and in a rash moment offered to help.

'You know, this would be so much easier if you computer-ized it. It would save you hours.'

Kevin nodded. 'But, Theo, you know I'm no good with computers.'

No, I thought, but you don't have much trouble operating the games console, do you?

'Well, would you like me to set it up for you?'

'Great! I thought you'd never ask. Here's all the details. I'm just nipping over to see Mum.'

And he shot out of the door before I could say a word.

I sighed, powered up my PC and found a simple book-keeping programme. It looked fairly straightforward – incomings and outgoings on a month-by-month spreadsheet, automatic calculation for VAT – a piece of cake. Or so I thought. My main problem was trying to make any sense out of the folderful of invoices, receipts and cheques. I got down on the carpet and played a gigantic game of patience with pieces of paper. Finally I sorted it and started entering the information into the computer. I was left with a pile of documents I didn't understand, and when Kevin returned a couple of hours later, we went through them. There seemed to be several parts ordered and paid for but with no customer invoice related to them. They were mostly small items, but added together they made up over 10 per cent of his turnover. Kevin 'couldn't remember' buying most of them.

'What's this for? Compression fittings – £2.76; brass hose union bibcock ½" – £1.61; straight washing machine tap 15 mm ...'

'They're just odd bits. I probably used them on other jobs. Or maybe I just thought I'd get them in case they came in handy.'

'Well, where are they, then?'

He shook his head. 'I dunno. I must have lost them.' He was avoiding eye contact. He was obviously telling porkies.

'But it doesn't make sense. You seem to be buying these things and not charging people for them. You can't run a business like this! Come on, Kevin. What's going on?'

'Okay, I'll come clean. The compression fitting was for Mrs Fry. Her pipe burst last January, and I found her standing in her front garden crying her eyes out because her house was flooded and she was scared stiff she couldn't afford to have it fixed. The others were for Elsie and Bert Nelson. Their washing machine started leaking, and I saw Bert dragging Elsie's bedsheets back and forth to the laundrette in a shopping trolley. I know I should have accounted it properly, and I'm sorry if I messed up your system, but that's what I did.'

'So you've been doing jobs for elderly people who can't afford it, buying the materials out of your own pocket?'

'Yup, that's about the size of it. I just didn't want to see them struggling – or getting ripped off by some unscrupulous cowboy. I figured Jesus was a tradesman, and I thought about what he might have done. I reached the conclusion he'd have helped them out. That's why I did it.' Kevin looked at me sheepishly. I threw my arms around his neck and gave him a bear-hug.

'And that's why I'm glad I married you.'

Monday 21 August

Bought a book about having babies. It's a good thing I didn't buy it before I fell pregnant. It all looks so complicated, I'm sure I would never have managed it if I'd known.

Getting pregnant in the first place is no tea party. The sperm's journey to the egg sounds more hazardous than travelling from Canary Wharf to Goldhawk Road in the rush hour during a tube strike! Even if the fertilized egg gets there and the cells start to divide, it doesn't mean the pregnancy's a certainty. In fact, it's a wonder any of us are here at all!

Wednesday 23 August

Dinner with Ariadne and Tom tonight. Made small talk about the weather, work (Kevin's), lack of work (mine), church (me) and football (Kevin). During the work bit, Ariadne grilled me about my plans to find a new job.

'Come on, Theo, here you are, reasonably young and healthy and not completely stupid, and you're still unemployed after three months. It won't look good on your CV, you know.'

'I'm not strictly "unemployed". For one thing, I'm not getting any benefit ... And another thing, I'm still working for the vicar a day a week. I've been busy with the wedding and the new house and ... everything. Anyway, I haven't wanted to do any of the crummy old jobs I've seen advertised.'

'If you don't like the "crummy old jobs", you could retrain – or start your own business ... Unless, of course, you've got other plans.'

She and Tom exchanged knowing glances. I was practically bursting to tell Ariadne about the baby, but we had agreed to wait till the fourth month. I changed the subject.

'Are you going away for the bank holiday?'

We finished Tom's delicious Toad-in-the-Hole, and Tom opened the oven door and got out the most enormous chocolate pudding and placed it on the table in front of me.

'Especially for you, dear sister,' said Ariadne. I swallowed hard a few times then took off for the bathroom. Ariadne looked at Tom and said, 'I told you so.'

Thursday 24 August

Ariadne rang me this morning.

'C'mon, spill the beans.' (An unfortunate choice of phrase considering the effect of the chocolate pudding.) 'You're sprogged up, aren't you?'

'Okay, you're right. Yes, I'm nearly eleven weeks pregnant.' There was a little scream from the other end of the phone. 'Only keep quiet about it. No one else knows, so I don't want you blabbing it all round the village.'

'You've told Kevin?'

'Of course, but no one else, not even Mum. We're waiting until I'm twelve weeks.'

'Ooooh, this is so exciting, a little playmate for Phoebs. How are you feeling? Don't answer that. I witnessed exactly how you're feeling last night. If you want to borrow any maternity clothes ...'

'Thanks, I'll bear it in mind.'

I hadn't thought of that. My midriff hasn't really started expanding yet, but by Christmas I'll be able to get a job as a department store Santa. Here I am, still revelling in the fact that for the first time in my life I've got boobs that enter the room several seconds before the rest of me.

Friday 25 August

Kevin has just come in from work and told me to pack a suitcase and grab my passport as he's whisking me off for a surprise romantic long weekend. Sorry, diary, you'll have to stay on my desk; you've been banned!

Tuesday 29 August

Back from a lovely weekend in Bruges. We stayed in a beautiful little hotel near the Market and the Burg and spent the days wandering round the museums and taking trips on the river, and spent the evenings in quiet little restaurants. Just one disadvantage – being surrounded by Belgian chocolate and not able to eat a crumb!

Wednesday 30 August

Round to Mum and Dad's for dinner to announce our impending arrival. After the initial shock I could see Mum calculating the dates by counting on her fingers.

'No, Mum, we didn't have to get married.'

She took a breath to speak.

'Yes, Mum, it's a honeymoon baby.'

Mum's mouth opened to ask the next inevitable question.

'Yes, I'm positive it's Kevin's.'

I held up my hand to stop her speaking again.

'No, Mum, we should have sorted something out before the honeymoon, but we didn't.'

'Actually,' said Mum, 'I was just going to say congratulations, love.'

And she hugged me tight.

SEPTEMBER

Friday 1 September

Sorting out some more boxes in the spare room today, I found a shoe box labelled 'Privite – Keep Out. Kevins Secrit Stuff'. I was about to peep inside, but guilt got the better of me. Kevin's been very good by putting up with me writing the diary, so I don't want to stick my nose into his 'Secrit Stuff'.

At supper, I impressed Kevin with my Fisherman's Pie from Tom's book. The book helpfully informed me that the pie 'contains no fishermen'. Even I'm not that much of an idiot! He wandered in from the garden after mowing the lawn just as I was serving up.

'Sorry, love, is dinner ready?'

'Perfect timing – come and sit down.'

'Only I wasn't sure it was cooked. The smoke alarm didn't go off.' He narrowly dodged the tea towel I flicked at him.

After dinner I showed him the 'Secrit Stuff' box.

'Oh, wicked! I've had this since I was six. It's got all my best stuff in it. All my happiest memories.'

'Shouldn't that be your "Bestist Stuff"?' I laughed. But Kevin was too busy rummaging. He brought out a tatty and faded football programme.

'This is the first match Dad ever took me to. I was five years old, and he put me on his shoulders so I could see over the crowds. He'd bought me my own little scarf and shown me how to wave it above my head. It was the best day ever. I can still remember the noise of all the supporters cheering. I'd never seen so many people before, all in red and white. It seemed that the harder I waved my scarf, the better we played, so I waved and waved till my little arms felt like they were going to drop off. We won 2–0, and I was convinced it was because of me waving my scarf. Afterwards Dad took me to the edge of the tunnel and got the players to sign my programme. I remember sitting there on Dad's shoulders just grinning and grinning.'

'You miss him, don't you?'

'I wish he'd been at the wedding ...' He replaced the lid on the box. 'Anyway, this won't get the gardening done.'

I finished clearing up and went out to help Kevin deadhead the roses and pull up the dandelions.

10 p.m.

Just got back from Kevin's mum's house. Eloise ushered us in. She looked anxiously from Kevin to me and back again.

Kevin took a deep breath. 'Mum, there's something I have to tell you. You're going to be a granny again.'

To my amazement her eyes filled with tears.

'Eloise, aren't you happy? I know we're only just married, and it's a bit sooner – actually, much sooner – than we'd intended, but we're really delighted about it.'

She started mumbling something I couldn't hear.

'Pardon?' I couldn't work out if she was laughing or crying. Kevin and I exchanged glances.

'Mum, do you want me to get you a glass of water?'

'A baby! Oh, a baby!' She took out her handkerchief and started fanning herself. Then she kissed each of us on the forehead.

'I jus' wish mi George was here.'

We stayed for tea and cake; all the while, Eloise was muttering to herself and laughing and crying alternately. Eventually we decided it was time to leave her to phone her sisters with the news.

'I think she was pleased,' Kevin said.

Saturday 2 September

Chrissie called round with some grapes and flowers. I was washing the car at the time.

'Feeling better, I see.'

'Yes, much, thanks.'

'You won't be needing these, then.'

'Come in. I'll make a cuppa and we can share the grapes.'

I sat Chrissie down in the kitchen and pulled up a chair opposite her. I took her hands across the table.

'I'm sorry to have been mysterious about all this. I've been back to see the doctor, and it's good news.'

'The blood test was clear?'

'Better than that. I'm not ill at all. I'm pregnant.'

'Oh!'

Her bright red lips smiled, but her eyes didn't.

'Aren't you pleased for us?'

'Of course! I'm delighted. Come here.' She wrapped her long arms round me and pressed me into her magnificent bosom (although these days mine is competing in the magnificence stakes). When she released me from her grip, we sat down again on our respective sides of the table and she studied me.

'You're um ... looking well.' She looked down at her hands, searching for something else to say. 'Um ... when's it due?'

'Middle of March.'

'Oh. That'll be nice. Spring baby.' She smiled weakly.

The rest of the conversation continued in the same stilted manner. After about half an hour of parish small talk, the Reverend Christina Monroe glanced at her watch, adjusted her dog-collar and made her excuses, leaving me wondering what I'd done wrong.

Sunday 3 September

Chrissie seemed to be avoiding me in church today, but the rest of the congregation made up for it. The news, it seemed, had spread around the parish like wildfire. Slimy, oily Roger Lemarck kept winking at me, Alfreda Polanski from the Post Office asked me if I wanted to order any pregnancy magazines and Miss Cranmer presented me with a pair of knitted booties which looked to be about adult size 8. They should fit the baby when it's about twenty-three. I wondered what irascible Jeremiah Wedgwood would have had to say, had he not moved on to St Umfridus' after a monumental hissy-fit. Charity sidled up to me.

'Well, well, well, Theodora, who'd have thought it? You wasted no time in starting a family. Are you quite sure you are ready for the challenges of motherhood? Would you like to borrow the triplets for a bit of practice? I'm assuming you will be like your sister and return to work after the baby is born.'

'Of course,' I said. Why did I say that? I haven't got a job now; why should I be any more likely to get one after the baby comes?

'Kevin will be staying at home to care for it? I believe that's the modern way,' she said.

'Possibly; we haven't decided yet.' Kevin had no intention of staying at home, but I didn't want Charity to know that.

'Oh, and you'll need some maternity dresses. I'll drop a few round to you, now that I won't be wanting them any more.'

'Thanks, Charity. That would be ... lovely.'

Fortunately, Nigel came to the rescue by asking Charity where he'd left the keys to the van.

Help! I don't want to become Charity Hubble.

Tuesday 5 September

Had a bad dream last night. Dreamed I was turning into Charity 'The Power of a Nagging Wife' Hubble. I dreamed I was wearing a huge flowery frock and that I'd started enjoying ironing underpants.

Wednesday 6 September

Going through Kevin's boxes again, we discovered a cassette tape with a photocopied picture of Kevin, Jez and two other guys I didn't recognize on the cover. The title on the cassette was 'Tent of Calves'.

'What's this?' I waved the cassette at Kevin.

'Oh, awesome!' He snatched it from my hand. 'It's our demo tape. I haven't seen this for ... goodness knows how long.'

'And who exactly are "Wee 3"?'

He studied the cover of the tape. 'That's me, DJ Kevin; that's Big Mike, Jay-Jay Jazzy and Paul, the keyboard player. You know Paul – he ran your youth group. We used to practise in Big Mike's dad's garage. We even played a gig once.'

'You were in a band?' My mouth hung open. I couldn't believe it. Kevin even refuses to sing in the bath in case the neighbours hear him. I couldn't imagine him standing up in front of a room full of people, warbling away.

'Yeah, I used to spin the discs and scratch. Sometimes I used to do a bit of rapping, but I always felt a bit too suburban for that. After a pint or two of Old Brindled Cow, I've even been known to break-dance.'

'When did you do that? I don't remember it.'

'Must have been that year you were at college; do you remember? Your mum wouldn't let you see me, and I'd picked up that knee injury that stopped me playing that season.'

I nodded. But Kevin in a band ... ? The thought still refused to embed itself in my brain.

'Well, that bloke from your church suggested we create some kind of Christian rap band – you know, to do youth clubs and that sort of thing.'

'Why Wee 3?' I asked. It sounded like the number of toilet-breaks I'd need on a trip to the seaside.

'It was near Christmas. We were all sitting in Paul's front room deciding what we should call ourselves ...'

'And you heard carol singers – "We three kings of Orient are!"'

Kevin looked puzzled. 'No, at the time there were three of us, and we weren't very tall.'

Kevin played the cassette, and I understood why Wee 3 had never made it big. It was the most appalling racket. The drummer (Big Mike) sounded like a man with drumsticks trapped inside a washing machine, and the vocals (falsetto verging on castrato) and the over-enthusiastic keyboard made them sound like a punk version of the Bee Gees. I couldn't hear Kevin's 'scratching' or emceeing at all.

'Oh, they never let me plug in the decks or my mike. There were too many plugs for the extension socket.'

The track changed to something equally frantic and high-pitched. Kevin saw my pained expression and pressed the stop button.

'We were much better live,' he assured me.

Somehow I doubt it.

Thursday 7 September

Tried out one of the bread-makers today. It actually worked. I baked one batch of white and one of wholemeal for Kevin and me and made a poppy seed and oregano one to take to my parents.

I drove to their house after supper, and we sat around the dining-room table like wine-tasters checking the texture, flavour, colour and bouquet.

'Mmm.' Dad chewed thoughtfully. 'It's good. Not the best I've ever tasted, but good.'

'What's wrong with it?' I asked.

'A little too much yeast, I think. But then, as far as bread is concerned, I've been spoilt.'

'By whom?' Of course, Mum is an excellent cook, but as far as I know, she buys all her bread.

'Evans, the bakers back in Newport. Best bread anywhere in Wales. Folks would flock in from England just to catch a sniff of those loaves baking. And if you were lucky enough to get him to sell you one ...'

He drifted off on a little ecstatic daydream.

'I tell you, if I could have just a slice of one of Evans' crusty cobs, I'd die a happy man. Do you know, his loaves were so widely renowned, they even wrote a song about them.'

'Really?'

'Too right. You've probably heard of it.'

'Go on!' I had the inkling this was one of Dad's 'stories'. He tuned up his voice with a scale or two then started singing in his best Welsh baritone.

'Bread of Evans, Bread of Evans, feed me now and evermore ...'

Friday 8 September

Word has definitely got round about my 'condition'. Chrissie was away on a clergy conference all day, but that didn't mean I got any more work done. People kept popping in and telling me all their maternity horror stories. If they are to be believed, I can expect at least a four-day labour which will inevitably end in either a forceps or caesarean delivery, which will result in the baby being distressed/blue/taken away from me for a fortnight and I'll never be the same 'down there' again.

Went to the village green at lunchtime and sat near the play area for a change. There were mums and dads and child-minders pushing toddlers on swings, helping little ones to ride their bikes, clapping with glee as a head appeared over the top of the slide and a pair of pudgy little legs squeaked their way to the bottom of the metal chute. The sound of the children's squeals and laughter drifted over to me as I ate my sandwiches. If it's so difficult, I thought, why do women have babies? And why do so many of them have more than one? I thought of Charity and her brood. Surely she would have something more positive to say about her birth experience than cracked nipples and epidurals.

Saturday 9 September

Kevin has gone round to his mum's house to do some gardening, so I am taking the opportunity to sort through the files, papers and old parish magazines that have been sitting in the boot of my car for the last four weeks. I think perhaps I'll make a scrapbook of parish events: village fêtes, births, marriages and deaths, and, with any luck, a bit of juicy local gossip. The records go back to the early 1960s and cover everything from the ridiculous to the touching and compassionate. They provide an image of parish life as unmistakable as a photograph. I read with relish about the 'delightful new altar-cloth knitted by Mrs Milton in practical polyester' and with a lump in my throat as I learned about the prayer and support group started for the victims of the Aberfan disaster and their families.

I put the rest of the magazines and papers into a couple of box files and dumped them in the spare room. I'll finish sorting through them when I have time.

Monday 11 September

Feeling a bit tired this morning, so Kevin offered to put the washing in the machine before he went to work. Got up to find that he'd included my best lambswool jumpers. I generally manage to resist the urge to call him at work, but today I made an exception.

'What are you playing at? You've ruined two perfectly good jumpers.'

'I'm sorry.'

'Is that all you can say? Didn't you read the labels?'

'Of course I did. They said 100 per cent lambswool.'

'And you still stuck them in the washing machine?'

'I didn't think there would be a problem. After all, sheep don't shrink.'

Tuesday 12 September

Had to go and sign on for my non-existent unemployment benefit. Saw a completely different woman (Kulbinda) who asked me exactly the same questions and proceeded to tell me that I should have signed on as soon as I became unemployed. I managed not to scream. Then I told her about my pregnancy and asked if it would make any difference to my claim. Apparently, it wouldn't at the moment, but in four months' time I will need to come back and fill in another batch of forms to claim Maternity Allowance. Oh joy! While I was there, Kulbinda insisted on looking through the current vacancies with me. They consisted of telesales clerk, data entry operator or a job as promoter at a race track. I said that I felt I wasn't sufficiently qualified or experienced for any of those jobs. Kulbinda lowered her eyebrows and warned me that I am obliged to take suitable employment when it is offered or my Jobseeker's Allowance may be withdrawn. Withdrawn? I haven't even received it yet!

Wednesday 13 September

My first scan today – appointment at ten o'clock. Kevin has taken the morning off work, and I've started on the recommended water binge to ensure I have a full bladder so the scan picture is clear.

10:30 a.m.

Still waiting for the scan. Have read every magazine here, including the golfing ones.

10:41 a.m.

Still waiting. Kevin is drinking tea, something that is completely out of the question for me. After all those gallons of water, I am at saturation point.

10:48 a.m.

Still waiting. Kevin has just been to ask if they've forgotten about us. Apparently they haven't; they are simply running late. Mustn't think about waterfalls or fountains or even dripping taps.

10:52 a.m.

Still waiting. Bladder like a blimp. Can't hang on much longer.

10:58 a.m.

Oooerrr!

11:29 a.m.

The scan was the most brilliant, wonderful, amazing thing I've ever seen!

I had given up and was on my way to the ladies' when the nurse finally called us in. I had to lie on a bed while the sonographer, who introduced herself as Julie, chatted constantly about last night's episode of *Coronation Street*, squirted some cold gel on my tummy and ran a transducer over it. At first it just looked like a mass of fuzzy grey blobs.

'Look,' said Julie. 'There's Baby's head, and the spine.'

And sure enough, out of the grey fuzziness appeared some shapes that did indeed look like a little head and something like a string of beads that must have been the baby's spinal column. Kevin and I were transfixed.

'Baby's heart's beating strong and fine. I'll just take some measurements to check the dates,' Julie said.

I was captivated watching this little wriggling thing with a head, a spine and a heart. My baby! I was so overwhelmed I nearly forgot how badly I needed the toilet. Fortunately, Julie wiped off the gel and I clambered off the table, leaving Kevin to talk details, and managed to get there in time.

When I returned, Kevin was sitting outside the scanning room studying a black-and-white photograph. When he looked up, I saw he had tears in his eyes.

'Look, Theo, our baby. Isn't it beautiful?'

I gave the big softy a hug, and we went off to show Eloise.

Thursday 14 September

Eloise was delighted when we showed her the scan photograph. She was baby-sitting Kevin's four-year-old niece, Kayla, who has the concentration span of a goldfish, the memory of an elephant and the vocal abundance of a parrot.

'What's that, Grandma?' Kayla climbed up onto Eloise's lap.

'Uncle Kevin and Auntie Theodora are going to have a baby. Here's the photograph.'

Kayla studied the image for several minutes, turning her head from one side to the other. Finally she wrinkled her nose.

'It's not a very good photograph,' proclaimed Kayla. 'I could do better than that.'

'That's because the baby still inside Auntie Theodora's tummy,' explained Eloise.

'How did it get in there?' asked Kayla.

Kevin glanced at me and grinned. 'Over to you, love.'

'Did she eat it?' Kayla turned from me to Kevin to Eloise. 'Did she? Did she?'

'Not exactly ...' I hesitated.

Eloise jumped in. 'Look at the photograph. There the baby's head and there it backbone.'

I breathed a sigh of relief. Kayla will start school after Christmas, and I'm sure someone, at some point in her school career, will tell her where babies come from.

Friday 15 September

Chrissie was out visiting parents who wanted to have their babies baptized when I arrived at the church office today. She'd left me a rather curt note detailing the work she wanted me to do. It included the inevitable *Church Organ* and some orders of service for a wedding and two of the baptisms. As I typed out the babies' names on the baptismal certificates, one

Shannon and one Jordan, I wondered what we would call our baby. Is it now compulsory to name your child after a river?

Chrissie returned at two o'clock to proofread my typing and to check for urgent messages.

'Typing's fine, nothing urgent. See you later.' And she left.

'Chrissie!' I called.

She didn't respond. I called again. Still nothing. I trotted out into the car park as Chrissie was unlocking the door of her Mini.

'Chrissie!' That time I knew she'd heard me. Still she didn't look up, but carried on getting into her car. I went over and crouched by her car window.

'You seem in a hurry.'

She smiled weakly.

'Chris, what have I done to upset you?'

'Nothing. You've done nothing. It's not you; it's me.' She waved her hand to dismiss me.

'No, I'm not having this.' The force of my words surprised me. 'Get out of the car. We're going to get a coffee, and we're going to talk this through.'

Chrissie looked stunned. People don't talk to her like that. She meekly got out of the driver's seat and locked her car, while I went to get my handbag.

We found a table at Chez Shaz, a little café in the High Street, and I ordered two coffees and some carrot cake. Diplomatic negotiations are always more favourable if carried out over carrot cake.

'Chris, tell me honestly, have I done something to offend you?'

'No.'

'Have I hurt your feelings?'

'Not exactly.'

'Is it something I've said?'

'Not at all.'

'Well, for goodness' sake. Why are you treating me like a traffic warden? Every time you see me, you jump in your car and drive away.'

'It's difficult to explain. I just feel ... betrayed.'

'How come?'

'Theo, you are one of my closest friends. You never criticize me, you go along with my mad schemes and you support me when I'm in trouble. You made me stand up to Jeremiah Wedgwood. You believed in me when the Press was determined to ruin me. You helped me to distribute all those Christmas trees. You're the Robin to my Batman, the Jerry to my Tom, the Dr Watson to my Sherlock Holmes.'

'The Mr Hyde to your Dr Jekyll? Come on, Chrissie, what is your point?'

'I know that things are going to change between us, and at the moment I feel angry that I'm going to lose something very precious and there's nothing I can do about it.'

'Do you mean that because I'm having a baby it is going to affect our friendship?'

'Yes.' Her voice sounded weak and slightly trembly.

I was about to launch into a speech about how nothing needs to change between us, how things would always be the same, when I stopped. She was right. Things would be different. I would have less time to spend with her, for a start. And more than that, my whole status would change. We'd gone from being two single girls with no ties to me being a wife and soon-to-be mother in a matter of months. The friendship would have to change. Chrissie had just sensed that particular door closing sooner than I had. In spite of my pregnancy-hormone-induced hyper-emotions, I managed to keep the tears from falling.

'Chrissie, you're absolutely right. I don't think our friendship will be exactly the same, but there's no need to throw out the baby with the bathwater.'

Chrissie managed a little smile.

'I'll still be your sidekick, and I promise to back you up. Admittedly, we won't be able to spend so much time together ...'

'It's not just the time. You're simply going to have different priorities. The baby and Kevin will have to come first – and quite rightly – but you'll have responsibilities now. You couldn't just drop everything to accompany me on a mission visit to Kathmandu or go walkabout in the Australian bush.'

'We never did those things anyway.'

'No, but we could have. And now we can't. That's my point.'

'But what about the everyday things? I could still work in the office; we could always put the world to rights in our coffee break; I could still be your press secretary, bodyguard and personal detective.'

'No, you can't. Not in the same way. Seems God has given you a new job to do.'

'Great. I never really got the hang of the old one!'

'And ...' Chrissie looked bashful, a demeanour that did not suit her. 'It reminds me of everything I don't have. I'm a priest and all that goes with it, and most of the time I wouldn't have it any other way. But sometimes, just sometimes, I wonder what it would be like to have a husband and children ... Then I snap out of it and think ... nah!'

We both laughed. Six months ago I would have had exactly the same thoughts. It's funny how things change.

Saturday 16 September

To my surprise Kevin woke me up with a cup of tea at eight o'clock this morning.

'Come on, lazybones, rise and shine! We're going out.'

'Where?'

'Marsford Manor Theme Park.'

'Why?'

'We're taking Kayla. Give Mum a rest. It's a beautiful day. I've made the sandwiches and the car's packed. Come on.'

I groaned, drank my tea and got out of bed. I dragged myself off for a shower and stood under the torrent until I felt partially human. I lay on the bed struggling to zip up my jeans. For something that is only 10 centimetres long, that baby's taking up an awful lot of space. To add insult to injury, I couldn't find a top that minimized my matronly bosom, so I'm compelled to go around looking like Dolly Parton's curvier sister. I went downstairs to find Kevin consulting a map and Kayla sitting on a kitchen chair, grinning.

'Hello, Kayla.'

'Hello, Auntie Theodora.' She looked me up and down. 'Did you know you're getting fat?'

'She's not fat; she's expecting a baby,' offered Kevin, seeing my look of disapproval.

'Well, the sooner it arrives the better. If she gets much fatter, she'll have to go on a television programme like *Fat Camp*.'

I scowled at Kayla and took Kevin by the elbow, steering him into the garden.

'Why have we got her?' I jabbed my finger in the direction of the kitchen door.

'I told you, to give Mum a rest. She's having her thyroid trouble again.'

'Is that what she told you?' I folded my arms.

'Don't be so cynical. I thought if we take Kayla out for the day, Mum could put her feet up for a while. Anyway, it will be good practice for us.'

'If our baby turns out anything like that –' I jabbed towards the door again – 'I'm resigning.'

'It won't ...'

'Anyway, why didn't you tell me we were baby-sitting the Petulant Princess?'

'Because I knew you'd react like this.'

'But remember what happened last time we took her to the zoo? She ran off and nearly gave both of us heart failure. And her little souvenir! When most people p-p-p-pick up a penguin, they mean the chocolate variety.'

'This isn't a zoo; it's a theme park. And we've learnt our lesson; we won't take our eyes off her. Let's go. You'll enjoy yourself once you get there.'

'I suppose so.' I hauled my bulk back into the kitchen, ready for Kayla's next round of cross-examination.

We all strapped ourselves into my car and headed off for Marsford Manor Theme Park. As Kevin had offered to drive, I sat back listening to the radio and letting my thoughts drift.

Poor Kevin, he's only trying to help his mum out. Perhaps I should be more encouraging. And Kayla's a whole year older than the last time we took her out ...

'Did you know that a frog uses its eyeballs to help it to swallow?' My reverie was broken by a chirpy little voice from the back seat.

'No, I didn't know that, Kayla.'

'My daddy told me.' She folded her arms and looked smug. 'And did you know that a frog sheds its skin, then eats it?'

'No, I didn't know that either.'

'And did you know ...'

'How do you know so much about frogs, Kayla?' I was getting desperate for a change of subject.

'Because I've got a pet one called Malcolm. My daddy says ...'

'Um, you didn't bring Malcolm with you, did you?' Kevin gulped nervously, not, as far as I could make out, using his eyeballs.

'Of course not!' Kayla was incredulous. How could we have been so silly? Frogs hate theme parks. Everyone knows that. Kevin and I exchanged glances in relief.

'He's at home, swimming in your sink. I moved all the washing-up first.'

'That's it. Turn the car around!'

'What? We can't. We're nearly there. Look, I'm sure Malcolm will be fine in the sink until we get back.' Kevin was not to be deterred.

This trip promised to be even worse than the zoo escapade. At least penguins aren't slimy.

When we arrived at Marsford Manor, Kayla dragged Kevin out of the car and pleaded to go on the highest, fastest, scariest rollercoasters. Fortunately for me, pregnancy had ruled out all but the most sedate rides.

After nearly four hours of trudging round – holding coats and watching Kayla and Kevin get soaked on all the water rides, shot into the air and dropped on the gravity machines and tipped upside down on all the rollercoasters that Kayla was tall enough to go on – I felt about ready to drop. They decided to go on one last Ferris wheel called the Disc of Death while I stood waving safely from the ground.

Suddenly, there was a screeching, grinding sound. The big wheel lurched to a halt, and sparks started to come out of the engine part. The people on it stopped screaming with pleasure and started screaming in panic. Kevin and Kayla's car was up at the highest point of the wheel, some twenty metres in the air. I went over to the operator, who looked almost as panicky as the people on the ride.

'What's happening?' I asked, not sure I wanted to know the answer.

'Er ... it's a minor technical problem which will be resolved as quickly as possible.' Sounded like an official response if ever I heard one.

Just then the big wheel started creaking again, and more sparks shot out. The crowd that had gathered around it gasped as the structure lurched round, the cars swinging wildly with the momentum. Kevin and Kayla were now about halfway up. A dozen attendants, officials and security officers came running up and began shooing people away from the base of the wheel. Some teenage boys were standing up and rocking their car, oblivious of the danger. My heart was beating so fast I thought I was going to faint. I sat down on a bench, my eyes fixed on the two metal towers holding up the steel spider's web of the wheel.

'Ladies and gentlemen,' shouted one of the theme park officials, 'there is a slight technical problem with the Disc of Death. An engineer has been called, and the problem will be resolved as quickly as possible.'

The Disc of Death had died.

I could just about make out the expressions on Kevin and Kayla's faces from their eyrie. Kevin looked as if he was barely suppressing hysteria, while Kayla chattered away, indifferent to their precarious location.

Ten minutes later an engineer drove up on what looked like a mutated golf cart with the face of a giant chimpanzee on it. He chatted in a very unhurried way with the attendant, looked up at the wheel, did that little intake of breath that all tradesmen do when asked for an estimate, sauntered back to his golf cart and got a tool bag out of the chimp's chin.

Half an hour later nothing had changed. The riders were still perched in their little baskets, enjoying their views of the countryside. Concerned friends and relatives craned their necks, shouted messages of support, then – imminent disaster seemingly on hold – drifted off to get burgers. I was about to drift off too when I noticed the sky had darkened and the first drops of rain started to fall. There was a distant rumble of thunder.

The fat raindrops continued to plop down, and the riders were beginning to get drenched. No sense in all of us spending the rest of the day soaking wet, so I ran to shelter in the gift shop and got rather engrossed in the cutest little baby outfits with ears and tails to make the baby look like a jungle animal. There were tigers, bears, monkeys and ... My diversion was brought to an abrupt end by a flash of light, shortly followed by a thunderous crash from outside.

Everyone in the shop ran out to see what was happening. It became obvious that we were in the middle of a violent thunderstorm – and my husband was sitting on top of a lightning conductor. I know he's spiritually degenerate, but I thought God was gently bringing him round. I had hoped for something a bit more subtle than a lightning bolt!

I closed my eyes and prayed. I prayed for God's mercy and grace for the safety of those people stuck on the wheel. I prayed that they would stay calm and that no one would do anything silly. I prayed for the skill of the engineer to mend the motor quickly and for the competence of the person who connected all the nuts and bolts on that giant steel cobweb in the first place. I opened my eyes. The rain had eased off a little bit and the storm had passed over. The mechanic had disconnected the engine of the giant wheel, and a team of seven or eight park attendants was turning it around by hand, hauling on its huge spokes.

One by one, the newly earthbound occupants alighted from their cars and hugged their families and friends. It was like watching the end of *Apollo 13*. Slowly, the cars descended and I could see Kevin and Kayla. Both looked half drowned, but Kayla was still smiling and chatting. Finally they reached terra firma, and I threw myself at Kevin. He was wet and cold and shaking slightly, but they were both safe. I hugged Kayla too and whispered a prayer of thanks. One of the park stewards handed Kevin a meal voucher and a free return ticket – as if we'd want to come back. As we sat and chewed our burgers, Kayla was still bouncing.

'That was brilliant fun, Uncle Kevin. When can we do it again?'

Sunday 17 September

It took Kevin a couple of hours to stop shaking after yesterday's little adventure. Kayla was returned safely to her grandmother, along with Malcolm the frog whom we found sitting in a frying pan. Poor Eloise had to sit and listen to Kayla tell of her exploits, at breakneck speed with hardly a pause for breath, all the way through her bath. I swear that child attracts trouble. No wonder Kevin won't tell me when we're baby-sitting.

Monday 18 September

I started bleeding last night. I'm frantic with worry. Should I tell Kevin? There's no point in us both being worried.

Tuesday 19 September

Still bleeding a little bit. Told Kevin, who rushed straight to the phone and called the doctor.

2:30 p.m.

Dr Edison came. She said bleeding isn't uncommon in pregnancy, but usually happens in the first three months.

'Don't worry,' she said, sounding worried, 'it isn't always the sign of a miscarriage.'

She told me to rest and booked me in for a scan on Thursday.

I might lose the baby. Help me, God.

Wednesday 20 September

Kevin has taken a couple of days off to wait on me hand and foot. I might have enjoyed it if I hadn't been so concerned about the baby. Mum brought over a moussaka for our dinner, and Chrissie brought flowers and a card. Ariadne phoned from work and prayed for me, which was very kind. Most of the time Kevin and I have just sat and held hands and talked. Waiting ... waiting ... waiting ...

Thursday 21 September

The bleeding has stopped.

It was hard walking down the same corridor, sitting in the same waiting room, reading the same magazines as I did a week ago, wondering if my baby is dead or alive. This time I didn't care how much water I had to drink. I just wanted to be told that everything was all right.

My knees nearly gave out as we entered the scanning room. It was a different sonographer this time, who introduced himself as Mr Shen. He read my notes and invited me to lie on the bed. Kevin looked as if he wanted to run away. He probably did. So did I. Mr Shen was less cheerful and chatty than Julie was. In fact, he was so taciturn I wondered if he was ever going to speak at all. I watched his face, trying to read his thoughts. I held my breath. Finally he spoke.

'The scan shows a healthy heartbeat and no other problems I can detect.' He looked at our anxious faces and added, 'You can breathe now.'

Both Kevin and I exhaled loudly. Then we both laughed. I wanted to kiss Mr Shen but decided against it. Even he was smiling. I felt like dancing and shouting but restrained myself on that front too. Kevin shook Mr Shen's hand and said a heartfelt 'thank you'.

Saturday 23 September

It feels as if I've been holding my breath for the last few days. Kevin hasn't dared to ask how I am. Even though the scan on Thursday was very reassuring, I need one every day, just to make sure. I've got an appointment with the midwife on Tuesday, so that should put my mind at rest. Told Chrissie and Ariadne, who both insisted they were certain that everything would be fine. I know we are not supposed to worry, but I feel so protective of this little life growing inside me. I can't help wondering if even the Virgin Mary fretted a little over her firstborn.

Sunday 24 September

Even though this pregnancy wasn't planned – in fact, there was a time when I doubted that I ever wanted children at all – I have come to realize that this baby is the most precious thing in the world to me. I don't know if it's hormones or what, but I am developing a maternal instinct so strong that I would cheerfully tear limb from limb anyone who tried to harm my baby. I would literally give up my life for it if I had to.

Kevin came rushing down the stairs holding a Bible. He read me a section from Psalm 139:

> *For you created my inmost being;*
> *you knit me together in my mother's womb.*
> *I praise you because I am fearfully and wonderfully made;*
> *your works are wonderful, I know that full well.*

'Isn't that amazing? God already knows everything about our baby, even before it is born.'

'Yes, it's one of my favourite psalms.'

'Oh, you mean you've read it before.' The disappointment showed in his eyes. He thought he'd made a discovery, only to find I'd come across it first.

'But I'd never really thought of it like that,' I added.

He hugged me. I'd never seen him more contented. This baby has got to be the best thing that has happened to us.

Tuesday 26 September

Appointment with the midwife today. She could hear the baby's heartbeat clearly again and told me not to worry about the threatened miscarriage. She'd had a similar experience with her third baby, who was now a pilot in the RAF. I'm going to stop worrying and trust God.

After measuring my height and weight, she asked me about any potential genetic problems in our family. I didn't think being Welsh counted, so I said I couldn't think of any. She also asked me some very strange questions, including my shoe size. Why? Are they planning to fit me with a pair of maternity sling-backs?

Friday 29 September

Ariadne and Tom came round for dinner today with little Phoebe, who is walking and chatting away – she's transformed every time I see her. With her bunches and tiny denim dress, she's more like a little girl than a helpless baby.

Kevin and I cooked roast chicken with all the trimmings as a co-operative effort. He was a sort of head chef – Gordon Ramsay with a lot less swearing – and I was his skivvy. He shouted instructions to me and I chopped vegetables, put things in and took them out of the oven and washed up. We even managed home-made apple crumble from the trees in the garden. We make a great team. Kevin cooked the crumble … and I peeled back the foil lid on the carton of cream.

OCTOBER

Sunday 1 October

Kevin and I are not speaking. At the moment, he's sitting in the lounge pretending to watch a film, and I'm sitting here in the bedroom writing this. When I've got it out of my system, I suppose I shall make him a conciliatory cocoa. But at the moment I'm furious with him. It started last week when Paul, Jez and Kev 2 invited him out for a day's fishing.

'What? You're going out for a jaunt with the Three Musketeers and leaving me here, all alone and pregnant?'

'It's only one day. Surely a man's entitled to the odd Saturday out with his mates.'

'Not if he's married, he's not.'

Kevin flicked his eyes towards the ceiling, opened his mouth to say something, then thought better of it and closed his mouth again.

'What if something happens while you're away? What if there's a problem with the baby? Anything could happen ... I could end up in hospital.' I was starting to whine.

'Relax! We're only going to be twenty minutes away. I'll take my phone. If you're worried about anything, I'll come back.'

I carried on sulking.

'But, Theo ... They've got me a permit and everything. I really do want to go. You could spend the afternoon shopping with your sister.'

'She's on holiday.'

'Go to the pictures with Chrissie.'

'She's got weddings.'

'Oh, I don't know, go and have your toenails waxed or something.'

'Don't be so patronizing.'

'What can I do? What can I suggest? Come on, Theo, you've got to help me out here.'

'You could take me with you.' I gave him a coy smile.

'What!' he exploded. 'I let you have your space. I never go out with you and your mates!'

'You could if you want. I don't mind.'

'I don't want.'

'But I do. So where's the problem?'

By now, Kevin was looking punch-drunk and defeated. He wiped his hand across his face.

'Okay, Okay, do what you like. You can come. But we're *fishing*. There won't be anywhere to buy a magazine or a nice little ladies' room for you to powder your nose in.'

'I know that!' I gave a laugh which verged on the hysterical. Actually, I hadn't thought of that.

'Okay,' he said with a sigh, 'you win.'

So yesterday we woke up to a beautiful balmy autumn day – an Indian summer, I think they call it. I decided it was too hot for the jeans and sweatshirt I'd laid out ready. Besides, the jeans really are getting a bit snug. So I chose a loose-fitting summer dress and put a flask of tea and a lacy cardigan in my bag. I filled the picnic basket with goodies for Kevin and me to nibble on the bank whilst the fish nibbled the bait in the water. I was just about to load them into Kevin's van when he sidled up to me, smiled ingratiatingly, then begged to use my car as he'd promised that we'd pick up Paul and Kev 2 on the way.

I sighed, then concluded that, as I was fortunate enough to be allowed to come on this boys' jamboree in the first place, I'd better not push my luck.

I'd only ever met Paul and Kev 2 at our wedding, when they looked reasonably smart and civilized. Today, Paul looked as if he had spent the night sleeping in a gorilla cage, and Kev 2, despite looking fairly respectable, smelled as if he'd slept in a gorilla cage. They grunted to acknowledge me and climbed into the back seat. I wound down the window.

The twenty-minute journey took forty due to an overturned lorry on the by-pass. My legs were feeling cramped, and I needed the loo. The half-mile drive across a ploughed field didn't help, and on top of that I was beginning to have doubts about the resilience of my car's suspension. We finally parked in a shady spot next to Jez's car, and I started to unload the boot. I took out all the fishing tackle, then the rug and the picnic basket. When I looked up, Kevin and his mates had disappeared. I scanned the horizon. Apart from the way we had come, there was a thick hedge on three sides of the field. In one corner was a gap in the hedge, blocked by a barbed-wire fence. I leaned over the fence and saw three figures vanishing into the distance. I put my finger and thumb between my lips and summoned my most unladylike whistle. The figures stopped, appeared to be having a conversation, then one of the figures started jogging back up towards me.

'What's the problem?' panted Kevin.

'The problem is how I am going to get this lot over the fence!' I pointed to the hamper, the rug and my bag. Kevin shrugged, and I passed them over to him. I stood there in disbelief as he began striding across the field again with my things.

'Oi! Haven't you forgotten something?'

'What?'

'Me!'

There didn't appear to be a stile, so Kevin prised the strands of barbed wire apart so I could climb through the fence. I gathered up armfuls of floaty fabric and bent double to clamber through. The vicious barbs snagged my cardigan and ripped the hem of my dress. The ground was rough and full of cow-pats and thistles. I staggered towards the river in my new canvas espadrilles, trying not to tread in the dung or break my ankle in a pothole.

Jez, Paul and Kev 2 had already settled themselves down in their portable armchairs and were baiting their lines. I placed my rug in a thistle-free, cow-pat-free area and started rummaging through my bag. I took out my flask of tea and my book.

Jez called out, 'Have you got all your equipment, love, or would you like to borrow some of my maggots?' He held up his hand, which was full of hideous white wriggling things.

I was determined not to rise to the bait.

'I've got the only equipment I need, thanks,' I said, brandishing my book and flask. Mind you, a portaloo would come in very handy right now, I thought as I went off to find a secluded spot with fewest nettles.

When I returned, they'd already started raiding the picnic basket. My daydream of Kevin and me reclining on the rug surrounded with wild flowers and butterflies quickly evaporated. I slammed the wicker lid shut, narrowly missing Jez's hand as he made a grab for another egg mayonnaise roll. Paul, Jez and Kev 2 propelled themselves a few hundred metres down the bank. I didn't care if I'd upset them.

I sat guarding the basket, reading my book, or trying to, as I seemed to be spending more time swatting gnats with it than following the story. Finally I put my book to one side and lay down in the softish, sweetish-smelling grass. I must have dozed off, but a sudden yell from the riverbank startled me awake. I trotted over to see Kevin wrestling with what looked like a giant wet black snake.

'Yuk! Is that an eel?' I asked, keeping my distance.

'Sure is. And it's a beauty. Must weigh ten pounds!'

'Throw it back. It's horrible.'

'I'm not throwing it back. We came fishing to catch fish.'

'That's not a fish!' I wrinkled my nose. Fish, by my reckoning, are pleasant-looking scaly things with fins that stare back at you from the fishmonger's counter.

'That thing's evil!'

'Of course it isn't. And I'm keeping it.' Kevin could not have sounded more like a petulant child if he had stamped his foot and stuck out his bottom lip.

'Well, it's not coming home in my car!'

'It can't walk.'

'I don't care.'

'The fish goes in the car. If you don't like it, *you* can walk.'

Our little contretemps was cut off by the arrival of Paul, Jez and Kev 2. We could finish the "eel-in-the-car" discussion later. The boys decided it was time for lunch, and Kevin magnanimously invited them to share our picnic. As it happens, I'd made enough to feed an army. Unfortunately, the moment I opened the lid of the basket, we were joined by several dozen wasps. As if three unwanted lunch guests weren't irritating enough! Kev 2, Paul and Jez looked a little crestfallen when they saw Kevin's eel. So far, between them, they had managed to snare an empty Coke tin and an old washing-up bowl. I couldn't resist a little gloat.

Kevin grabbed Kev 2's (empty, ha-ha!) landing net and started swinging it to shoo away the wasps. It worked better than I would have anticipated, and we managed the pork pies, crisps, little tomatoes and Marks & Spencer coronation chicken with only the occasional wild flapping from Kevin. However, when I opened the fresh cream and strawberry jam scones, we were engulfed in a cloud of yellow-and-black-striped monsters, bent on sharing their smarting poison with us. I stuffed the food back in the hamper as Kevin thrashed away with the net like some demented lepidopterist.

Wasps were buzzing round my head while Kevin's swings sounded like a helicopter rotor getting closer and closer. I should have known better. I should have headed back to the car and let Kevin and his friends finish packing up, but I didn't. Kevin's final swipe trapped my head inside the net. Unfortunately, my head wasn't the only thing he trapped. He had also managed to catch the Incredible Hulk of the wasp world, an evil stripy beast with a body like an unshelled peanut (and I should know – the thing was an inch from the end of my nose) which stung me several times on the face and the neck.

Howling with pain and indignity, I finally fought the landing net off my head and started marching back towards the car. Kevin, Paul, Kev 2 and Jez collected their tackle and the picnic basket and trailed after me. Another rip in my skirt climbing back through the fence, but I was too furious to care. I got into the driver's seat, my face and neck throbbing and starting to swell. Kevin sent the others away and coaxed me to open the window.

'Theo, love … I'm really sorry. Now I'm just going to open the door and check on those stings. We really ought to get you looked at. Stings on your face and your neck can be nasty.'

I locked the door, trying not to cry with the pain and anger. It didn't work, as the window was open and Kevin put his arm through and unlocked it. I fell on him, sobbing, and he gently led me to the passenger seat and took my keys. The others silently stacked the paraphernalia back in the boot with stealth and efficiency, then tiptoed round and climbed into the back seat of my car.

No one said a word as we drove to the hospital. I sat glowering, my face feeling as if it had been sandblasted.

I would like to put it on record that there is no special treatment under the NHS for pregnant women with wasp stings. Four and a half hours after arriving at the hospital, by which time the stings didn't sting any more, the doctor advised me to go home and bathe them with vinegar. Still, as Kevin pointed out, several times, if there had been a problem, I would have been in the right place.

And that is why I am not talking to Kevin.

Monday 2 October

And yes, the eel came too.

Tuesday 3 October

Had my first free trip to the dentist today. I was expecting my usual dentist, Mr Kahn, a pleasant man who fills your mouth full of scrap metal then asks you where you've been on holiday. In his place was a Mr Macadam, who gave me a blow-by-blow account of his recent divorce. I didn't know whether to 'open wide' or give him legal advice, so I settled for sympathetic nods and shakes. He finished the examination, warned me my gums might bleed a little, advised me to brush thoroughly – and always to sign a prenuptial.

I went out to see the receptionist and settle the bill. She just asked me to provide proof that I am pregnant (as if mammoth boobs and expanding waistline aren't proof enough) and sign a form.

The one situation when I don't have to pay for dental treatment, and my teeth are all in perfect working order. Typical!

Thursday 5 October

Came home from a visit to the supermarket to find what I can only describe as 'eel-wrestling' going on in my kitchen. The eel, christened Eric, which had been living in a bucket under the sink since the weekend, was involved in a fight to the death with Kevin. And the eel appeared to be winning.

Kevin, I learned later, as the true hunter, had decided to turn Eric into a gourmet dish of jellied eels. His first problem was how to kill the leathery little blighter. He had decided that the most humane way to polish Eric off was by means of swift decapitation. He had taken out the breadboard and the electric carving knife that Auntie Gladys had given us for a wedding present, and the Sidcup Chainsaw Massacre had commenced. He made a grab for the writhing creature, which succeeded in slipping from his grasp and jumping clean out of the bucket. After pursuing it around the kitchen floor, he managed to grip it just behind the head. With a writhing wet creature in one hand and a mini power saw in the other, Kevin had his work cut out to behead Eric without electrocuting himself and while remaining in possession of all his fingers.

He had finally managed to pin the eel down and, in one swift move, to end Eric's slithering days for ever. He'd been moderately successful in one respect – Eric's head was no longer attached to Eric's body. However, Kevin didn't know until that moment that an eel's body goes into a sort of spasm, and Eric's torso had coiled itself firmly around Kevin's wrist.

That was the point at which I entered. Kevin was flailing around the kitchen trying to release his eel tourniquet.

'Get this thing off me!' he yelled.

I just stood there, shopping bags in my hands, seeing my husband locked in mortal combat with the Creature from the Black Lagoon's baby brother. A pregnant woman should not be exposed to this sort of thing. I wondered if there was some old wives' tale about the baby suffering some calamity because the expectant mother had been frightened by an eel.

Coming to my senses, I dropped the bags and unplugged the electric carving knife in the interests of damage limitation. Kevin had already inflicted a large gash in my rustic pine breadboard.

'Um, aren't you supposed to drop them into a pan of boiling water?'

'That's lobsters,' shouted Kevin, who was now bashing the unfortunate creature against the work surface.

I did the only thing I could think of under the circumstances and phoned Dad.

'Now, Dad, this is an emergency. I don't want any stories about great-aunts or any of your awful jokes; I just want to know how to get a headless eel off of someone's wrist.'

When he had finished laughing, he explained that the only thing Kevin could do was to sit and wait till the spasm subsided.

'As soon as it goes limp, he can unwrap it. May take awhile, though.'

So Kevin, most of Eric and I sat down to watch television. We ate a Sainsbury's lasagne, cleaned our teeth (well, we let Eric off that bit) and got ready for bed.

'I'm sorry. You are *not* coming to bed with that.' I pointed at Kevin's eel bracelet. Kevin looked dejected and went downstairs to play some soothing classical music to try to get Eric to relax. As he trailed off down the stairs, I hadn't the heart to point out that Eric couldn't hear because Eric no longer had ears.

Friday 6 October

Tried to explain the "Eric the Eel" incident to Chrissie, who nearly fell off her chair laughing. I also described Kevin psyching himself up to eat Jellied Eric, complete with vinegar, salt and pepper. Eric had finally released his grip a little after midnight and had spent the night languishing in the fridge before being immersed in a pot of boiling water. The smell when the eel was cooking was just indescribable. Kevin the budgie almost fell off his perch with the fumes. Kevin, however, was a man on a mission. With Eric cooked and allowed to turn cold, he offered me some. Even with my hormones and strange pregnancy cravings, I couldn't bear to put a forkful of wobbling Eric-jelly anywhere near my mouth. Disgusting!

'That's not fair,' commented Chrissie, wiping away her tears, 'you shouldn't speak eel of the dead!'

I think she's turning into my father.

Monday 9 October

Diana phoned this evening. After all the small talk about the taverna, her grandparents and her church, I told her my news.

'Of course, it's sooner than we planned. I don't really know how we're going to cope.' I gave a little laugh.

'You're keeping it, then?'

'Of course!'

What other option is there? A baby isn't like an unwanted Christmas present. You can't just send it back with the receipt if you change your mind. Then it dawned on me: she meant terminate the pregnancy.

'I could never think of having a termination!' I snorted. 'It's funny, I was so shocked when I found out I was expecting, but now that baby means the world to us. How anyone could even think of ending a little life like that is beyond me.'

I thought of Psalm 139 that Kevin had brought to me all shiny-eyed.

'We don't all have a choice,' she said harshly.

'I know it's not always convenient to have a baby, but that doesn't mean you should just kill it because it doesn't suit your lifestyle or would mess up your figure. What kind of a monster would do that?'

'A young, single, broke, depressed one who has just been dumped by the guy who promised he'd stick with her for ever no matter what happened and with no family support and no way of bringing up a baby on her own.' Diana's voice trembled. She was obviously close to tears.

'Oh, Diana! I'm so sorry.' Me and my big mouth. Here I was with all my pregnancy hormones pumping away nineteen to the dozen, shooting off like some placard-waving abortion-clinic groupie.

'You don't need to tell me what a monster I am. I have been telling myself that for years.'

'I didn't mean ...'

But it was too late. A click at the other end told me I had more than blown it. Of course the idea of abortion was sickening, but that was no reason for making my friend feel like scum. I had behaved inexcusably. I should be praying for her, not cutting her into little pieces and dancing on her feelings.

I tried to phone back, but there was no answer. I e-mailed my apology and sat there waiting for her reply. It didn't come. After half an hour Kevin came to find me, and I told him what had happened. He let out a low whistle.

'You've really blown it there.'

'I know. What can I do?'

He shrugged and went back into the lounge.

I spent the rest of the evening surfing around some post-abortion counselling sites. They were full of heartbreaking stories. Poor Diana.

Help me, Jesus. I don't know what to do.

Tuesday 10 October

Dropped into the church to see Chrissie to ask her what to do about Diana. I found her in the vestry sorting out the harvest gifts. Her reaction was similar to Kevin's. I felt about two inches tall.

'I didn't know Diana had had an abortion. How could I? She never told me. It never came up in conversation ... Well, it wouldn't ...' I paced the floor. 'I suppose if I'd been a little more sensitive, I could have guessed.'

'I should imagine she did it with the best of intentions. She felt it was her only option at the time with no family and support. She was vulnerable and let down by the man she obviously loved. It's only now that she looks back and sees what she has lost. Oh, the poor girl!'

Chrissie's eyes filled with tears. They began to stream down her cheeks. I had never seen her like this before.

'Excuse me,' she croaked and practically ran into the church.

I wasn't sure whether to follow her and see if she was all right. I decided to give her ten minutes alone. I sat and prayed.

I prayed for Diana and our friendship. I prayed for the baby she lost and for other young women in her position. Finally I prayed for Chrissie. I'd seen her hoot with laughter playing with the young Hubbles and weep with the mourners at a funeral, but I'd never seen her this distraught. Surely Chrissie had never had an abortion. She hadn't even mentioned a boyfriend.

I found two mugs and heaped a spoonful of instant coffee in each. I put the kettle on to boil. I couldn't find any fresh milk, so I unscrewed the lid of a jar of coffee whitener which looked as if it could have been packed by Mrs Noah just in case the cow went on strike. I slopped the boiling water in and grabbed a mug in each hand. I managed to scoop up a box of tissues under my arm and reversed into the church. Chrissie was on the steps in front of the altar, not just kneeling but curled into a tiny ball, her long legs tucked under her and her arms clasped round her knees. I couldn't hear what she was saying. The tissue box slipped from my armpit and crashed onto the tiled floor. Chrissie looked up, startled.

'Sorry, I didn't mean to disturb you. I just wondered if you were all right.'

She got up and stretched. She swept up the tissue box, took out a tissue and blew vigorously. Her face was pale with red blotches, and her mouth looked strange without her red lipstick. We both sat down on the front pew. I gave her a coffee and held her hand.

'Do you want to talk about it?'

'I ... find it ... I can't always put into words how I feel. When I see suffering ... A child dies, a woman's life is devastated by abortion, war, famine, violence, inhumanity ... and I just want to weep.' She took a sip of coffee. 'I'm the sort of person who wants to put things right. I'm a fixer. If I can do or say something to make it better, I will. It's as if God allows me a little glimpse of what is happening through his eyes and, oh, the compassion, the love, the deep well of grief …' She started to weep again.

'But you're not God … and some things can't be fixed. Not by you, anyway.'

'I know that. So I pray. I plead and beg and paw at God's trouser leg, and I get angry with him for letting it happen and not doing anything about it, and I pray some more. Sometimes I do what I can, if there's anything to be done. I write letters, I phone the radio stations, I wave banners and go on protest marches. I sit with the bereaved, I visit the prisoners, I visit the sick in hospital, I listen to the elderly, I go to clubs and bars where young men and women try to find love and happiness through drink or a one-night stand … but it's not enough.'

It sounded like an awful lot to me.

'When I see what God sees, I want to … I don't know what I want to do. It's all so frustrating. And when you try your best to help and it all goes wrong …'

'It sounds like a gift – to see people and situations as God sees them.'

'Sometimes it feels like a curse.' She blew her nose again and gave me a weak little smile. I sat and looked at this amazing woman, feeling blessed to call her my friend. She took another swig of coffee.

'Theo, this has got to be the most disgustingly awful coffee I have ever tasted.'

I took a swig of mine. She was right.

Wednesday 11 October

I prayed for both Diana and Chrissie, then I sat and wrote to Diana yesterday. I don't know if she will write back. I just hope it represents an olive branch.

Thursday 12 October

Chrissie phoned me at the unearthly hour of half past six this morning.

'Wha' do you want?' I groaned.

'Get up, you lazy moo. You've just got a job.'

'What?'

I shot upright, flinging the duvet onto the floor. Kevin grunted and pulled it back over him.

'You are no longer unemployed. Tell the Employment Office to take a running jump and the Tax Office to start celebrating – P-A-Y-E is B-A-C-K!'

'What are you talking about? What job?'

'Well, it will suit you down to the ground. Eight forty-five to three thirty, so there's time for an afternoon nap if you need one, five days a week, in the village so no commuting, and the money's not bad. The job's temporary, just for a month but maybe longer, and possibly with the opportunity to go back part time after the baby's born.'

'Chrissie, you're an angel – it sounds perfect! How can I thank you?'

'Auntie Chrissie would be easily thanked if it meant you would wipe that sour look off your face and start smiling again.'

'I'm smiling already. When do I start?'

'Today!'

'Oh! What do I wear?'

'Anything practical. Smartish. Whatever you can get round your burgeoning belly.'

'Thanks! Oh – you haven't said where I'll be working or what I'm doing.'

'No, I haven't, have I. As I said, it's only temporary, filling in at short notice for Mrs Williams, who has had to go into hospital unexpectedly for an operation. The head teacher phoned last night. You'll be working at St Swithun's Primary.'

A school secretary, eh? My mind raced. I wondered what kind of computer system I'd be using. Would my accounts experience be up to scratch? Never mind, I'm sure I can pick it up.

'So I'll be typing letters, sorting out dinner money and that sort of thing?'

'Not exactly. It's more sort of hands-on than that.'

I shifted uneasily, accidentally kicking Kevin in the knee.

'What do you mean? You haven't got me a job as a dinner lady, have you?' I was getting more and more suspicious by the minute.

'It's Midday Supervisor, not dinner lady, and no, I haven't.'

I breathed a sigh of relief. Slopping out semolina to a crowd of poisonous little ankle-biters was not my idea of a fulfilling career.

'You're going to be a Teaching Assistant.'

'And what is one of those?' My voice squeaked.

'You assist the teacher.'

She didn't add the word 'bozo', but she might as well have.

'You mean I'll be working with children?'

This time she did use the word 'bozo'.

'I am just not a children person,' I protested. 'I don't understand them. They're noisy, smelly, demanding and unreasonable.'

'I know a few adults like that. Come on, get dressed. It's time you were going.'

'B – but I don't even know if I want this job.'

'Too late. I've already told her you'll do it.'

'Thanks!' I wondered if Chrissie could detect my pout down the phone.

'Don't mention it,' she chirped, oblivious, and hung up.

'Great! This fantastic new job that Chrissie has volunteered me for is working in a school – with children!' I grumbled. 'What am I going to do?'

'Take it, of course. It will be good practice.'

'Why do you always say that?' I scrambled out of bed, stomped across the room and started rummaging through my wardrobe to find something childproof to wear.

6:30 p.m.

Well, I've just survived my first day in Class 2B – just. It's the sort of day when I really *need* a bar of chocolate. If only the baby agreed. Made do with a bag of jelly babies. It wasn't the same. It felt like cannibalism.

Saturday 14 October

Two days at work and a day off. That's definitely the way to do it. Have been too busy or too exhausted to write in my diary. Here I am sitting with a cup of tea and a digestive or two (one for me, one for the baby) and scribbling away while Kevin is at a home match. It certainly is a shock to the system, working again. I have to admit, sceptical as I was, I'm actually enjoying the job. That wasn't the way I felt on Thursday morning as I drove down the hill in the rain to St Swithun's Primary. I think the word is ... 'daunted'.

The school is in a road just off the High Street, and I struggled to find anywhere to park, what with the yellow zigzags and the parents driving their children to school in four-wheel-drives. Why does anyone need a vehicle with off-road capability in Sidcup? My guess is the furthest off road most of these people would get is Sainsbury's car park. St Swithun's is a small school with extensions stuck like barnacles to the Victorian red brick.

Mrs Thomas, the teacher, came out to meet me and bustled me along a corridor to the tiny staff room to get a cup of tea. Mrs Thomas is a short, compact woman with a warm, friendly smile but glacial eyes that could freeze a child across the classroom. I bet nobody throws paper aeroplanes in Mrs Thomas' class.

She took me along a labyrinth of corridors, pointing out places of interest on the way – the school-keeper's cupboard, the trophy cabinet and, most importantly, the ladies' loo.

The empty classroom was decked with children's paintings, letters of the alphabet and numbers. There were low coat pegs with drawstring bags hanging from them. The chairs and desks and cupboards were brightly coloured. It was as if a rainbow had exploded in the room. I also noticed that everything was labelled. I sat down on a tiny 'chair' next to the 'computer', and Mrs Thomas, who obviously moved too quickly to have a label stuck on her, gave me a piece of paper. She asked me to help Blue Group with their story writing, then to assist Green Group with their number bonds to ten. Didn't like to admit that I wasn't 100 per cent sure what number bonds are. The orderly calm was soon broken as twenty-nine six- and seven-year-olds streamed in, all wearing little blue sweatshirts. How was I ever going to remember all their names? They filed past, put their lunch boxes on a cabinet and their nylon mini briefcases into a red plastic box, then most of them sat expectantly on the floor. One serious-looking little girl with long dark plaits and deep brown eyes stood directly in front of me.

'Who are you?' she asked.

'Yes, what are you doing here? Where's Mrs Williams?' the other children chorused.

'Ummmm ...' For a moment I couldn't remember what I was doing here or even who I was. Perhaps I should have had a label – 'idiot'. Then Mrs Thomas rescued me, and a bell rang to signal the start of the day.

Sunday 15 October

Cornered Chrissie outside the vestry after Communion this morning. I was still worried about her after Monday.

'How's life at the chalkface?' she asked breezily.

'Fine, thanks,' I replied with equal breeziness. 'In fact, I owe you a proper thank-you.'

'Pub!' we said simultaneously.

Settled at a table with a beaten copper top in the Red Lion, with an orange juice each in front of us, I pulled out my mobile phone.

'Better just let Kevin know I'll be late back.'

Chrissie made an 'under the thumb' gesture and went to the bar to buy crisps. I stared at the row of horse brasses over the fire until Chrissie returned.

'I didn't really bring you here to talk about the job.'

Her face fell.

'Although of course I wanted to do that too.' We clinked our glasses in a half-hearted toast.

'Don't tell me ... You're running off with the milkman ... You're really a man ... That's not a baby at all, just a bad case of wind ...'

I didn't smile. 'What happened on Monday?'

'Oh. It's nothing.' She brushed some invisible dust from her black velvet trousers. 'It all gets on top of me sometimes – the job, things back at home. And I guess I'm just a sensitive soul.'

'Come on, Chris. I've never seen you like that before. Did I do something wrong?'

She gave a sigh that seemed to start in the soles of her black stiletto boots.

'It just touched a nerve, that's all. And coming when it did.'

'Will you tell me about it?'

'Nothing to tell, really. It's all in the past. Got to move on.'

'I can't force you to talk to me, but something was going on there. I was about to send for the men in white coats.'

'Well, I'm all right now.' She smiled broadly. 'Your round, I think.'

Monday 16 October

Number bonds are pairs of numbers that make ten, like six and four or two and eight. Easy, really!

Tuesday 17 October

I'm feeling a little more confident today. I am beginning to learn the children's names and how to approach them. I was surprised at how many children seem to need extra help. There's Axel who is dyslexic, Rowan who has Attention Deficit Disorder and Marcus who has Asperger's Syndrome, which makes it hard for him to cope in a social situation. The day passes in a flash, starting with hearing children read in assembly through supporting them in lessons, sorting out play-time squabbles, opening yoghurt pots at lunchtime and helping to locate lost wellies at home time. The children are friendly, polite and extremely curious. Today's questions have ranged from 'Which football team do you support?' to 'How do you spell "brachiosaurus"?' – I had to look that one up!

Thursday 19 October

Finally found out the reason I got this job. Turns out the head teacher owed Chrissie a favour, something to do with a mix-up over Harvest Festival gifts where the donations to the local elderly and needy got confused with donations to the local animal rescue centre. Chrissie had to go and pour oil on troubled waters. Apparently the residents of 'White Chestnuts' weren't too happy when instead of corned beef and tinned peaches they received Whiskas and Winalot.

Saturday 21 October

After an exhausting trek round the local supermarket this morning, Kevin offered to help me put the shopping away. No wonder I can never find anything. And he is so inconsistent. He puts ketchup in the fridge and brown sauce in the cupboard. Come on, condiments should be served at room temperature – everyone knows that!

'Ketchup belongs in the cupboard, next to the cornflakes.'

'Of course it doesn't; it goes in the fridge.'

'Why?'

'My mum puts it in the fridge.'

I thought of Eloise and her hot pepper sauce that can strip the skin from the roof of your mouth, and realized it would probably explode if you didn't keep it in the fridge.

'Well, that's fine for your mum,' I said with just a hint of irritation, 'but I put ketchup in the cupboard.'

'It will go off.'

'No, it won't. It's got vinegar in it. Vinegar is a preservative.'

'It says here on the label, "Keep refrigerated".'

I had to admit, that was a bit of a blow. I muttered under my breath while continuing to unpack the rest of the shopping. I went to put the cucumber and tomatoes away only to discover the salad tray full of cans of lager.

'What's this?' My voice had shot up by two octaves.

'Beer.' He grinned sheepishly. 'The rest of the fridge was full. I had to put it somewhere.'

'Get it out of my salad tray. Beer is not salad.'

'It's got hops in it.'

'Out.'

He took the cans and went out of the front door. Incredible! How could anyone be such a slob? I would have to work on re-educating Kevin to wean him off his bachelor habits. Oh well, it could be worse. He could be dismantling a motorcycle in the dining room. I had more or less forgiven him until I opened the cheese compartment ... and found his socks.

Sunday 22 October

Nigel was preaching today. His sermon title was 'Christianity – Boring, Old-Fashioned and Irrelevant?' Halfway through I felt like shouting, 'It is, the way you preach it!'

Unfortunately, there wasn't even a *Church Organ* to relieve the monotony. Chrissie has obviously not managed to find a replacement for me. Perhaps I should offer to come in on Saturday mornings. I do rather miss it – the collapsing chair, the phone calls from the bishop's snooty secretary, the endless stream of parishioners complaining about something or other. On the other hand, perhaps not.

Monday 23 October

The children had PE today. I have never untied and re-tied so many shoelaces in my life. It's getting a little difficult to bend down now. A slightly dreamy child named Katrina had got rather carried away when getting changed. I heard a flurry of giggles, then Mrs Thomas' voice rang out, 'Katrina, dear, there's no need to take *all* your clothes off!'

Poor Katrina ran red-faced into the toilet and quickly re-garbed but refused to come out. As I sat there with a special teddy bear dressed as a fairy princess (the bear, not me), which normally sits on Mrs Thomas' desk and only comes

down for a hug under very exceptional circumstances, I discovered yet another duty of the Teaching Assistant – bribery.

Wednesday 25 October

Nipped into the supermarket on the way home from
work – yes, another 'ready meal'. Tom's *Cookery for Complete
Morons* hasn't made it off the shelf for the past fortnight. There
were rows of menacing costumes – witches, skeletons, devils
and Count Draculas. I know there will be sweet little children
(in most cases) inside the costumes, but it still made my flesh
crawl. I decided to buy a packet of the least repulsive-looking
sweets to give to any children that turn up on the doorstep to
avoid having the house or car egged. I wonder if Nigel will be
arranging another All Saints' Eve party this year.

Thursday 26 October

Had the afternoon off to see the midwife. All is well. I am
nearly twenty weeks. Hooray, I'm almost halfway there. Told
Kevin.
'Twenty weeks, is that all? You're less than halfway there!'

Friday 27 October

Today is a staff training day and so I don't have to go in,
and next week is half term. This is the life!

Monday 30 October

Decided to take this week to devote to relaxation and
pampering.
'Hmm! Fine for some,' grumbled Kevin as he braved the
dark wet morning and I snuggled down under the duvet with

another cup of tea and a magazine. *Babyworld* magazine proclaims 'New Baby, New You. How to renew yourself in mind, body and spirit during pregnancy'. It sounded right up my street. There are bits of me that could certainly do with renewing after bending double over those pixie-sized chairs and tying all those shoelaces. My back and feet are beginning to suffer, and my brain feels even more fuddled than usual. Must be the lack of chocolate. I feel I deserve a bit of pampering – and I've earned the money to pay for it! So I put on the only pair of trousers that still fit and my flattest sandals and set off for Tranquil Lagoon, the local giant 'retail experience'.

After an hour wandering around, I finally bought a pair of baggy black trousers with an elasticated waist that even my mother wouldn't wear on the grounds that they were too old-fashioned and a tee shirt that would have gone round Dawn French twice. I gave the flowery maternity frocks a wide berth. I may be 'breeding stock', but there's no way I'm dressing like Charity Hubble.

I rewarded myself with a milky latte with whipped cream (I still didn't dare risk the hot chocolate) and added caramel syrup. Calories – who cares? I could live on lattes with caramel syrup and my baggy pants would still fit.

On with the shopping – this was even harder on the feet than the teaching! I was browsing round Boots, oohing and aahing at the sweet little itsy-bitsy baby clothes and dreading the maternity bras and breast pumps. I decided I needed a new look, perhaps some jewellery or lipstick to draw the attention away from my mountainous boobs and rapidly expanding waistline to my face with its glowing complexion and flawlessly perfect skin. Actually, my skin looks dull and I've got acne for the first time since I was fourteen, but I'm going with what it says in the magazine. I bought a pillar-box-red lipstick to rival Chrissie's and some dangly silver earrings which were reduced to £6. Then I saw it: a huge sign which read 'New Colour – New You'. Underneath was a display of every kind of hair colour you could think of – from platinum blonde to raven black. Just what I needed. My highlights had faded and grown out, and I was back to my usual mouse. Now what colour would the new me be, Riotous Red or Dazzling Damson? In keeping with my new impetuous, emotional personality, I decided to go for something with a reddish tint – Confident Copper, in spite of sounding like a rather brazen police constable, seemed to sum it up. I grabbed a packet then ran to the checkout before I could be tempted to fritter any more of my hard-earned cash.

Seized by a compulsion I hastened home, flouting the speed limits in my rush to become confidently copper. Somehow I'd managed to convince myself that to change my hair colour was to change my life. Rebirthing by Garnier.

3:45 p.m.

I now have bright orange hair.

Tuesday 31 October, All Saints' Eve

Nigel has come up trumps, and Kevin is helping at the All Saints' Eve party. They decided to hold a mini Olympics to divert the local little darlings from their trick-or-treating. So far we have had only two groups of teenagers knocking at the door.

'Like yer hair! You look just like a pumpkin!'

I scowled at them, doled out the sweets, gave them an invitation and sent them off to St Norbert's to join in.

Pumpkin indeed!

NOVEMBER

Wednesday 1 November, All Saints' Day

Kevin came back full of it last night. They'd had over seventy children from the village, and there were no reports of vandalism or intimidation. Chrissie gave a talk about being 'a champion', Charity arranged some craft activities and Kevin and Nigel set up some games. Perhaps this is a way of getting Kevin to church. I can always hope …

Thursday 2 November

In spite of the fact that Kevin has nicknamed me 'Duracel', I am determined to continue with my self-improvement. Ariadne and I had arranged to go for a swim at the local leisure centre. I look and feel like Shamu's overweight cousin. I'm sure everyone is going to be staring at my midriff.

'Theo! Whatever have you done to your hair?' she asked, circling me, staring in astonishment.

'It's supposed to draw attention from my bump.'

'So would setting fire to your hat, but I wouldn't recommend that either.'

I gave her a withering look and put on my rather tight swimming costume. I've got a figure like Santa Claus but without the beard and red suit. I must buy a new swimsuit. I slid into the water as surreptitiously as possible and started to swim. Ariadne, who looks disgustingly sylphlike in comparison, came and joined me, and we chatted as we swam. I reached the deep end and dived in. I surfaced and trod water while I waited for Ariadne to catch up. I became aware of the people around me pointing and laughing. I felt sure they were exchanging *Free Willy* jokes.

'What's the matter with them?' I asked Ariadne.

'You are just great entertainment value,' she said with a laugh. 'If you weren't my sister, I'd hire you to cheer me up.' She pointed to the water around me. I realized I was swimming in a circle of orange water which spread out to a greenish tinge near the edges.

'My hair!' I screamed and doggy-paddled to the changing room with visions of emerging from the waters with green hair. Fortunately, the pool water had simply washed the colouring out, leaving my normal mousy colour. I'm probably paranoid, but when we'd got changed and gone for a coffee in the little restaurant, I could swear that everyone had started looking at my belly.

Saturday 4 November

It moved! I felt the baby move today. I called Kevin down from sorting out the spare room and got him to put his hand on my tummy. We stood silently for an eternity until I felt a little bubbling, hiccupping movement.

'Cool!' he said. 'It feels like it's about to burst out, just like the creature in *Alien*.'

Urrgggh!

Sunday 5 November

Since I left the church office, the standard of *The Church Organ* has reached a new low. I don't know who is doing it now, but the spelling, grammar and content are all over the place. I don't wish to sound critical, but I've a mind to offer to at least cast an eye over it on Saturday mornings.

This week alone we were treated to a note from the WI asking for furniture to be donated for their pensioners' afternoon teas.

'The Women's Institute would like to request some more small tables as they are growing so fast.'

Monday 6 November

After fireworks poems, Guy Fawkes videos and 'Remember, remember ...' poems all day at school, I'd had just about enough 'gunpowder, treason and plot' for one night. Kevin invited his mates and got together his usual selection of fireworks to let off in the back garden. I opted to stay indoors on the pretext of making sure the budgie didn't get frightened. It was a great excuse to stay in the warm in front of the television. I agreed to check occasionally on the baked spuds and bangers that were sizzling away in the oven. Unfortunately, our tiny lawn is rather smaller than Kevin's mum's garden, so there wasn't as much distance to retire after lighting blue touchpaper. I glanced out of the window to see Kevin, Kev 2 and Jez standing in the smoky drizzle. Kevin had just put a match to a particularly evil-looking rocket when it started fizzing, spinning and twisting itself out of the piece of tubing and launched itself up the garden towards the house. The three men stood frozen to the spot for a moment, then I heard Kevin yell, 'Run!' They dashed towards the house, the three of them becoming wedged in the doorway like some very bad slapstick comedy. They fell through the door, slamming it shut behind them. There was a terrific explosion from the back garden. The glass door shook, and I could see a shower of sparks. Kevin was trembling slightly, and Jez had gone completely white.

'He, he, he. That was amazing!' said Kev 2, laughing. 'Can we do it again?'

'No,' I said firmly.

I stood there with my arms folded. 'I prefer my house in one piece, thank you very much.'

They stood there like scolded children.

'Can't we have our sausages and potatoes?' asked Jez.

'Afraid not,' I said. 'Bangers, of both kinds, are off.'

It was at that point that Kev 2 and Jez decided to go home.

Tuesday 7 November

Went outside this morning to discover there were scorch marks up the door, and the garden gnome that Auntie Dilys gave us as a wedding present had been decapitated. When I say decapitated, the poor little chap had actually been truncated just below the knees, and all that remained in the flower bed were his little blue wellies. The rest of his body lay under the bird-bath. He was still smiling and still clutching his little fishing rod. I shall have to ask Kevin to cement him back together.

Wednesday 8 November

Decided to have another sort through the papers from St Norbert's and add some more to my scrapbook. I started making piles of the papers, one for each decade, then sorted through the best stuff and started to stick it in. My eye was drawn to an old copy of the *Sidcup Herald* from 1962. The headline read: 'Former Striker Finds God'. The story was about a professional footballer who had renounced his sex, drugs and rock 'n' roll lifestyle when he became a Christian. A photograph with the caption 'From Striker to Server' showed a young man in a server's robes but with a quiff and long side-boards – and a very familiar-looking face.

I took the paper to the window to study the photograph better. There was no mistake. It had to be him. The article read,

> Saint Norbert's church celebrates with a celebrity addition to its team. Former three-times-capped striker Jerry Wedgwood's lifestyle has been transformed overnight after attending a gospel rally by well-known evangelist Bobby J. Milligan. After quitting while at the peak of his career, Wedgwood (27) claims to have 'no regrets' about the decision. Wedgwood reportedly sold both his houses and all of his cars after having a 'dream' from God, donating his fortune of tens of thousands of pounds to the Church. When asked if he'd consider re-joining the world of professional football, Wedgwood remarked, 'I've had my share of fame and fortune. Now I want to live quietly and follow Christ.'

Unbelievable! Jeremiah Wedgwood a professional footballer!

Thursday 9 November

Nigel Hubble came round to talk to Kevin about 'a little proposal' today. When he arrived he handed me his coat, ordered a cup of tea and shut the lounge door. It was obvious he didn't want me to hear their discussion. How dare he! This is *my* home, and Kevin is *my* husband. I have a right to know.

I could hear their muffled voices from the next room, but I couldn't make out what they were saying. My curiosity had got the better of me, and I had to find out what they were talking about. I tried the subtle approach – bringing in cups of tea, biscuits and serviettes. Then I tried feeding the budgie, pretending to look for books, even dusting. That didn't work. They just sat in silence whenever I was in the room. I gave Kevin a pleading look, but he just shrugged. I went out to the garden and fiddled with the dustbins. I peered through the window. There was a crack in the curtains, and I could see Kevin listening and nodding as Nigel spoke. I pressed my face against the glass. Kevin spotted me and waved me away.

I decided on the more direct approach. I marched purpose-fully in and settled down in the big armchair. Nigel and Kevin just stared at me.

'Oh, don't mind me,' I breezed. 'Just carry on.'

'You don't object to Theo being here, do you?' Kevin asked.

'Actually, I'd prefer it if she wasn't.' He looked at me. 'If it's all the same to you.'

'Oh, okay,' I said meekly and went back to the kitchen where I belonged. Truth is, I did mind. I minded very much. Why did I let him treat me like that in my own house? Why didn't I just refuse to leave? How dare he! Why didn't Kevin stand up for me?

I was still fuming when Kevin brought the empty cups into the kitchen.

'It's all right. You don't need to use a glass to listen through the wall any more – he's going,' Kevin said. I sheepishly put the glass back in the cabinet.

'Couldn't hear anything through these walls anyway.'

He gave me a hug.

'So what was he talking to you about that wasn't fit for my womanly ears? Was he sharing the secret of his great fertility, or was there some kind of Stepford Wives initiation going on?'

'Nothing like that. He just asked me what I thought of the idea of starting up a St Norbert's football team. Following the success of the games on All Saints' Eve, he thought it might be a good activity for the kids in the village. Apparently the vicar is all in favour.'

'A football club! Is that all? Why didn't he want me to hear?' I was incredulous.

Kevin shrugged. 'You know what Nigel is like.'

All that effort, and they were just talking about football!

Friday 10 November

Yet another Teaching Assistant duty to add to the list – wildlife relocator. Mrs Thomas was talking to the children about Florence Nightingale and Mary Seacole when a kerfuffle broke out on one side of the classroom. The children dashed over to see the cause of the fuss while Mrs Thomas carried on bravely, trying to regain their attention. Eventually, she too gave up and came over to see what was wrong. There, making a web between two desks, was a spider. It wasn't a particularly big spider or a particularly fierce-looking one, but it might as well have been a funnel-web for the commotion it was causing. Ashley had turned deathly pale, Parvesh was hiding under the computer desk and Junior wanted to know if he could pull its legs off.

'Would you mind?' Mrs Thomas indicated the spider.

I found a jam jar and a history book, scooped up the offending arachnid and carried it carefully towards the window.

'Can't we keep it?' called out Mei. 'We could name it "Incey-Wincey" and it could catch all the flies in the classroom.'

'No, dear, it's a wild animal. It needs its freedom,' replied Mrs Thomas.

'Oh please, can it stay? We could keep it in a cage,' suggested Katrina.

'It would escape through the bars and run away,' said Manny.

'Not if I pulled its legs off,' said Junior.

I opened the window and dropped the little creature out. The children ran over and watched as it scuttled across the playground.

Natalie waved it goodbye, wishing it a safe journey. At last Mrs Thomas could resume her history lesson. Without missing a beat she pronounced, 'Right, a little change of plan here. Now let me tell you the story of Robert the Bruce.'

Later, when the children were writing and drawing their own version of the story, she drew me to one side.

'Thanks for removing our little friend, dear,' she whispered. 'Anyone would think they'd never seen a spider before!'

'First rule of the classroom,' she said. 'Spiders, wasps, ants, dogs – anything with more legs than you – is automatically more interesting than you.'

Saturday 11 November

Tried on my old swimming costume today. It hardly covered my rear, and the front pulled so tight it looked rather obscene. Ariadne wants us to go swimming again on Monday evening, so I will have to buy one. I guess that means another trip to Tranquil Lagoon.

Rummaged through the 'end of season' lines in Debenhams. To my amazement there was a rather vivid lime-green maternity costume with thin olive green stripes. Not a colour scheme I would have chosen, but it was reduced to only £5. As it was in the seconds basket, I thought I ought to check with the rather superior-looking shop assistant that it wasn't going to unravel or turn transparent as soon as I got into the water.

'Um, this was in the seconds basket. I just wondered if there was anything wrong with it.'

'Wrong with it? Wrong with it?' sneered the assistant, looking as if she wouldn't even deign to blow her nose on it. 'It's lime green, that's what's wrong with it!'

2 p.m.

Kevin came home raving about the football. Apart from the usual selection of Hubbles, eighteen youngsters from the village turned up on the green. Nigel and Kevin were overwhelmed.

'I tell you, love, if this keeps up, I'm going to need some help.' He looked me up and down. 'How are your coaching skills?'

I gave him a withering look. He was joking – I think.

Sunday 12 November, Remembrance Sunday

Now the dwelling of God is with men, and he will live with them.
They will be his people, and God himself will be with them and
be their God. He will wipe every tear from their eyes. There will
be no more death or mourning or crying or pain, for the old order
of things has passed away.

(Revelation 21:3–4)

Monday 13 November

Went swimming with Ariadne and little Phoebe after school. Time to test out the new costume. Ariadne burst into peals of mirth when I emerged from the changing room.

'Well,' she said, looking me up and down, 'that's the first time I've ever been swimming with a giant gherkin!'

Tuesday 14 November

Woke up in the middle of the night with one of those mad thoughts that sneaks past the barriers of sanity in that twilight zone between being asleep and being awake. The idea was that perhaps Kevin could ask Jeremiah Wedgwood, who was, after all, an ex-professional, to help him out on Saturday afternoons. I could see Jeremiah and Kevin getting on about as well as Popeye and Bluto, but experience tells me that God sometimes puts the unlikeliest people together. After all, it was Charity, the British Martha Stewart, who helped Ariadne through her post-natal depression. I have decided to pray about it before I suggest it to Kevin.

Dozed off on the sofa in front of *Match of the Day*. I've read that it is common for pregnant women to have vivid and bizarre dreams, but I had the strangest dream that I was watching a match where both teams were made up entirely of Jeremiah Wedgwoods. The commentary was certainly odd:

'Wedgwood passes to Wedgwood, who gains possession. Ooh, a tackle there from Wedgwood; it was a nasty one, but the referee has allowed it. He clears ... he passes to Wedgwood ... he shoots ... he scores ...'

I woke up with the unpleasant image of a dozen Jeremiah Wedgwoods hugging and kissing each other in celebration. The Bible is full of occasions where God speaks to people through dreams but they are always sensible things like thin and fat cows, wheels within wheels or the Four Horsemen of the Apocalypse, not footballing fundamentalists.

Perhaps I should set up a little test to see if the idea really is from God. I know – if I bump into Jeremiah Wedgwood in the next week, it is a sign that God wants me to talk to him.

Thursday 16 November

Got home from work to find a letter with a Greek postmark. I had a cup of tea and waited until my hands had stopped shaking before I opened it. It was from Diana. Quite a short letter considering the impact. It said that she had been doing a lot of thinking lately and was not sure that Christianity was the right thing for her. She went on to say:

> I have tried so hard to be like you, Theo, and have
> faith in God like you have, but it is just too much of a
> struggle. The house church has disbanded, although I'm
> still in touch with Brad and Lori. It's as if I'm waiting for
> something to happen, to feel different, but nothing ever
> happens and I still feel the same disgusting, contempt-
> ible old me.

> Well, there you have it. I don't want you to feel sorry for
> me or blame yourself in any way. You're a good friend
> to me, Theo, and I hope that won't change. I just have
> to be honest.

> Love to Kevin and congratulations on the baby.

... and she signed off. Poor Diana. The truth is I do blame myself. I kicked her when she was down. What am I, some kind of anti-missionary who goes up to Christians and un-converts them?

I was still crying when Kevin came in. He hugged me and said, 'God's got a way of hanging on to those people he wants to keep. Don't worry about how it seems now. Things can change.'

Don't worry! Don't worry, when I'm a good candidate for the role of Antichrist! How can he say that?

Friday 17 November

I was in such a state that I wasn't looking properly when I crossed the High Street on the way to the vicarage to see Chrissie about Diana and narrowly avoided getting run over by a red sports car. Chrissie reassured me that in interviews for the post of Antichrist, I wouldn't get past the initial application.

'She's obviously lonely. How do you think that you would have coped over the last year without us, your chums, around you? Anyway, she didn't say that she'd stopped believing in God, just that she couldn't keep up with being a Christian. Don't you ever get days like that?'

'Weeks, more like!'

'And it's easier for you. You've been a Christian for so long that you don't really have a life to go back to. She does. It is good that she's thinking and being honest with herself.'

'What if my Mrs Tact and Diplomacy act over her abortion was the thing that pushed her over the edge?'

'What if it was? The worst it could have done is to make her face up to some things she needs to get sorted out. These things can mess you up if you don't deal with them, and I should know.' She looked as if she was about to cry again. 'You need to write back and encourage her. Just be a friend. She doesn't blame you ...'

'She said that she didn't want me to blame myself. Not quite the same thing.'

'Maybe not, but she still wants to keep up the friendship. Write to her. Encourage her. Love her.'

Saturday 18 November

Kevin came home from football shattered today. He was covered from head to toe in mud and exhausted from running from group to group supervising all the children. His old knee injury was playing him up, and as he shoved his kit into the washing machine and headed off for his shower, he said, 'We've got to do something, Theo. We had thirty-five kids today.'

I decided to tell him about Jeremiah. I can't wait any longer for a sign. Sometimes God just needs a gentle nudge in the right direction.

Sunday 19 November

Snuggled up in bed before church this morning, I decided to tell Kevin that Jeremiah Wedgwood had a secret past.

'Jeremiah who?'

'You know, looks like an undertaker ... watery eyes ... "The end of the world is nigh ..." You must have met him when he used to go to St Norbert's. He probably informed you that you were on your way to eternal judgement and damnation and may have offered you a bag of potatoes.'

'I don't remember him ...'

'You must have come across him at Miss Chamberlain's funeral.'

'Which pub does he drink in?'

'He doesn't.'

'Which team does he support?'

'I don't know.'

'What car does he drive?'

'I don't know!' I was beginning to get exasperated, when it hit me – well, narrowly missed me. 'Yes, I do! He drives a little red sports car!'

'1976 MG MGB V8 roadster, tartan red with black leather trim and alloy wheels? I know him. Great car!'

I proceeded to show him the newspaper cutting and suggested that we try to get in touch through the vicar of St Umfridus'.

Monday 20 November

I am getting bigger by the minute. The clothes that fitted yesterday are too tight today. Even my feet seem to be growing. I have a definite 'bump' now, if I stand in a certain way, and people are starting to pat it. Why do they do that? I am not public property! If this carries on, I'll have to think about taking up residence in Pets Corner at the local zoo.

I will be twenty-four weeks pregnant at the end of this week – nearly six months. If the baby was born from now onwards, he or she would have a chance of surviving. I just hope it doesn't come yet. I'm not ready. I haven't even bought a rattle.

Tuesday 21 November

Mrs Williams, the lady I am replacing, will be off for another two weeks, and Mrs Thomas has asked me to stay on. Even though I am getting very tired in the evenings and my back aches from sitting in those small chairs, I would actually miss the children.

I was helping Nisha write about her family when I was called away to help Marcus, who was finding it difficult to cope in the role-play area. I returned to find that Nisha had written this:

In my family there are six peeple. My mum is nice and fat. She has brown hair and brown eyes. She is very pritty.

She works at the hopital. My dad is tall and sometimes grumpy. My mum says he makes smells in bed. He plays with me to cheer him up. I have two brothers Bharat who is ten and Ravi who is two. Bharat is nice. He only punches me jently. My dad works in a sticky place. I don't know what he does there. When he comes to get me at home-time. He sais don't hug me Im all sticky. My granny lives with us to. She is very old and has ~~dench denjur~~ teeth that come out at night. I love my family becus they are very very very nice.

I've met Nisha's family, and she's absolutely right.

Thursday 23 November

Kevin went to see Jeremiah after work today. To my amazement, Jeremiah has agreed to help out with the coaching. I found some details of his career on the Internet, and Dad says he can remember him playing. I can't quite take it in. You think you know someone …

Friday 24 November

Went for dinner with Kevin's mum. I was rather surprised when the door was opened by a very tall man with a deep, booming voice and bottle-bottom glasses. He shook my hand, and Kevin introduced him as Brother Moses. I remembered him as the man we'd seen in the garden last year. Eloise explained that he was an elder at her church and she thought it would be nice for us to meet properly. Kevin behaved as if he was dining with his headmaster. He even called him 'sir' when he asked Kevin to pass the callaloo.

I was beginning to get a bit fed up with being called 'Sister' Theodora, so I resorted to the pregnant woman's prerogative

and claimed a few twinges. The situation was even more difficult because it was obvious that Eloise not only liked him a lot
but desperately wanted us to like him too. I found him pomp-
ous and irritating, and Kevin looked terrified of him.

'I have the horrible feeling your mum is getting serious
with Brother Moses,' I said when we were back in the car.

'You don't think it's *that* serious, do you?'

'She was very keen for us to get to know him, and the gossip will start if he keeps going round to her house. I wouldn't
be surprised if they announced their engagement soon.'

'If he's an elder, he'll have to be a married man.' Kevin
looked disgusted.

'You don't think she's having an affair, do you?'

'Of course not,' he snorted. 'He's probably a widower.'

'What's the problem, then? Why don't you like him?'

'He's just so different from Dad. I can't imagine her with
someone else.'

'I think he will treat her well, and he's obviously smitten.'

'I'm just a bit worried. You see, Dad left her quite well
off. Oh, she never spends it – we were still using the backs of
envelopes for notepaper, and she always darned my socks until
there was more darn left than sock. She's got it all stashed
away in the bank. "For a rainy day," she used to say. Well, it
never rained that hard, so with her pension and her job and no
mortgage or expenses and my wages coming in' – he pursed
his lips and puffed out his cheeks – 'she must be worth over
half a million, not including property.'

'What property?'

'As well as the house, she's got an apartment near Port
Antonio that Grampa left her and a flat in Spain that Dad
bought before the timeshare thing kicked in.'

'So what are you saying, that Moses is after her for her
money?'

He looked at me over a pair of imaginary glasses. 'Why else?'

'You cynic! She's an attractive lady, independent, outgoing, popular.'

'Exactly, so why does she need him?'

'They could be in love.'

He looked away and started the engine.

'Well, they could,' I protested. 'Not everyone thinks like you. You really should give him the benefit of the doubt. Anyway, it's her life and her money ...'

'And for all we know, he could be lying in wait until he can get his hands on it. I told you, she really is a little gold mine.'

I shook my head. 'Why did you never tell me all this before?'

'I wanted to be sure you weren't marrying me for my money.'

Now there's a thought ...

Saturday 25 November

We started clearing the spare room so that Kevin could make it look more like a nursery than a walk-in glory hole. I finished sorting through the papers and documents and finally assembled the scrapbook. I will present it to Chrissie tomorrow. Then I helped Kevin paint the whitewashed walls a sunny shade of primrose yellow.

By lunchtime I was in need of some fresh air, so I decided to go with Kevin to his football club on the village green. I could always walk back up the hill if I got too cold standing there. I pulled on my boots and to my horror found that my heavy winter coat wouldn't do up around my middle. I borrowed a couple of Kevin's jumpers instead, which just made me look fat.

I helped Kevin unload the footballs and cones from the van while Nigel got the youngsters warmed up with a jog around the field; then I settled myself in a slightly more sheltered spot near some trees. I was just wishing I'd brought a flask of steaming coffee when a red MG pulled up, leaving two brown scars across the grass. A familiar figure climbed out of the driving seat. Tall and gaunt as ever, he made an unlikely professional footballer. I watched, fascinated, as he started to remove his long black greatcoat and trilby to reveal a vivid scarlet tracksuit. He folded his coat carefully and laid it on the passenger seat with his hat on top. He took out some folded pieces of paper and tucked them into his tracksuit pocket. The biting wind whistled across the scrubby grass. Jeremiah removed a handkerchief the size of a tea towel from his pocket and dabbed at his eyes and nose, then he began warming up, stretching his legs and twisting his torso. He was mid-twist when he spotted me and jogged over.

'Ah, Miss Llewellyn. It's been a long time.'

'It certainly has, and I'm not Miss Llewellyn any more. I got married in June. You've met my husband, Kevin.' I waved across the field. Kevin put down the cones he was carrying and waved back.

'Indeed, indeed.'

'It's very good of you to help out, Jeremiah. Kevin has told me how much he appreciates your input.' I tried to smile, but an icy blast froze my lips into a sort of grimace.

'So you've been married since June, have you? Was it a hastily arranged wedding?' He glanced at my midriff.

'Yes, it was rather.' I laughed. 'You see, what happened was ...'

'I fully understand. Relentless lasciviousness will always have its way.' He turned around and started to walk towards his car.

'Hey, just a minute!' I called at his back. 'I don't like what you're insinuating here.'

He turned back and shouted, 'You young people today. I don't care about your complete lack of morals; it's just when you dress it all up and parade it as Christianity ...' The wind stole the end of his sentence. He unlocked his car and climbed in. I stood there open-mouthed as he drove away. Kevin loped over to me.

'Where's he going?'

'I don't know. We were having a chat, and suddenly he started prattling on about morals and stomped off.'

'What did you say to him?'

'Nothing! Honestly!' Kevin looked at me suspiciously.

I stormed home, my cheeks blazing with anger and the cold. How dare he?

After the football finished, Kevin came in, and I was still fuming. Kevin looked at me and went to pick up the phone. I wrenched the receiver out of his hand and slammed it down.

'Hey, calm down. I was just going to give Jerry a ring to see if I can sort out this misunderstanding.'

'Misunderstanding? It was not a misunderstanding. He was suggesting – no, implying – no, insinuating – oh, whatever the word is that is stronger than insinuating but not quite declaring – that ours was a shotgun wedding.'

'It's an easy mistake to make.'

'No, it isn't!' I was ranting now. 'I'm amazed you can take the way he's insulted me so calmly. We did everything by the book, and now he's dragging our reputation through the mud.'

I paced the floor, tears burning down my cheeks with the injustice of it all. 'And of course he won't keep his thoughts to himself. Oh no! It will be all round the village.'

'Well, if anyone asks, you can tell them what's what.'

'But they won't ask, will they. They'll just assume ...'

'Does it really matter?'

'Yes! It matters to me. I want you to go round there and put him straight. Use violence if necessary, but let him know that he can't get away with insulting us like that.'

'It was you he insulted. You go and sort him out.'

Some kind of roar, something primeval, came from deep inside me as I put my hands in the small of Kevin's back and literally pushed him out of the door.

He came back rather sheepishly about twenty minutes later.

'Well, did you explain?'

'I don't think he believed me. He's decided he isn't going to help on Saturdays any more. Something about "unevenly yolked". So I guess it's back to square one. Just Nigel and me again.'

Sunday 26 November

Kevin and I had made up by bedtime. It's just impossible to win with the poisonous Jeremiah Wedgwood. Fumed all the way to church but did my best to forgive him before Communion. It just makes it feel as if there was no point in waiting until we were married. We might as well have gone ahead and slept together. After all, most people do, but as Kevin said, we wanted to make the first time special. I suppose we know, and God knows, and that's all that matters.

Monday 27 November

Mum rang me to ask if we had chosen a name for the baby yet. To be honest, I haven't even thought about it. I don't know what she was angling for. I reminded her that Ariadne had already stated quite clearly that we didn't want 'ridiculous Greek names or silly Welsh ones'.

'I'm aware of that.' She sounded rather hurt. 'I wouldn't interfere; you know me.'

Yes, I thought, only too well, and I wasn't intending to name the baby Doreen after Mum or Dai after Dad either.

'We're sort of keeping it a secret, until after the baby's born,' I said.

Such a good secret that even Kevin and I don't know.

Wednesday 29 November

Sent a silly e-mail to Diana today, just one of those that were doing the rounds. Added a little attachment to say that I was thinking of her and left it at that. She sent back an e-mail full of smilies, so I guess she is feeling a bit better.

I still haven't got to the bottom of why Chrissie was so upset. I know she doesn't have to tell me, but I thought in some sort of pre-adolescent way that we were best friends.

Thursday 30 November, St Andrew's Day

Ariadne has been nagging me for weeks to drop into the office where I used to work, if not to lay some ghosts to rest (I did leave under a cloud), then to parade my pregnancy. I didn't need their rotten job. I had my own little manufacturing operation going on. There was to be no questioning my productivity.

I had a nine-thirty hospital appointment for a check-up and more blood tests, so I asked the head teacher for the rest of the day off as unpaid leave, intending to go straight from the hospital up to London to meet Ariadne for lunch.

The wait at the hospital was interminable, so I got to the bistro rather late. I found Ariadne sitting at a table tapping her foot and flicking furiously through the *Guardian*.

'Where have you been?' she snapped.

'You know where I've been.'

'And it took that long?'

'Yes!'

She seemed to calm down a bit. 'And how was your journey?'

'What is this, a job interview?'

'Sorry. Actually, I have been interviewing all morning. Is it that obvious?'

My look must have said it all, because she took my hand and squeezed it. 'I truly am sorry. How are you?'

'Do you really want to know about my journey? The train ...'

'Not particularly,' she interrupted. 'I want to know how you are. Are you over the morning sickness yet?'

'I've not really had morning sickness; it's just this terrible feeling when I smell chocolate. In fact, I don't even need to smell it; just seeing a bar in the newsagent's sets me off. Or even a chocolate advert on television. Just talking about it now makes me feel quite ...'

'WELL, DON'T TALK ABOUT IT, THEN!'

'All right. Just calm down. What is the matter with you? You're more crabby than a seafood platter.'

'It's work. It's got me all tense. I'm sorry. I shouldn't be biting your head off.' She took a deep breath. 'We're having – well, they're calling it a restructuring. That's why I've been interviewing. There are rumours of redundancies here and an office move to Paris. Quite frankly, I feel as if I'm fighting to keep my job.'

'But that's terrible!'

'You're telling me. Poor Tom is terrified he's going to have to go back to work, and I'm terrified I'm going to get stuck at home.'

'Could you get another job?'

'Trouble is, it's a bit specialist. Six months ago I was getting head-hunted left, right and centre, but now ...' She let out a loud sigh. 'I've followed up a few contacts, but nothing yet.'

I smiled feebly. 'I know of a nice Teaching Assistant job, if you want it.'

She squeezed my hand. 'Don't worry about me, Theo. Something will turn up.'

༺༃༻

It was nearly three o' clock by the time I reached my old office. I was astonished to find the third floor almost deserted. It was unlike Myrna Peacock to leave so early. Her office door was open, and her chair was tucked neatly underneath her desk. Her in-tray was empty, and there were half-full cardboard boxes all around. I went back to where my beloved slogbrot, 'a rhapsody in light ash with azure faux-leatherette cushioning', had stood. All that was left were four little dents in the carpet and a worn patch where I used to scoot up and down between my desk and the coffee machine. Most of the filing cabinets that had formed a wall down the centre of the office had also disappeared. One person I didn't know sat mournfully in the former 'gossip factory' of the accounts department. I went up behind him and coughed politely. He ignored me, staring out of the window and muttering to himself.

'Excuse me,' I said, coughing a little louder. It was only when he spun round I realized he was talking on one of those attachments on his mobile phone. He pulled out the earpiece and said, 'Can I help you?'

'Yes, have you seen Mrs Peacock? I think she still works here.'

'Ummm ...' he scratched his chin thoughtfully. 'She's probably up a floor doing some filing. Would you like me to ring up?'

'No thanks. I'll go and find her.'

Myrna filing! The only filing she did when I was there was her nails. I entered the elevator and pressed the button for the fourth floor. The doors dinged open, and I came face-to-face with Myrna carrying armfuls of files.

'Oh! Theodora Llewellyn! What are you doing here?'

'Just visiting. I was up in town, so I thought I'd pop in and say hello.' I tried to make it sound as casual as possible. Things had obviously changed a lot in the last seven months, and Myrna was bound to be rather sensitive about the fall of her empire.

'Come back down and have a coffee. I don't think the machine's been packed yet.'

We settled ourselves back in the bleakness of Myrna's office.

'So what's new?' I knew it! I just knew it! The place would fall apart without me! As Jeremiah would say, "I call this place Ichabod – the glory has departed."

'We're moving,' she said brightly. Stating the obvious, I thought, glancing around.

'Oh, where are you moving to?'

'Umm ... Rickmansworth,' she said, swallowing hard. 'It's really very nice there. Watford's good for shopping ...'

I managed to restrain myself from punching the air. This was comeuppance indeed.

'And Covenant Blake, is he still here, or has he gone to Rickmansworth too?'

Covenant Blake – Super-Christian! He probably named and claimed my desk as well as my job. I really can't believe he used to say grace before drinking his coffee.

'Er, no. He left not long after you did. He got "the call" and went off to do something or other in Kathmandu.'

Poor Kathmandu, I thought.

She poured the coffee, and I told her my news. She made all the right noises and asked all the right questions.

We sat down near her desk, and she handed me some envelopes, one from the union, one from the Pay and Pensions Department, and two from an office supplies company.

'These came for you. I saved them in case they were important.'

They weren't, but I thanked her anyway.

'Oh, and someone rang up asking after you. I took his phone number and said I'd pass it on to you. I can't remember his name, Dermot or something ... Declan, his name was Declan.'

'That's right – used to work here.'

'Here's the number. Pity I didn't have yours to give him.'

'Thanks, that's fine.'

I took the number and shoved it in my pocket. I made my farewells and took the lift back to the ground floor. I held the piece of paper very tightly in my hand inside my pocket for a long time. Then I took it out, tore it to confetti and threw it in the nearest bin.

DECEMBER

Friday 1 December

Kevin has bought me a chocolate advent calendar. A lovely idea, but the smell of chocolate still makes me heave.

Sunday 3 December, Advent Sunday

Charity sidled up to me after church.

'You're looking well, Theodora.'

'Thank you. I'm feeling well.' My mind flitted back to the chocolate advent calendar. 'Mostly.'

'Remind me, when is the baby due?'

'Third week of March.'

'Fourteenth?'

'Seventeenth to be precise. Look, what is this all about?'

'Married life is suiting you well, I trust?'

'Yes, thank you. Charity, why all these questions ...?'

'And when did you get married, exactly?'

'Seventeenth of June.'

'Thanks.'

And she scuttled away and sat in one of the pews next to the choir stalls. My curiosity aroused, I crept up to the organ loft where Gregory Pasternak budged over mid-anthem to let me sit on the edge of his large wooden organ-stool. I peered into the little rear-view mirror that is strategically placed so the organist can see when members of the choir are picking their noses. I swayed and swivelled until I managed to see Charity in the mirror. She had a pocket calculator. She seemed to be trying to work something out ...

'No!'

The few people left in church looked up at the organ loft. Gregory stared at me horrified. I made my apologies and ran down the steps as fast as I could.

I half ran, half walked home, trying to hold back the tears. Jeremiah Wedgwood couldn't have started spreading his venom around the village already!

I don't know why it mattered so much, but it did. Kevin knew straightaway that something was wrong. I told him about Charity.

'And you wonder why I don't go to church! People like them make me sick! No one else would care less if we were married or not, only that bunch of so-called Christians. Hypocrites, that's what they are. How many single parents go there? How many pregnant teenagers, how many people struggling with their sexuality?'

I couldn't think of any that I knew. I shook my head.

'Is it any wonder? If they treat other Christians like this, what kind of welcome would there be for those who don't normally go to church? I don't know, talk about shooting your own wounded! Jesus didn't treat people like that, so why do they?'

I'd never seen Kevin like this before, not even when he was sounding off about a bad refereeing decision.

'They're not all that bad …'

He wasn't listening. 'And to think I actually took to that Jerry Wedgwood. It shows how wrong you can be!'

Monday 4 December

We have started preparations for the school nativity play. Most of the children want to be involved, even the ones whose parents follow other religions, which seems a bit odd. The only ones that opted out were the Turners, who live in a house called Somostusovejas for some reason, and who have started a church in their garden shed. They make the Hubbles look like a bunch of heathens. Apparently they don't 'do' Christmas because of its pagan origins. That's as may be, but I definitely saw Mrs Turner buying satsumas in Tesco's.

Mrs Thomas and I started to make a shortlist of children to play the various parts. I always thought it seemed a mite unfair that when I was at school, the little girls with long blonde hair got to play angels while their brunette counterparts ended up as shepherds or innkeepers. I once played second innkeeper's wife. I was relieved to find that all that has changed now and children of all races and both genders are bestowed a tinsel circlet and shiny wings and get to stand on tables pointing towards Bethlehem.

We decided to start with the main parts. We got the register and went through methodically, eliminating all the unsuitable children.

'Imran can't be Joseph – he picks his nose then eats it. Freddie's too shy, and Carlos – well, he's Carlos.' We eventually decided that Joseph should be played, coincidentally, by a boy called Joseph.

'Makes things easy. At least he'll know who we're talking to.'

'What about Hazel or Katrina as Mary?' I suggested.

'As long as Katrina doesn't burst into tears and run to hide in the toilets. She's been doing that a lot lately.'

We ended up having a discussion about Katrina's parents' rather acrimonious divorce and decided it would give her a little boost to be cast in the leading role.

After picking suitable 'wise persons', two male, one female, we turned our attention to the background artistes and sorted the shepherds from the goatherds.

Thursday 7 December

Saw a smug Charity Hubble in the playground this morning. Wanted to go up to her and shake her and shout, 'My child is legitimate,' but I managed to restrain myself. As Kevin said, I don't know why it's so important to me. It just is.

Perhaps I should put an announcement into *The Church Organ* to staunch the rumours once and for all.

> Kevin and Theodora would like to announce that their baby, due on 17 March, was conceived on their honeymoon. No shenanigans took place before their wedding night whatsoever.

That should do it.

7 p.m.

Unfortunately, Kevin didn't see it the same way as I did and banned me from putting the notice into the magazine.

'Let them think whatever they want. We know, and more importantly, God knows.'

Of course he's right.

Friday 8 December

The head teacher called me into her office as soon as I got in this morning. She told me that Mrs Williams will be off until the end of term and I am welcome to stay for the next couple of weeks. She told me that Mrs Thomas is delighted with me and if I want a job after the baby is born, I'll be first on their list. I felt quite emotional. Apart from my initial misgivings, I have loved working with the children – and the money has been very handy. I found out later that two other Teaching Assistants are off with the flu, so I really am indispensable.

We spent the afternoon making Christmas cards, and by home time there was more glue and glitter on the children, the furniture and the carpet than there was on most of the cards. As the children lined up with their lunch boxes, clutching their sparkly handiwork which was still shedding all over the floor, Mrs Thomas whispered, 'We've got to do something about all this glitter; the cleaners will be here soon.'

If the cleaner at St Swithun's Primary was anything like the cleaner at St Norbert's, we were in trouble. Any sort of mess is enough to send him into paroxysms of protest. I could never work that out. After all, if nothing ever got dirty, he'd be out of a job. After one particularly glittery Sunday school lesson, I remember helping Chrissie to sweep up the church hall before the cleaner came. We brushed and mopped and scrubbed, but the glitter just wouldn't budge.

'Oh well,' she said with a sigh, running glittery fingers through her hair, 'I shall just have to try to pass it off as a manifestation of the Holy Spirit.'

Saturday 9 December

Kevin went to a home match today so couldn't run the football club. Now that Jeremiah has left and Nigel has the flu, the club was cancelled. That didn't stop three little boys knocking on the door to ask if Kevin could come out to play.

Sunday 10 December

E-mail from Ag to say that he and Cordelia are coming back from Calcutta (I thought they were in South America) and that they have a surprise for us. I hate Ag's surprises. Last time he surprised us, it cost me a wedding present, a new outfit and a fortune in car repairs and cleaning bills, and ended up with me embarrassingly legless followed by a three-day hangover.

Monday 11 December

Weekly phone call from Mum tonight. After giving me the rundown of who has succumbed to this rather nasty flu outbreak, we had the usual 'what are you going to do for Christmas' conversation, and I rather rashly offered to host Christmas lunch. So it will be Mum and Dad, Ariadne, Tom and Phoebe, Ag and Cordelia, Kevin and me.

Oh my goodness! That's nine people to cook for. It will cost a fortune, and our dining room is minuscule. What have I done? We only have four chairs. Kevin will go ballistic!

Tried to break the news gently.

'Cool,' said Kevin. 'Can we invite Mum and Moses too? I'll cook.'

Whew! The only problem now is where to put them all. Eleven people – that's 2.75 people per chair.

Tuesday 12 December

Tried to go Christmas shopping after work today, but my back and feet ached, the stuffy, overcrowded shops made me feel faint and I needed the loo every twenty minutes. I was worried that I was coming down with this flu that seems to be doing the rounds, so I came home with just a pair of earrings for Cordelia and a tub of cashew nuts. I've been feeling faint rather a lot recently. If it's not flu, it must be a chocolate deficiency.

10 p.m.

Kevin has just ordered most of our Christmas presents and other necessities online. He even ordered some fold-up chairs. What would I do without him?

Wednesday 13 December

Feeling fine today until I got to work. Another rehearsal for the nativity play. As much as I love Christmas carols, if I hear Bethlehem pronounced 'Bef-lee-hem' one more time, I'm going to scream.

Thursday 14 December

Desperate visit from Chrissie tonight to ask me to attend a meeting in the vestry to help plan the Christmas services while she got home for an early night. After the interminable nativity rehearsals, the last thing I felt like was helping organize a carol service. Chrissie was looking so stressed that I took pity on her. This flu epidemic means that she is getting called out day and night to visit her ailing parishioners.

'Pleeeease help me sort out this service, Theo. I'll do anything. I'll ring the pope on his mobile phone and arrange immediate canonization.' She was practically on her knees.

'Okay, you get home to bed,' I said. 'When is the meeting?'

'Now,' she wheedled.

I patted her shoulder, jumped into my car and drove the 300 yards up the hill to church. I made my way into the vestry and sat down with Doris Johnson, Charity and Nigel just as the opening prayers finished.

There followed much discussion about what form the Christmas services should take. Nigel wanted to focus on the genealogy of Jesus, while Doris wanted to do the whole thing from the point of view of the donkey. Charity suggested re-enacting the flight to Egypt, which, we decided, would be rather difficult considering the width of the aisle and the position of the Christmas tree and the lectern, not to mention the font. It would be more of a 'carefully manoeuvre your way around obstacles to get to Egypt'.

Finally we settled on asking the playgroup and the Sunday school to make a nativity scene complete with the obligatory Holy Family, shepherds, innkeepers and animals, all made out of plasticine and cotton wool. We agreed we could display it in the hall and the parents could stop by after the carol service. Charity agreed to make the stable out of a shoebox, and Gregory offered to produce a 'starry night' effect with one of the glitter balls he uses for his mobile discos.

Friday 15 December

Kevin and I were 'summoned' to Eloise's house this evening. Kevin had said that his mum had sounded evasive on the phone. He looked uneasy as he washed and dressed in his best jeans and football shirt. When we arrived, it was Brother Moses who opened the front door, not Eloise, and I was starting to worry that she might be ill. I was relieved to find her in good health and smiling, albeit nervously. Her hair was neatly styled, and she was wearing a smart black dress and jewellery. She sat very upright in a chair, and Moses took up a position behind her with his hand resting on her shoulder. They looked as if they were posing for a Victorian photograph. Kevin looked terrified. Moses spoke first.

'Um, Kevin, I wonder if I might see you for a moment ... in the kitchen.'

Moses opened the door and ushered Kevin through. Kevin glanced back at me, and I gave him a reassuring wink. It felt more like a nervous twitch. Kevin trailed out into the hall, and Eloise jumped up and closed the door.

Eyes shining, she clasped my hands. 'Oh, darlin', he's only gone and aksed me to marry him.'

I feigned surprise. 'Oh, Eloise, that's wonderful news. When's the big day?'

'Boxing Day. We're goin' to honeymoon in Montego Bay, then we'll be living here until we can find a place to buy together.'

I hugged her and asked all the usual questions about dresses and flowers. I was just about to ask whether they needed a rather pregnant bridesmaid when the door swung open and Kevin stormed in.

'Come on. We're going, *now*.'

Too stunned to protest, I gathered up my bag, and Kevin half escorted, half dragged me to the car.

'What is the matter with you?'

'I told you this would happen. We've got to stop it.'

'Kevin, what has got into you?'

'That ... gold-digger!'

'Moses?' I laughed at the idea. A more upright person would be more difficult to imagine. 'Oh, Kevin, are you sure? I think he really loves her.'

'Oh, that's what he says. Smooth-talks his way into her life then cons her out of everything she has.'

'You've absolutely no evidence that he's not genuine. I can't believe you jumping to conclusions like this. You're normally so open-minded about other people.'

'Other people are not my mother.'

'Well, did you challenge Moses about it?'

'Of course not. What was I going to say? "Excuse me, Brother, but are you some kind of con artist who is trying to take my elderly, gullible, rich, widowed mother for a ride?" I could hardly do that, could I?'

'It would have been more honest than what you are doing now.'

'Look, I don't want to talk about it. She's not marrying him, and that's final!'

Tonight when we lay in bed you could have driven a bus between us. We certainly did let the sun go down on our anger.

Saturday 16 December

Went round to see Eloise while Kevin was at the match this afternoon. Fortunately, formidable Brother Moses wasn't there. It felt dishonest going behind his back, but I had to try to sort this out. Eloise was, quite understandably, upset and bewildered by Kevin's behaviour.

'It like the boy don't want to see me happy,' she wailed.

'It's not like that. He just feels very ... protective towards you. He doesn't want to see you get hurt.'

'But it's him who is hurtin' me. No one else.'

I could see I wasn't going to get much further without accusing Moses of being a swindler. She handed me a cream envelope. It was an invitation to their wedding at Rivers of Glory Church on Tuesday 26 December.

'Will you persuade him to come? It would make me so happy to have all mi children there on the big day.'

I hugged her. 'I'll do my best.'

Sunday 17 December

Kevin was still asleep when I got up to go to the carol service, so I couldn't tackle him about Eloise's wedding.

Before the service I went to see the crib scene. Apparently the idea had gone down brilliantly with the youngsters, and there in the hall was a rather rickety-looking shoebox with twigs glued to the outside of it and filled with straw. It looked as if the innkeeper had gone for the cheap 'self-assembly stable' and found that half the screws were missing. There was also a throng of multi-coloured plasticine people and animals. The sheer number made the Terracotta Army look like the annual picnic for agoraphobics anonymous. There also seemed to be several Holy Families, with four Marys and at least half a dozen baby Jesuses.

'I know,' giggled Doris, 'they just got a bit carried away.'

'And what about the sheep?' There were sheep in a spectrum of colours. 'Look!' I pointed. 'There's a purple one!'

'Ready-coloured sheepskin?' she ventured.

'But it looks silly,' I persisted. 'We can't have that on display. It's a special time, one of the holiest celebrations of the year, and what are we going to treat the congregation to? The Virgin Mary quads and purple sheep!'

'Nobody will mind. They know the children made it. After all, Christmas is for the children.'

So it went on display. Gregory had duly produced his mirror ball as requested, along with some multi-coloured disco lights that whirled and spun and changed colour.

It proved a great talking point; the ramshackle stable and the multitude of shepherds, innkeepers and other assorted hangers-on contributed to the atmosphere. That, coupled with the flashing illuminations and spangles of revolving light from the mirror ball, made it look like Bethlehem's most popular discotheque. All it needed was the Bee Gees' 'Night Fever' and the effect would have been complete.

Monday 18 December

No, Christmas isn't just for the children. It's for adults too! If we didn't have Christmas, we'd have to buy our own bath salts and novelty socks.

Tuesday 19 December

Last day of term and my last day at St Swithun's Primary. I was invited to the staff Christmas meal tonight, but I just need to go home and put my feet up. The nativity scene went relatively smoothly with the exception of Joseph and Mary having a little domestic over who was going to hold the baby Jesus. After the play and the carols, the PTA had provided mince pies and coffee. Little children kept coming up to me, hugging me and telling me how much they were going to miss me. They brought their parents up to introduce them to me. They gave me drawings, home-made cards – mostly with pictures of me with an enormous belly – and presents. I don't know if it is the hormones, but my eyes went all misty and I seemed to have a lump in my throat.

Wednesday 20 December

Mr Singh, the father of the woman who bought my old flat, came round today with a handful of Christmas cards and junk mail. I ditched the junk mail and opened the cards from people who hadn't updated their address books. To my consternation there was one from Declan. It was a dancing Santa and a penguin. The message read:

At Christmastime, bring in some cheer,
Serve up the food and pour out the beer.

It joined the junk mail in the bin.

Thursday 21 December

I invited Eloise to dinner tonight without telling Kevin. I was reluctant to go behind his back, but I felt I had to try to at least get them talking. After all, the wedding is only a few days away. Kevin's over-zealous concern for her welfare has continued all week, with each of my attempts to reason with him ending in either an argument or stony silence. At the end of the day, she's a grown woman and Kevin can't stop her marrying Moses.

He came in from work and, after washing his hands, walked into the kitchen where we were already eating.

'What's she doing here?' he spluttered.

I stood in front of the door so that he would have to rugby-tackle me to get past. Eloise looked hurt, but she took Kevin's hand and guided him to sit across the table from her. I stood by the door like a sentry, with my arms folded.

'Tell me, son,' she said gently, 'what's weighing on your heart?'

'Okay,' he said wearily. 'I don't like Moses, I don't trust him and I don't want you to marry him. That's all.'

'But why?' Tears welled up in her eyes. 'It like you trying to rob me of mi happiness.'

'It's not that, Mum. I just can't work out what's in it for him. All I know is that Dad provided well for you and you have Grampa's place in Port Antonio. He's got to be some kind of con artist.'

Eloise threw back her head and roared. 'Cha! Moses after me fer mi money!'

Kevin looked gobsmacked.

'Well, yes. Why else would he want to marry you?'

'Because he love me,' she said quietly.

'Well, he would say that. He's smooth-talked his way into your life, and as soon as he gets into your bank account, he'll be off, leaving you penniless and broken-hearted.'

Eloise sucked her teeth. 'What would it take to convince you?'

'Nothing. Nothing would convince me.'

'What if I told you that the hotel we going to for our honeymoon belongs to Moses?'

'He owns property in Montego Bay? Get out of here!'

'Not just in Jamaica. You know them new flats down by the river? Moses own them too. He rent them out. When the church needed new chairs, him just got out a chequebook an' write a cheque fer all the cost. I'm tellin' you, Brother Moses is a rich man. Now what you got to say?'

Kevin looked mortified. 'Sorry, Mum,' he mumbled. She looked at him over her glasses. He squirmed in his chair. 'No, I really am sorry. I jumped to the wrong conclusion about Moses and interfered in your life. I had no business, and I'm sorry.'

He sat there like a scolded puppy as Eloise stacked the plates in the sink, gathered her handbag and coat, and headed towards the front door.

'Now I expect to see you both at mi weddin' on Boxing Day all suited and booted an' with your church demeanour on. Do you understand me?'

'Yes, Mum,' he muttered again.

I hugged Eloise, and Kevin planted a dutiful kiss on her proffered cheek as she made her way out to the car where Moses was waiting to collect her.

'Did you see her kissin' her teeth at me like that? I was only trying to save her feelings.'

'Save her feelings? You told her in so many words that the only reason you could see for anyone wanting to marry her was for her money. She's an attractive woman. She spent years bringing you and Deyanna up on her own. Now you're both married off, it's her turn for a bit of life. Be happy for them.'

'Yeah, you're right, I suppose.' Kevin pulled me close and kissed me.

Friday 22 December

- ✓ make list
- ✓ shopping – wedding present for Eloise
- ✓ cleaning
- ✓ chop wood for fire
- ✓ wrap presents
- ✓ bed

In bed, I remembered that we haven't bought the turkey, the tree or the Christmas crackers yet. I've nothing to wear to the wedding, half the presents haven't arrived and although we now have enough chairs, they won't all fit in the dining room.

Saturday 23 December

Another day of running around sorting things out. I think we're finally ready. A fire is laid in the grate, and I've cleaned the house from top to bottom and aired the bedding in the spare room. Mum rang yesterday to ask if we could host Ag and Cordelia, as their guest room is taken up with freezers full of Aphrodite's Greek Delicacies. Not only has she expanded into Cypriot cuisine but has also just introduced a new range of vegetarian classics, replacing the lamb in the moussaka with soya, replacing the meat in the souvlaki with haloumi and presumably replacing the squid in the kalamari with rubber bands.

Ag and Cordelia arrived just before seven. After spending hours in the kitchen with Tom's book, I'd produced a very passable Toad-in-the-Hole followed by Spotted Dick to welcome them back to England. I hadn't had time to get changed out of my baggiest old joggers and one of Kevin's jumpers. I tidied my hair and brushed most of the flour off the jumper. It may not be the front cover of *Vogue*, but it's comfortable and it covers up my bump. I helped Kevin and Ag bring their luggage in from the taxi while Cordelia floated in on a wave of chiffon, announced that she was exhausted and asked for her meal to be brought to her on a tray.

'Poor thing,' said Ag. 'She found the flight rather gruelling. I'll settle her in, then I'll be down.' He disappeared up the stairs with a suitcase.

'Poor thing,' I echoed sarcastically. 'So she's been on a plane. She could at least say hello and eat with us.'

I served up the food, which didn't look as bad as I thought it would, and put Ag's and Kevin's on the table, left mine in the oven, and prepared a tray for Cordelia.

I struggled up the stairs and knocked on the bedroom door. Cordelia was sitting up in bed, wearing some kind of frilly bed-jacket. I began to wonder if I had misjudged her and she really was ill, but her bright eyes and healthy complexion didn't seem to substantiate it. She took one look at the tray and said, 'I'm sorry, Theodora, I can't eat this. Do you have something a little lighter? Perhaps some toast and Marmite?'

'I'll see what I can do,' I said and lifted the tray off the bedside table.

'Oh, leave the tray,' she said. 'I may just pick at it.'

I stomped back downstairs, where Kevin and Ag had already started eating.

'Where's the gravy, love?' Kevin asked.

'In the packet,' I growled and slammed some bread into the toaster.

I scraped what would seem an adequate amount of Marmite onto the toast and once more scaled the stairs. Cordelia's 'picking' had led to both the sausages, all of the potatoes and carrots, and most of the batter finding their way down Corde-lia's gullet. I delivered the toast rather unceremoniously into Cordelia's lap and turned to go.

'Oh, and do you have any tea? Preferably herbal.'

I grunted and went downstairs again, hoping that my meal hadn't been cremated in the oven while I was dancing attendance on Cordelia. I opened the oven and found it empty. Kevin and Ag had left the table and were slumped on the sofa in front of the television.

'Oi, where's my dinner gone?' I demanded.

'Oh, sorry, love,' said Kevin. 'We finished it off. I didn't realize you hadn't eaten. It was very nice. I think there's a little Spotted Dick left.'

'Well, thanks very much! Now would one of you make Cordelia some tea while I scrape together something I can eat?'

Ag jumped up and came out into the kitchen with me. He filled the kettle, and I found some camomile tea bags I'd bought once while on a health kick.

'Was she all right?' Ag asked.

'Seemed fine to me.' I slung some more bread into the toaster. Toast and Marmite would have to do me too.

'I've been worried about her, not sure if this trip would be too much for her.'

By now, all tact had departed. 'Why? What's wrong with her?'

'Oh, you'll find out on Christmas Day.'

I sat on my own in the kitchen and munched my toast and rock-hard Spotted Dick. I crawled up to bed, nursing indi-gestion, without saying goodnight to anyone and fell asleep wrapped in a big blanket of self-pity.

Sunday 24 December, Christmas Eve

Woke up feeling a little more charitable towards my nearest and dearest until I discovered that they had used all the bread, drunk all the milk and taken themselves off on a walk along the river. Kevin cooked me eggs and bacon to make up for last night, then rubbed my tense shoulders. It was while I was at his mercy that he reminded me that he, Ag and Tom were going to a football match this afternoon. 'It'll give you and Cordelia a chance to catch up.'

I tried to explain that I didn't want to catch up with Cordelia, that in fact all my instincts were telling me to run in the opposite direction. An afternoon alone with Wimbledon's answer to Alan Wicker was not my idea of fun. I rang Ariadne, who (bless her) invited us both over. She's a little more cheerful since the big shake-up in her company is over and she hasn't been shaken out. She even got a Christmas bonus. It turns out that she and Tom have done a substantial amount of preparation for tomorrow's meal to help me out.

Cordelia returned from her walk and had a little rest while I prepared sandwiches for lunch. Then Kevin and the others set off in his van, and I drove Cordelia to Ariadne's house. It was only when I got out of the car that I realized I was still wearing my baggy old clothes. Oh well, I needed to keep the only decent dress that fits me for Christmas Day and Eloise's wedding. Phoebe was toddling round, bringing us all in turn imaginary cups of tea in a red plastic tea set. She said, 'Ta,' every time she handed us a cup, and we said, 'Ta,' back. She also presented us with each of her teddies and cuddly animals and showed us how to hold them properly. She wore a denim dungaree suit and had her hair up in two bunches. She looked every inch a proper little girl.

After a relatively pleasant afternoon (I'm afraid to say that I dozed off in the middle of Cordelia telling Ariadne about their media project in India), the boys picked us up and we drove to the local Indian restaurant for a curry. Of course, Cordelia, who seemed to have regained her appetite, insisted on ordering in Bengali, which slowed us down considerably as the waiter had to keep asking her to repeat the order. I presume he didn't normally have to deal with a Wimbledon-Bengali accent.

I sidled up behind my brother and leaned over the back of his chair. 'Go on, Ag. What's the big secret?' I asked.

He tapped the side of his nose. Cordelia giggled. 'Wait until tomorrow,' he said.

After an excellent meal, I decided to brave an After Eight. I nibbled cautiously at the edge, and to my amazement it didn't make me feel too sick. Perhaps I'll be able to eat chocolate again – the best Christmas present ever.

Ag, Cordelia, Tom and Phoebe went home while Ariadne and I set off up the hill to the midnight service at St Norbert's. It is my favourite service of the year, and although I was tired, I didn't want to miss it. The air was crisp and clear, and the only sound seemed to be a muffled rumble of bonhomie coming from the nearby Red Lion.

St Norbert's was almost in darkness. We found seats in a pew near the pulpit. The only light came from the ushers' lanterns, which were reflected occasionally as a breeze caught them by the twinkling decorations on the Christmas tree. The air was tingling with expectancy. I could feel vigorous movements from the baby inside me. I pulled Ariadne closer and placed her hand on my belly. She grinned at me as she felt the kicks.

Then the ushers extinguished their lanterns. The church was in complete blackness. I heard the heavy oak doors swing open and felt an icy blast. I could just make out a child's voice singing 'O Come, O Come, Emmanuel', and I could see the flickering golden light of a candle. The rest of the choir followed, also carrying candles. The light and sound seemed to expand until the whole building was illuminated, and the harmonies echoed from the ancient stone walls as if centuries of praise were resounding in agreement. Chrissie followed at the back, the golden embroidery on her stole glimmering in the candlelight. The choir filed into the stalls as the organ thundered the last verse. As the sound died away, Chrissie stood on the altar steps and read from Isaiah 60: 'Arise, shine, for your light has come, and the glory of the Lord rises upon you.'

I remember singing 'O Come, All Ye Faithful' as Nigel and Roger lit the candles on the pew ends, soaking the church in liquid gold. I remember kneeling at the altar rail and receiving the Communion, but the combination of the late hour, my general weariness and the large meal meant I dozed through much of the rest of the service. It was only as Ariadne steered me out into the cold air that I woke up a little. Chrissie stood at the door, sniffing miserably. It looked as if she was succumbing to the flu bug.

'Well, I'm glad the service was so scintillating,' she snapped. I apologized, and she seemed to forgive me. I pushed a gift and a card into her hands, and she gave me a weary smile.

'Happy Christmas,' we said and both went home to bed.

Monday 25 December, Christmas Day

I woke up later than I'd intended, threw on a clean baggy jumper and joggers, and slouched downstairs to find Kevin wrestling with a turkey on the kitchen table. It was like Eric the Eel all over again. It turns out he was trying to stuff it with chestnut stuffing, and according to him, 'the stupid thing kept sliding all over the place', so I held it down while Kevin, elbow-deep in a turkey's backside, inserted the stuffing. Eventually he enveloped it in foil, put it on a tray and threw it into the oven. He slammed the door shut and leant against it as if he thought the turkey would fight its way out.

We decided to forgo church this morning, so we sat round the fire and took it in turns to open presents. I managed to jam all the chairs around the dining-room table, but it looks as if we are going to need to practise synchronized breathing. The turkey seemed to be cooking nicely, and Ariadne and Tom arrived just before eleven with Phoebe and a Christmas pudding. They also brought some ready-prepared potatoes for roasting and a huge tub of homemade brandy butter.

'Nice to see you made the effort and dressed up for us,' she said, glancing down at my shapeless apparel. I stuck my tongue out at her. As soon as I'd closed the door, Moses and Eloise arrived with gungo peas and yams. I rushed round taking coats, fetching drinks and putting the food in the kitchen. I took another tray of drinks through to the living room to see Cordelia sprawled in my favourite armchair and Ag on the floor next to her, rubbing her feet. Why did her feet need rubbing? As far as I could work out, she'd hardly used them since she'd been here.

'A little help with handing round peanuts would be nice,' I said, directing the comment at Cordelia.

'Oh, okay,' said Ag, getting up. I glared at her, but she didn't seem to notice. That woman is really annoying me. Would it kill her to help out a bit? I just about managed to resist the urge to strangle her with a piece of tinsel.

Mum and Dad arrived loaded down with presents, mezze and gliko. After several more rounds of drinks and trips to check the dinner and lay the table, I just wanted to go back to bed. Unfortunately, the turkey had other ideas, and at one o'clock we squeezed ourselves into the dining room and launched into the dolmades (or Koubebia) and Tzaziki before indulging in a more traditional main course. The conversation centred round Eloise's wedding. Once again, Cordelia didn't lift a finger to help while the rest of us bustled back and forth. I seemed to spend most of the time with my hands in the washing-up bowl. We had Christmas pudding, coffee and Glikis, and I was just planning to sneak off for a little nap while everyone else watched the Queen's speech and polished off the wine when Ag tapped his glass with his teaspoon. The conversation stopped, and Ag stood up – well, as near as he could get to standing up, as he couldn't push his chair back far enough to fully straighten his knees.

'I have an announcement to make. Firstly, I'd like to thank my lovely sister, Theodora, and her not quite so lovely husband, Kevin, and everyone else who contributed to this wonderful repast.' Everyone murmured their approval and applauded politely. 'Secondly, I would like to congratulate Moses and Eloise on their big day tomorrow and wish them health and happiness.'

'Don't do it,' called Dad. 'It's not too late to change your mind.' Mum kicked him under the table, and everyone laughed, even Moses.

'Finally,' continued Ag, 'I have the delightful duty to announce that Cordelia and I are pregnant! The baby is due in August.'

Everyone started to congratulate Ag and Cordelia and, as it was too cramped to get up, blew kisses across the table. They were all asking how she was feeling, and she sat there glowing and gestating like a Botticelli Madonna. I felt as if I was going to explode with indignation. What was the 'we're pregnant' bit about? Perleeze! Does Ag have the morning sickness or megaboobs? No, he just does all the work while she sits on her lazy backside. I felt like standing up and shouting, 'Hey, everybody,

I'm even more pregnant than she is!' but I realized that I'd had my moment and I should let Cordelia and Ag have theirs. I collected the plates and forced myself between the wall and the back of Ag's chair. 'Congratulations,' I whispered in his ear. I didn't intend to whisper, but I couldn't take a deep enough breath to speak properly.

'Thanks,' he said. 'That's why Cordelia couldn't help as much as she would have liked to. It's very important she gets all the rest she needs. We can't have her too tired.'

'Of course not! That wouldn't do at all.'

'Would you like me to take these through for you?' He nodded at the pile of plates. 'You must have a ton of washing up to do.'

And he disappeared before I could enlighten him. Fortunately, Mum, Dad, Tom, Eloise and Ag washed up and cleared the kitchen, and I took the opportunity to disappear upstairs for a bit of peace and quiet. I sat on the bed and prayed for Ag and Cordelia and the baby. And rather grudgingly repented of my churlish attitude. I felt a hand on my shoulder.

'You all right, love?' Kevin sat down next to me.

'Fine, just a bit tired. It was a great Christmas lunch.'

'Thanks! Hey, do you want me to rub your feet?'

'No, I don't!' I tucked my ticklish feet under me. 'You can make me a cup of tea, though.'

I must have dozed off, because when Kevin came up with my tea, my feet had gone dead and he had to rub them anyway to get the circulation going.

'Have you seen this?' he said, pulling back the bedroom curtains. It was dark outside, but by the street lamps I could see huge white flakes floating down like feathers. The pavement and cars were already dusted in white, and the few cars that cautiously drove past were heaped with snow.

'A white Christmas!'

'Come on. We're going outside for a snowball fight.'

I scrambled off the bed and ran downstairs, grabbing Kevin's coat and my scarf from the end of the banisters. Mum and Dad, Eloise and Moses had gone home, but the others were already outside, and we ended our Christmas Day pelting each other with icy snowballs and laughing until we cried.

Tuesday 26 December, Boxing Day

This morning it was Ag who woke me up with a cup of tea.

'I've just been chatting with Kevin. Why didn't you tell me?'

'Tell you what?'

'That you and Kevin are ... expecting a baby too.' I was glad he didn't say 'pregnant'; otherwise I would have had to slap him.

'I thought you knew.'

'I haven't seen you since your wedding.'

'I'd have thought that Mum would have told you.'

'She probably assumed you would have told us yourself. She hardly ever e-mails, and we weren't always near a phone in rural areas.'

'What about the bump?' I pulled down the covers and patted my tummy. 'Did you think I'd been overdoing the Christmas pudding?'

'I couldn't tell with those baggy jumpers you've been wearing, and you're such a skinny little thing ...'

Skinny! Bless him. I kissed him on the cheek and sent him back downstairs so that I could get dressed and organize myself for the wedding.

The snow had stopped falling before we went indoors yesterday evening, but the churned-up snow had frozen overnight, turning the roads and pavements into an ice rink. Kevin helped me to the car, and we half drove, half slithered down the hill and around the ring road until we arrived at Rivers of Glory Church. The church was a huge building, a converted cinema next to a big roundabout. Smiling, suited ushers greeted us at the door, and we sat next to a large lady who appeared to be wearing an ostrich on her head.

Kevin looked pale, and a fog of perspiration had appeared on his forehead. He clutched my hand.

'What's the matter with you? You look like you're at the dentist.'

'I hate church. You know that.'

'You were smiling at our wedding.'

'Through gritted teeth.'

'Well, try to look a bit happier. Everyone will think you are spiritually degenerate.'

'Probably.'

'It's your mum's special day. Surely you can make the effort.'

'I know. I'll do my best.'

His expression didn't change. He still looked petrified.

There was no sign of Kevin's sister, Deyanna, but Floyd was sitting a few rows in front. He turned around and grinned, giving us a thumbs-up sign.

The choir started singing an enthusiastic gospel song, and in spite of myself I found that I was singing and clapping along. The minister welcomed us, and we sang another song. We sat down, and the minister gave a speech. People called out their agreement with what he was saying, which was basically that you had to be born again to start a new life with Jesus. All standard stuff, but I'd never heard Chrissie do an altar call at a wedding. Eventually the minister introduced Brother Moses, and he gave his testimony. We sang another song, then it all went quiet. The doors at the back swung open, and Eloise entered, followed by Deyanna and little Kayla. Eloise was beaming and radiant in a cream suit with a hat that looked as if it was made of white candy floss. Deyanna and Kayla were dressed like marshmallows in pale pink velvet dresses with pink fur collars and hats. All in all, I was starting to feel hungry. Eloise walked slowly up the aisle to the front of the church. Moses took her arm and looked at her as if she was the most precious thing he had ever seen. I wanted to cry. I looked round at Kevin, but he had his eyes tightly shut. Perhaps he was praying.

The vows were simple and beautiful, and we sang a few more rousing hymns and threw confetti before heading back to the community hall for the reception. We had a gorgeous meal, and the disco was great, but I was flagging a little. My back ached, my legs ached and my jaw ached from the constant smiling. I had never seen so many joyous, laughing, happy people in one place before. Fat ladies chuckled, old gentlemen guffawed, teenage girls giggled and young men grinned and slapped each other's backs. It made St Norbert's congregation, with the possible exception of Charity Hubble, look like a meeting of Depressives Anonymous. Kevin noticed it too.

'Shall we go home, love? I think I've had all the excessive happiness I can take for one day.'

We made our excuses and headed out to the car. Kevin breathed a sigh of relief. 'I couldn't stand one more minute in there. It was like being in the Kriss Akabusi Centre for the Terminally Cheerful.'

Thursday 28 December

Another heavy fall of snow last night. Kevin was out from six in the morning to seven tonight unfreezing people's pipes or mending their leaks. In theory we should be quids in, but I know for a fact he doesn't charge the elderly residents the going rate. Still, I wouldn't change a thing. I'd much rather be married to someone who cares about people than have a few more fivers lining the bank vaults. And when he gets home cold and tired, it's been fun unfreezing him.

Friday 29 December

Three days sitting on the settee watching television and eating up the Christmas leftovers has made me feel a complete Christmas pudding. Tried to drag Kevin out for a bracing walk this evening, but he insisted he wanted to finish watching *EastEnders*. Someone in the Square was threatening someone else in the Square, just for a change, when Kevin turned to me and said, 'These people are supposed to be your average working-class Londoners, right?' I nodded in agreement. 'So you'd expect them to do what ordinary working-class Londoners do, right?'

I nodded again, 'Like going to the pub, working in the market, taking their washing to the laundrette.'

'That's right. But they're not like proper, ordinary working-class Londoners, are they?'

'Why not?'

'Well, do you realize you never, ever see them sitting down and watching *EastEnders*?'

I suppose he has a point. *Friends* has got to be one of the best-known and most popular sitcoms, but you never saw the bright young things at 'Central Perk' discussing recent episodes. The *CSI* team could easily find out whodunit just by watching the episode, and the doctors in *ER* wouldn't need their fancy machines if only they tuned in to the series.

Saturday 30 December

Kevin came home jubilant from the match today.

'Two goals in injury time! Can you believe that?'

I tried to sound amazed.

'We were one – nil down at full time. Then Jones scored, then Degas put one in too. It's got to be the greatest comeback in the history of the world.'

Suddenly his face became serious. 'Actually, scrub that. I guess Jesus' resurrection counts as the greatest comeback of all time. But it's got to be the second greatest comeback ...'

I'm glad to see he's got his priorities right.

Sunday 31 December, New Year's Eve

It hasn't snowed any more, but the freezing temperatures induced a desire to stay indoors in the warm; to hibernate, almost. At least I don't have to worry too much about putting on weight.

Kevin's football club is holding a New Year's Eve disco, but we decided to stay at home and welcome in the New Year with just the two of us. Ag and Cordelia went to see her parents in Wimbledon the day after Boxing Day. They were both delighted when they discovered I was expecting too. We talked about how the little cousins would be able to play together. To say that Cordelia and I bonded wouldn't be strictly true, but as we flicked through her *Designer Baby* magazines and chose what crib and layette we would like (her for real, me in my dreams), I felt we had something in common. However, for the whole five days they were with us, she didn't lift a finger.

JANUARY

Monday 1 January, New Year's Day

Well, it's the start of another year, and I *still* haven't found my ministry. The way it looks, it will be a while before I'll even be able to think about it. I sometimes wonder what God's playing at. I've spent so much time and energy praying for some special task from God, and nothing has happened. I've asked him to make it so clear what he wants me to do there'll be no mistake, because I know I'm not very good at hearing him. Now I'm pregnant, and soon I'll have a baby. I'll need to put whatever it is on hold for even longer. It could be years before I finally find my ministry. How depressing!

Tuesday 2 January

Kevin has gone back to work today, and I hate to admit it, but I'm bored. Ariadne's at her office, Chrissie's busy and daytime television is all makeover programmes and chat shows. I miss working, and I am fed up with trying to make conversation with Kevin the budgie. There are only so many questions you can ask where the answer is 'Pretty boy'.

Wednesday 3 January

I have been reading my baby book. I am now terrified. I didn't know there were so many things that could go wrong during pregnancy, everything from German measles to pre-eclampsia, and you've got off lightly if you only end up with anaemia, varicose veins and piles.

2:30 p.m.

Obstetric cholestasis, polyhydramnios, gestational diabetes. I'm sure I've contracted them all – I've read through the symptoms and, just to make sure, looked them up on the Internet, so I should know. I phoned Kevin, who just told me to 'burn that blooming book'. So much for getting the support from those closest to you! Perhaps I should ring Ariadne for advice ... perhaps not.

5:30 p.m.

I'm really worried now. When I say 'worried', I mean that I'm worried in the Christian sense, where you are just legitimately very concerned about something, not in the other sense where you panic and read through the medical dictionary imagining that you have all the diseases, in alphabetical order. The difference is that I've checked with the medical dictionary, and I'm sure I really do have most of them, with the possible exception of prostate cancer. Perhaps I should get Chrissie in to lay hands on me.

8:30 p.m.

Just got back from my 'emergency' doctor's appointment. I had to sit in the waiting room for an hour and a half before

I was seen. Good job it wasn't a real emergency; I could have been dead in an hour and a half. The doctor was almost as dismissive as Kevin.

'It is possible to have too much information,' he grumbled. 'Those books can be a menace.'

However, it wasn't a complete waste of time – I did have one thing on the list, and the doctor has now given me a prescription for ointment for piles. Glad I didn't get Chrissie to lay hands on them.

Thursday 4 January

Charity Hubble has just given me an invitation to her Mothers Against Modern Alternative Lifestyles (MAMAL for short) meeting next Tuesday. She pointed out that it's for 'women who seek to return to traditional roles, based mainly around keeping the home spick and span'. Apparently they start with coffee and chat, maybe a visiting speaker on such fascinating subjects as 'how to make all your laundry glow with whiteness' and a road test of the latest turbo-ironing boards. They end by swapping recipes and household hints. Sounds like a desperate attempt to make housework seem faintly more interesting. Charity and her chintzy super-home-maker pals will try to brainwash me into believing that true happiness can only be found through a well-ordered sock drawer. I don't want to go on principle, but I am so bored that anything is better than sitting here discussing the merits of entering the European Monetary Union with the budgie.

Friday 5 January

Kevin has decided it is time to replace the bathroom suite. Our current one is the wrong colour and rather old. Now, all

shades ranging from rose pink to bright coral may be fine for
little old ladies like Miss Chamberlain, but for a young go-
ahead couple on the first tread of the escalator of marriage – it
just won't do! We spent ages over the summer decorating
the rest of the cottage, but we didn't have time to work on
the bathroom. Kevin has ordered a very refined white suite
including a bath with little lion's feet and Victorian taps that
will really enhance the cottage. He's installing a power-shower
in the corner of the room and under-floor heating. He's going
to start tomorrow.

Saturday 6 January

Kevin did quite well this morning. He's removed the old
bath and has started chipping away at the salmon-pink tiles.
We were just finishing lunch when the phone rang. It was
Nigel: had Kevin remembered that the football club resumes
after its winter break this afternoon?

'Sorry, love,' said Kevin.

Fair enough, but he'd turned off the water, so the central
heating didn't work.

Sunday 7 January

Charity bounced up to me after the service.

'Look,' I said, 'if you've got any more snide comments about
my baby's legitimacy, I don't want to hear them.'

'Not at all.' She shuffled uncomfortably. 'Theodora, I know
you have your shortcomings, but this time it's me who is at
fault. I just wanted to apologize for what I said about your
baby. I jumped to a conclusion, and I was completely wrong.
Will you forgive me?' She took my hand.

Did I have any choice?

'Of course,' I said.

'Super!' She bounded off again as if nothing had happened.

I suppose it took courage to apologize like that, unless, of course, you're like me and get things wrong nearly all the time. If they made saying sorry an Olympic event, I'd be going for gold.

When I got back from church, Kevin had removed the old toilet and washbasin. He'd also finished hacking the rest of the tiles off the walls, so he's making good progress. He grumbled a bit about chopping wood for the fire, but we needed it as we've still got no central heating. Ariadne and Tom invited us round for a Scrabble night, but Kevin stayed behind to plumb in the new toilet.

Monday 8 January

Scrabble night nearly ended in a punch-up. Ariadne kept concocting obscure words which Tom and I had never heard of – 'efts', 'azo' and 'aleph', to name but a few. She insisted they were real words, but Tom accused her of pretending to go out to the loo when really she was sneaking up to the computer in the bedroom and looking them up on the Internet. She denied this and implied that Tom and I were 'outside her intellectual class'. Tom called her a smarty-pants; she called him an igno-ramus. This led to a domestic during which Ariadne 'acciden-tally' knocked the Scrabble board over then stomped upstairs in a sulk. Tom went up to make peace, while I, who had been witness to Ariadne's temperament for the whole of my child-hood, decided to let her get on with it. I paid a quick call to the bathroom on my way out, just to be on the safe side, and admired the luxurious white tiles, the sparkling chrome taps and the washbasin that was firmly attached to the wall.

Tuesday 9 January

Good thing I did use Ariadne's loo last night. When I got home, Kevin had found a vital part missing from the new toilet and was unable to connect it. He promised to go out early in the morning to get the right one and have it fitted by the time I got up. I sincerely hoped he would manage it, and I hoped my pregnant bladder could last the night. He was as good as his word, and when I emerged from under the duvet, there was a working lavatory in our bathroom.

Have decided to go to Charity's mothers' group today. We may not be ideologically compatible, but at least her bathroom is warm and has a bath in it.

4:30 p.m.

MAMAL was everything I'd feared it would be, and worse! I arrived just before eleven wearing the only things that fit me – my baggy trousers and one of Kevin's old sweat-shirts – to be confronted by a group of women clothed in either designer casuals or twin sets and pearls. There was a fair selection of flowery frocks too, which would have looked more at home on six-year-old girls than middle-aged women. Charity beckoned me in and introduced me to the 'gals', as she called them. I thought that wildly inaccurate, as not one of them looked to be under thirty-five. There were also what seemed several dozen babies and toddlers milling around the floor. We drank our coffee, coffee substitute or herbal tea, and I was enjoying the warmth and thinking that it wasn't too bad when a particularly horsey woman who introduced herself as Alyson (with a *y*) Hughes-Churchill flopped onto the sofa next to me.

'Well, hello, Theodora, how nice to meet you. When is the happy event?'

I put my hand on the bump as if to check it was still there. 'March,' I said coyly.

'Oh,' she said, raising her eyebrows. I don't know whether she was surprised the date was so soon or surprised it was so distant. 'Mine too. Who is your consultant?'

'I don't know. I've only seen midwives and my GP.'

'Oh, you're going NHS, are you?' She looked sympathetic. 'I've heard some of them can be very good.'

I felt less than reassured.

'What have you got down in your BP? Are you going for an HD or an HB?'

'Sorry?'

'Well, are you having an epi or are you going to try to make it with just G and A?'

I felt as if I'd fallen into a tin of Alphabetti Spaghetti. I wished Ariadne was here. This woman would not dare try to bamboozle her with abbreviations. Alyson (with a *y*) sat there with her eyebrows so high they practically met her hairline. I would have to come clean.

'I'm very sorry, Alyson. I haven't the faintest idea what you are talking about.'

'Oh!' she said again. If her eyebrows had gone any higher, they would have started slipping down the back of her neck. 'Your Birth Plan – are you going to have a home birth or hospital delivery?'

'I'm having it in hospital ... and what's a Birth Plan?'

'You haven't got one yet?'

'No, should I have?'

'Of course!'

'Where do you get them?'

She threw back her head and brayed. 'You don't get them; you write them. Don't you have a copy of *The Totally Infallible Guide to Birth and Parenthood*?'

'No, I've got a book about pregnancy and childbirth, but I haven't read anything about Birth Plans yet. Mind you,' I said, laughing, 'my husband's hidden it at the moment. He's threatened to burn it!'

'The brute!' If it were possible for her to have looked any more astonished, she would have. 'And are you still intending to have him as your principal BP?'

'BP?' My head began to spin. Surely that meant Birth Plan. How could my husband be a plan?

'Birthing Partner! Someone to hold your hand, mop your brow and change your whale music CD.'

I excused myself from Alyson (with a *y*) and went and sat in Charity's bathroom for rather a long time ... admiring the fittings.

When I came out, there was a queue of ladies with their legs crossed. I went to the kitchen and helped myself to a flapjack. There were snotty-nosed, slimy-fingered babies everywhere, spreading their oozy trail all over Charity's perfectly polished pine. I noticed some older children around too. Alyson Hughes-Churchill reappeared. Drat! I thought I'd escaped. 'Your children not at school?' I commented.

'Home-schooled,' she returned.

'Oh, you've decided to teach them at home. How fascinating. I really admire people who choose to do that. You must be very dedicated. Still, it must be great to have the flexibility to suit the curriculum and methods to your child.'

'That's right, and we can be sure of who they are mixing with and make sure that they only learn what is biblically based.'

'Oh!'

'Yes, you see, we are Christians, so we couldn't possibly expose Esther and Josh to the corrupting rubbish you find in the state system.'

'Aren't you being a little harsh ...?'

'The schools are full of idolaters, pagans and atheists.'

'Most of the teachers I know are very nice and wouldn't dream of "corrupting" the children.'

'I didn't mean the teachers!'

'What, the children?'

'That's where the rot starts,' Alyson answered darkly.

I thought about the children I knew who weren't from Christian families: little Hassan, whose mum came in to explain about Eid celebrations, and Sacha, a little Sikh girl who was the 'good Samaritan' of the playground. Grazed knees, broken friendships – Sacha would have them sorted out before the teacher had even crossed the playground. Of course, these people needed to be shown the love of Jesus, just like everyone else, but they wouldn't 'corrupt' anyone.

'What about a church school?' I asked.

'As if I'm going to entrust my precious children into the hands of wishy-washy liberal compromisers...'

I glanced around to make an escape plan – I could see that Alyson and I were not about to become bosom buddies.

' ... of course, that could be good enough for some people.' She nodded in Charity's direction.

'You mean the Hubbles? But they're ...'

'Compromised – in every area. Their children run riot – that Nebuchadnezzar talks disrespectfully to his mother and goes about with some awful boys. I would never allow my Josh to do that.'

I glanced round. Josh was trying to stuff a giraffe from Noah's ark into an electrical socket. Little chips of paint were flying off, and the giraffe had lost an ear.

'Should he be doing that?' I said.

'It's made of wood; there's no danger.' She waved a dismissive hand. 'Mind you, look at this place,' she whispered. 'Could be a death trap. Nigel so busy, poor man, and with all those children, of course, she doesn't have time to maintain the house properly.'

'Hang on. Charity is one of the hardest-working people I know. She's devoted to her home and family …'

She leaned in towards me: 'And there are so many of them. You'd think they'd be able to control themselves.'

'Just because they choose to have a big family …'

'Like rabbits!' Alyson looked disapproving. I couldn't take much more of her poison. I know that Charity and I have had our disagreements, but I couldn't sit here and listen to this woman assassinating Charity while sitting in her kitchen and scarfing her prune flapjack.

'When you home-school your two children, do you teach about the Ten Commandments?'

'Of course. That's one of the reasons for doing it, so that they get a godly grounding. You wouldn't get that in a state school.'

'Have you read the ninth commandment lately? "You shall not give false testimony against your neighbour." You've just sat here and demolished Charity with your horrible gossip. And for the record, they do teach about the Ten Commandments in state schools. They are a crucial part of the Jewish and Christian religions, and the children learn about both. Now if you'll excuse me, I'm going to get some fresh air; I've started feeling rather sick.'

Alyson shrugged. 'It's probably the flapjack. I'm sure she doesn't clean her pots and pans properly.'

I got up and headed for the back door. I opened it and gulped in the icy air. Charity appeared behind me.

'Are you all right?' she asked.

'I am now.' And I gave her a hug.

Wednesday 10 January

Sat shivering and grubby all day answering phone calls from people who were quick to point out that they *don't* want to sell me double glazing/life insurance/a luxury-fitted kitchen/a conservatory. I couldn't help wondering what they'd do if they *did* want to sell me those things. No one offered to fit me a new bathroom. If they had, I'd have taken them up on the offer.

Thursday 11 January

Day six with no bath, no hot water, no proper washbasin, bare floorboards and no tiles on the walls. I haven't washed any clothes for nearly a week, and if Kevin doesn't do something soon, I'm moving in with Ariadne and Tom.

Friday 12 January

That's it! Kevin has decided to go to Manchester tomorrow for an away match with his mates. I've given him an ultimatum. If we don't have a working bathroom by the time I get back from evensong on Sunday, I'm leaving him – for good.

He laughed at me when I told him, but then I started sobbing hysterically and he knew I wasn't joking. I packed a case and stood it in the hallway after dinner. I'm going to Ariadne and Tom's so Kevin can get on with it in peace.

10:30 p.m.

Lying in Ariadne and Tom's spare bed staring at the ceiling and thinking about Kevin. This is our first night apart since we've been married. Over dinner, I talked to Ariadne about it.

'I'm worried that I've been too harsh on Kevin. After all, he works so hard ...'

She took my elbows and looked into my eyes. 'Listen, sis, you're seven months pregnant; it's January, so it's cold enough to freeze your eyebrows off; and your husband installs bathrooms for a living. He can do it in two days flat if he puts his mind to it. If I were you, I'd have contacted a divorce lawyer by day three!'

I suppose she's right, but I do miss him.

Saturday 13 January

Kevin had got up early to go to Manchester and rang me from the coach at half past nine. They'd just reached Leicester. He asked if I was all right and apologized for letting me down. I, in turn, apologized for nagging him, then his battery ran out.

Around teatime, curiosity got the better of me, and I decided to call into the cottage to sneak a look at how he was getting on. I unlocked the door, and the first thing I noticed was the warmth. The central heating was switched on again. Hallelujah!

There was a pile of letters on the floor, junk mail mostly – I would sort it properly at my sister's house. I stuffed the letters into my handbag, climbed the stairs and cautiously nudged open the bathroom door. There was a pristine white basin to match the toilet, with sparkling chrome taps – I could imagine the elegant soap and colour co-ordinated towels. The shower cabinet stood to attention in the corner of the room. I didn't dare open the door, as it all smelt of fresh grout and I didn't want to disturb anything. The floor felt warm under the new black-and-white chessboard of tiles – and the bath! It stood proudly on its lion's paws just waiting to receive the first bather into its bubbly jaws. The wall at the taps end of the bath was still bare plaster, although Kevin had completed the rows of tiles above the basin. I stood there in awe. How had he finished it so quickly? Perhaps his mates rallied round and helped him so they could all go to the match. Had Kevin, in a fit of guilt, worked all night to fulfil his promise, or did my threats of leaving him if it wasn't completed provide the catalyst? If it was the latter, I would have to remember that technique for future use, provided I didn't employ it too often, as Kevin might call my bluff.

On an impulse I grabbed a lipstick from my handbag and drew a huge heart on the newly installed mirror which almost covered one wall. Inside the heart I wrote,

I love you much,
I love you true,
Can't wait to share
This bath with you.

Then I headed back to Ariadne and Tom's to sample Tom's delicious Boeuf en Croute.

11:30 p.m.

I sorted through the post on Ariadne's spare bed. The only interesting item was a Christmas card from Diana which must have been rather delayed in the post. It had all the usual greetings and a handwritten note.

> ... and you'll never guess what. I've got a new boyfriend. He's called Steve. He's the brother of Esther who used to go to my old church ... He's great; we can talk about anything, and he's helping me to sort things out. Thanks, Theo, for your continuing friendship and prayers ...

Well, who'd have thought it? Isn't God brilliant!

Sunday 14 January

Fought the temptation to ring Kevin this morning. Chrissie is away all week at a clergy conference, so we had a visiting speaker from an organization that takes Bibles out to countries that don't have them and translates them into other languages.

It seemed a very worthy cause, and his message seemed to be 'It's best for everyone to be able to read the Bible in their own language.' An admirable ambition, but did he really need a forty-minute sermon to say that?

Also, it mystified me that, coming from a Bible organization, he had to ask to borrow a Bible.

Kevin popped round just after lunch to say that the bathroom was finished.

Tom said, 'My, that was quick.'

'That's because my husband's a genius,' I said, hugging him round the waist.

'Ah, well, it wasn't all down to me,' he said.

'What do you mean?'

'Well' – he made an 'I've got a confession' face – 'I sort of subcontracted it.'

'What?' How can a plumber subcontract the plumbing in his own house to another plumber? Where was his pride?

'I was really worried about getting it finished on time, so while I was in Manchester yesterday, I had Vague Dave doing the work for me. He owes me a favour after playing all those "break up" songs at the wedding reception. "I Can't Get No Satisfaction" followed by "Young Hearts Run Free" and "I Will Survive". I ask you – '

'I thought Vague Dave worked at the market,' I interrupted.

'He does, but he also does a bit of this and that – chauffeuring, DJ-ing ...'

'... and plumbing. I hope he's City and Guilds.'

'Ah, well, he was a bit vague about that, but I've checked it over and the proof's in the pudding. Come and see. It looks brilliant.'

'Actually, I have seen it. It looks very nice.'

'So you had a chat with Dave, then?'

'No, he wasn't there when I dropped in.' My mind flicked back to the lipstick heart on the mirror.

'Are you sure?'

'Why? Did he say anything?'

'Not really; he was as vague as ever. Just one strange thing. He asked if he should bring the rubber duck and loofah, or will you?'

Monday 15 January

Had a lovely long soak in my new bath this evening, almost managing to submerge the bump beneath the bubbles. I lit some candles, and Kevin brought me up a cup of tea. Kevin perched on the edge of the toilet lid, and we chatted for ages. I admitted that he and Vague Dave had done a fantastic job.

'Some things are just worth waiting for,' he said. 'Like mature cheddar and *Match of the Day* highlights on Sunday morning.'

I was just considering topping up the hot water and giving myself another half hour when Kevin said, 'You'd better hurry up and get out. I bought self-destruct grout – it dissolves automatically after an hour.'

He beat a hasty retreat, and I jumped out of the bath and pulled the plug.

I'm still not sure if he was joking.

Wednesday 17 January

As I opened the front door, a gust of icy January wind almost tore the handle out of my hand. There under the rose arch stood an elderly gentleman wearing a tweed jacket and a beret and leaning on a walking stick. His eyes were watering with the cold, and his lips looked blue.

'Oh,' I gasped as the draught swept round my ankles and sneaked inside to steal the warmth from my hallway, 'can I help you?'

'I'm looking for Estelle. Is she here?'

'I'm sorry. There is no one here with that name. Have you tried next door?'

'No. This was the address. Rose Cottage.' Despite the firmness of his words, his voice trembled. I couldn't tell if it was from age, the cold or emotion. 'I'm sorry to have bothered you. It was an outside chance I'd find her. I don't even know if she's still alive.' He gave what looked almost like a salute and turned painfully around.

'Wait!' I called. 'Perhaps someone else in the village knows her. Mrs Polanski at the Post Office might be able to help.'

He shook his head sadly. 'This was the address.'

I searched my brain to find some helpful suggestion. 'The only other person who lived in this cottage was Miss Chamberlain,' I added as an afterthought.

He turned back towards me. 'That's right. Estelle Chamberlain. Do you know her?'

'You'd better come in.'

He manoeuvred himself cautiously up the step and into the hallway. I bustled ahead of him into the lounge and fluffed up a cushion on our most comfortable armchair.

'Would you like a cup of tea?'

'I don't want to trouble you, love.'

'No trouble. I was just about to make one. My husband will be back soon.'

'White, two sugars, then, and thank you.'

I went into the kitchen and put on the kettle. Estelle Chamberlain! In all the years we'd been friends, I'd never known her first name. I suppose it must have been on the house deeds or on the solicitor's letter explaining she'd left the cottage to me, but I'd never noticed. Truth was, I was in such a state, I don't remember much about the whole episode. To me she was always 'Miss' Chamberlain. 'Miss' was as much a title of rank as Colonel and as closely linked with her profession as Dr or Reverend. And, like army officers and priests, she continued to use her title long after she had retired. She had been a teacher through and through. If you'd cut her in half, at her core you would have found chalk.

I made the tea, found the best china cups, unwrapped a fresh packet of biscuits and brought them, on a tray, through to the lounge.

The elderly man rose from his chair and helped me set the tray on the coffee table. The warmth had returned the colour to his face. I poured the tea and offered the biscuits.

'I'm sorry, I haven't introduced myself. I'm Percival Burns.'

'Pleased to meet you, Mr Burns.' I shook his hand. 'You were asking about Miss Chamberlain ...' I began, not sure how to end the sentence.

'She's dead, isn't she?' His voice quavered again.

'I'm afraid so,' I said as gently as I could. 'She died nearly two years ago. She had broken her ankle, and, well, she caught pneumonia and ...' My voice trailed off. 'We all miss her very much.'

The old man puffed out his cheeks and steepled his fingers as if he was praying.

'Were you a friend?' I asked.

'More than that. You might not believe it, but Estelle and I were engaged once.'

'I know. She told me about you. You were a fisherman,' I said.

'Only for a couple of years before the war. I joined up and spent the war with the 24th Lancers 11th Armoured Division. After demob, I worked on a farm until I met my wife,

Joanie, then I trained as a teacher. Taught in a boys' technical school for over thirty years. Estelle was a wonderful teacher – inspired me.'

'She inspired us all.'

It dawned on me that even I, who had despised children, had been sucked into the classroom. I don't think it is coincidence that Miss Chamberlain was the common factor.

'We had been engaged for a while.' His gaze drifted off to the corner of the room. 'Then she got a job in London, and we tried to think of all the ways we could keep it going. Her in the Smoke, me in Brighton. Jobs weren't so easy to come by then, and in the end she decided we should call it a day.

'This sounds selfish, but to be honest with you, it was a relief when the war came along. Gave me something else to think about. I had to go to London a few times for training, and each time I was tempted to look her up, but I said to myself, "No, Perce, she's made herself quite clear. You must respect that." And I have, for nigh on seventy years.'

'What made you come here now?'

'My Joanie passed away last year.'

'I'm sorry.'

'I decided I had nothing to lose. It was daft, really. To think she'd still be alive, to think she'd still remember me after all these years.'

'Wait there,' I said. 'I've got something that belongs to you.' I dashed up and down the stairs as quickly as the bump would let me.

'She didn't forget you.' I held out the gold engagement ring.

'Oh!' he gasped. He looked as if he was about to cry. 'She kept it all these years.'

'And she told me about you. She didn't forget.'

'Did she have any regrets?'

'Regrets, no. Memories, yes. I know she treasured the time you were together.'

'And she never married?'

'No.'

'Ah, well, at least it's settled now. Is there a grave ... ?'

'Just up the hill at St Norbert's. It's a bit late tonight ...' I got up to draw the curtains; the bitter wind gusted through a gap in the sash cord. 'I'll take you in the morning if you like.'

'That's very kind of you, dear, but I'll make my own way if you don't mind.' He squinted at his watch. 'My goodness, is that the time? I'm sorry to have held you up. Didn't you say your husband would be back soon?'

'That's right. Please stay and eat with us.'

'Wouldn't dream of it. Might I use your telephone to call a taxi?'

I heard Kevin's key in the lock.

'Where are you staying?'

'With one of Joanie's nieces in Bromley.'

'Hello!' called a voice from the hall.

I called a greeting back then turned to the old man. 'I'm sure my husband would drop you back.' Kevin is kind like that.

Kevin had his cup of tea, and it was quickly agreed that he would drive Percy back. I helped him on with his coat and shook his hand. I pressed the little box containing Miss Chamberlain's ring into his palm.

'I can't take this. She gave it to you,' he protested.

'No, she didn't. I was just looking after it until it could be returned to its rightful owner.'

He gave me a peck on the cheek and wished me all the best with the baby and God's blessing.

After they had gone, I sat and thought. Miss Chamberlain might never have told me the story, and I would just have sent

Percival Burns away without the ring. What if Miss Chamberlain hadn't left me the cottage in her will, or we had sold it to someone who didn't know that Miss Chamberlain was once engaged to a fisherman in Brighton?

Was it all coincidence, or does God have a way of working things out that shows us that, in his kingdom, things don't happen by chance?

Thursday 18 January

E-mailed Diana today to thank her for the Christmas card. I wasn't sure whether to mention anything about the baby or not. It still seems rather a sensitive subject. Instead, I gave her the saga of the bathroom, copying bits out of my diary. I desperately wanted to send her a Bible verse from Romans 8, 'And we know that in all things God works for the good of those who love him,' but I didn't want to seem too pushy. In the end, I just congratulated her on her new boyfriend and said I hoped it worked out well.

Thought about our visitor from yesterday. Miss Chamberlain once told me that she didn't have any regrets, but I can't help wondering how her life might have been different if she'd married Percival, or even if she'd lived long enough for them to meet again. So many 'what ifs'. How can we ever know that we've made the right decisions? What if I hadn't quit my job? What if I wasn't pregnant? What if I had married Declan instead of Kevin? What if I hadn't been born? Would the world be any different? My head feels as if it's going to explode with all these thoughts. Perhaps if I had a 'ministry' I would feel better. I thought I'd made progress; I've been trying so hard to pray and to listen and to read my Bible and to become more like Jesus. It doesn't seem to be working. The more I look at him, the less like him I seem. At the moment I feel like a piece of chewing gum stuck to the shoe of life.

Friday 19 January

Bravely volunteered to help in the church office today. Anything is better than sitting at home and contemplating my navel, which is actually worth contemplation at the moment as it has completely changed shape. Chrissie was out on her Special Constable duty again and had left me the work in a folder. As usual there were the corrections from the previous sheet, including the announcement that the PCC was to be held in the 'Parish Hell' this week due to heating problems at the vicarage. Oh well, at least they couldn't complain it was too cold there!

Gregory Pasternak came into the office in a state of animation. In spite of it being the middle of winter, he still wore his brightly coloured striped shirt. He wanted to speak to Chrissie about his wonderful idea for a Dickensian pageant in the village next summer.

'But Dickens has no connection with this village!' I sneered.

'Dickens lived in London ...'

'Yes, but ...'

'... and Dickens lived near Rochester.'

'So?'

'This village is between London and Rochester, so Dickens could have passed through here on his way between the two places.'

'There's nothing to say he did.'

'Ah!' Gregory said, tapping the side of his nose. 'But there's nothing to say he didn't!'

'True.'

'And my cousin's wife's sister is a member of some kind of Dickensian society in Arkansas. They're coming over in June, and I thought it might be nice if it sort of coincided with a pageant.'

Gregory was so excited by the prospect that he started wrapping his arms around himself in a sort of self-congratulatory hug. It had the unfortunate effect of making him look like a golf umbrella.

'This wouldn't be some kind of scheme to try to fleece a bunch of American tourists over a tenuous literary connection, would it?'

'As if!'

Gregory unfurled himself and pushed a piece of paper onto the already inundated desk. 'If you could just make sure the vicar sees it.'

And he went.

I settled down to work through the rest of the items Chrissie had left. Typing up the action notes for the building committee proved most entertaining. Here is the original list.

Hole in church roof – Maurice Johnson is looking into it.
New Neighbourhood Watch sign required – last one was
    stolen.
Lack of space in the churchyard – vicar to meet with rep-
    resentatives from parish council to discuss this grave
    problem.
Leak in ladies' toilet – permission granted.

Well, item 4 is a relief at least!

Saturday 20 January

Kevin and Nigel nearly got frostbite at the football club this afternoon. In spite of the icy mist that was drifting around the village green and the daylight that packed its bags and went home at four o'clock, Kevin insists he loves every minute of it. He's obsessed. Instead of sleep-suits, I think we should buy our little one a football shirt.

Eloise and Moses got back from their honeymoon yesterday, so they came round for a meal this evening. They both looked relaxed and happy and spent most of the time gazing into each other's eyes. Moses had been completely transformed by two weeks in the Caribbean sunshine. He had swapped his rather stuffy image with his black suits and stiffly starched white shirts for a gaudy peacock-blue Hawaiian shirt with scarlet hibiscus and green parrots. Kevin said afterwards that he didn't know whether to reach for his sunglasses or a bucket.

Giggling like a pair of teenagers, they extolled the delights of Jamaica, pointing out that it wasn't that warm, of course, being mid-winter – only twenty degrees!

When they'd gone home, I cuddled up to Kevin and suggested that we could visit Jamaica for our holiday next summer. He nodded.

'Yup, I could live with that. I can get used to supporting the Reggae Boyz.'

'Perhaps we could go sooner, escape this dreary, sodden, frigid British winter.'

'Yeah, somewhere really hot ...'

And he drifted off as I lay there imagining azure seas lapping golden sand ...

Sunday 21 January

I cornered Chrissie after the service to ask whether she'd spoken to Gregory Pasternak.

'Ah, our mutual friend!' she said.

'But do you think this proposal for a Dickens pageant is just some hare-brained, moneymaking scheme?

'Maybe, but since he was made redundant he may have fallen on hard times.'

'Perhaps, but that's no excuse for trying to rip off American tourists. I know they have Dickens festivals in Rochester and London ...'

'Hmmm, a tale of two cities that already benefit from an association with the great author,' Chrissie said, smirking.

'In fact, I went to the Rochester one once when I was little. It was just before Christmas, and I remember standing in the High Street with loads of people dressed as Dickens characters all singing that song.'

'A Christmas carol, was it?' Chrissie barely suppressed a grin.

'No, it was "Pick a Pocket or Two". We were staying down there, goodness knows why.' I racked my brains. 'Oh, I remember. We were having an extension built on our house, and Mum wanted to get away from the cold and the mess for a few days.'

'It must have been a bleak house?' Chrissie pursed her lips then looked away.

'It certainly was. We had no central heating or anything for a fortnight. Dad came close to suing the builders, they made such a mess of it.'

'Dombey and Sons?' Chrissie smirked.

'No, I think they were called Galloway. Mum was so disappointed; the extension didn't turn out anything like the plans.'

'They must have had great expectations.' Chrissie picked up a hymnbook and pretended to read.

'They did, but their dreams were ruined by those cowboys. Took them months to put it right. Mind you, they blamed the architect. Said the drawings were all wrong.'

'Sketches by Boz!' Chrissie collapsed into a little heap of hysterical giggles while I stood with my hands on my hips.

'Look, I know what you're doing,' I said, 'and you can just stop it now!'

Wednesday 24 January

Our first birth-preparation class tonight. The conflict started at breakfast time. Kevin sat there pulling the same face as when I am trying to make him go to church.

'Don't tell me you're going to be difficult over this.'

'All right, then.'

'What, you're not going to be difficult?'

'No, I'm not going to tell you.'

I scowled at him.

'Do I have to go?' he whined.

'If I have to, so do you!'

'But you're the one having the baby.'

'Excuse me, but you did have some "input". Come on. I need you there, Kevin. I need *you*. I don't need my friends or my sister or even my diary. I *need* you.'

'Okay,' he said reluctantly and went to work.

I sneaked the baby book out from under a pile of flowerpots in the shed where I'd hidden it when Kevin was threatening to burn it. I read the section on ante-natal classes. I wish I hadn't. Now I don't want to go. There's bound to be a bunch of women sitting around discussing breast-feeding, epidurals, their placentas and pelvic floors. Yuk! (Actually, I remember a few years ago nearly falling over with shock when my mother confidently announced to a crowded Chinese restaurant that she was going to have a new pelvic floor fitted in her conservatory!)

11 p.m.

The class wasn't as bad as I thought it would be. There were five other couples and a single lady in our group. I think that everyone else was as nervous as we were. I met a lady called Jan, and Kevin discovered a bloke he knew from football. We had a tour of the hospital maternity unit and met the midwives. It was scary and reassuring at the same time, and afterwards we had the opportunity to ask questions. Suddenly, the deluge of questions in my mind dried up. By the blank looks, everyone else was having the same experience. One rather earnest-looking young man with spectacles bravely volunteered. 'Um … I've heard that massage can be very beneficial in the later months.'

The midwife agreed and stressed the importance of seeking advice before using essential oils during pregnancy. 'I'm sure,' she concluded, 'that massaging the back and shoulders can be very useful in relieving tension and stress before and during the birth.'

'My wife might even want her back rubbed too!' quipped one of the men. And that sort of broke the ice. After that came a flood of questions on all sorts of subjects. At the end, Kevin and Gary and Jan and I swapped phone numbers. There was no doubt that we had joined a new club – one that we wouldn't be leaving for a very long time.

Thursday 25 January

Ariadne, Tom, Kevin and I booked a table at our local restaurant for a quiet evening of good food and good company. Actually, 'good food' is a slight exaggeration in a place where a steak sandwich is considered the height of sophistication and garnish invariably consists of one slice each of tomato and cucumber.

We had just settled down when a herd of rumbustious Scotsmen stampeded through the door and proceeded to serenade us with 'My Luve Is Like a Red, Red Rose'. I'd forgotten it was Burns Night, although why there were quite so many Scotsmen in Sidcup I'm not sure. They settled down at a table near us, and after their initial disappointment at the lack of haggis on the menu, they settled for a steak sandwich too. Our food arrived quickly, and it didn't look too bad. Our Caledonian companions received their food at the same time. To my horror, Tom sprang out of his chair and started tapping his glass with his knife.

'Pray silence for the Grace,' he cried.

I hoped the ground would open, but it didn't, so I had to make do with hiding as much of myself as I could behind the menu.

Tom spoke again in his 'toastmaster's' voice,

Some hae meat and canna eat,
and some wad eat that want it,
but we hae meat and we can eat,
and sae the Lord be thankit.

Ariadne, Kevin and I sat with our mouths open. The Scotsmen gave a cheer and toasted us heartily.

'Where did that come from?' Ariadne asked when she regained her composure.

'Grandpa Willie,' Tom explained. 'Every January when I was growing up, we used to go to Grandpa Willie's house. He was born in Burnside, near Aberdeen, but all I can remember is visiting him when he lived near my parents in Croydon. All my uncles, Dad's brothers and all my cousins used to gather to celebrate. Not easy to find a haggis in Croydon, I can tell you! That's how I learnt the Grace ... and all the songs and poems.' He grinned. 'But I'll spare you those.'

Ariadne looked relieved.

The Scotsmen started singing 'Auld Lang Syne', and everyone else joined in, linking arms. We stayed and chatted afterwards, the men nursing a fine single malt and Ariadne and I on the orange juice. It wasn't exactly the quiet evening I'd imagined, but we'd made some new friends. After all,

That Man to Man, the world o'er,
Shall brothers be for a 'that.

Friday 26 January

Back to the church office today. I'm going to have to quit soon, as I'm having difficulty getting near enough to the keyboard to type. Chrissie helpfully offered to fetch a hacksaw and cut a semicircle out of the desk to make room for the bump. I threw pencils at her, and she didn't make any more helpful suggestions.

Saturday 27 January

My cravings to date have included anchovies, apricots, Bovril crisps, marshmallows (only the pink ones), raw spaghetti, golden syrup (straight out of the tin) and pretzels. Oh, for the good old days when the only thing I craved was a huge slab of milk chocolate!

Monday 29 January

Bumped into Percival Burns, Miss Chamberlain's beau, outside the Post Office. He has decided to stay on for a week or two with his niece and had been visiting Miss Chamberlain's grave. He looked very sad and rather lost. I have invited him round for supper on Saturday. I think I'll make a trifle.

FEBRUARY

Thursday 1 February

Have mustered the courage to tell Chrissie that I'm not going to be able to help her with *The Church Organ* any more. I know it's not exactly a job, but it still takes a huge amount of time, effort and fortitude to cope with the demands of St Norbert's rather batty congregation.

To my surprise, Chrissie accepted my resignation. Gave me a hug and thanked me for all my hard work.

I settled down to type the folder full of notes, advertisements and announcements for the last time. I was delighted to see the entries were up to the usual standard, including the advertisement for the 'Prayer and Fasting Day' at a nearby retreat centre. The cost for the day was £10 – all meals included.

Friday 2 February

Kevin and I sat down this evening to try to make a short-list of babies' names. It needs to be done before Mum railroads us into something that sounds as if it comes from Jason and the Argonauts. We decided to each write down our favourite names then come up with a couple of possibilities each for a boy and a girl. I sat in the lounge while Kevin took himself off to the kitchen. After much pencil chewing, scribbling and crossing out, I had a list.

Boys	Girls
Charles	Grace
Matthew	Clarice
Mark	Faith
Luke	Hope
Paul	Tabitha

Kevin lurched in from the kitchen, his brows furrowed. 'That was hard,' he said. He handed me his list.

Boys	Girls
Kevin	Britney
Jez	Beyonce
Beckham	Theodora
Sven	Eloise
George	Annabelle

I laid both lists on the coffee table. There were no names in common, and he seemed about as impressed about my choices as I was about his. We decided to cross out the ones on each other's lists that we really couldn't stand. I voted that all the pop stars and those connected with football had to go. Also, although it was very sweet of him, I couldn't possibly inflict the name Theodora on another generation. Kevin was equally indifferent about my 'virtue' names for girls and thought my boys' names belonged 'on a set of apostle teaspoons'.

So we were left with Charles, Clarice, Tabitha, George, Jez, Kevin, Eloise and Annabelle. Having yet another Kevin in the house would be beyond a joke, and Jez isn't a proper name, so that was out.

We sat and stared at the remaining list and decided that neither of us really liked any of those names, so we agreed to leave it until the baby is born. That way, if it looks like a Timothy or an Abigail, Timothy or Abigail it is!

Saturday 3 February

Kevin and Nigel almost got frostbite once again overseeing the football club. Kevin picked up a nasty bruise on his shin from a tackle from an eight-year-old thug.

'Why do you do it?' I asked.

'I enjoy it.' He grinned and went off to thaw out in the shower.

At six o' clock the doorbell rang, and Percival Burns stood on the doorstep looking dapper in a navy blazer with a red-and-yellow-striped tie with a British Legion tie pin. I welcomed him and rushed into the kitchen to check on the roast chicken. When I returned, Percy was sitting there with a glass of sherry, and he and Kevin were engrossed in conversation.

'Percy was telling me about the Remembrance Day parade at the Cenotaph last year,' Kevin said.

I thought I remembered catching a glimpse on the television of column upon column of soldiers, many elderly, marching up Whitehall while the Queen laid a wreath to remember the fallen.

'I was very honoured,' Percy continued, 'to be given a special distinction at this year's parade.'

'What was that?' I asked.

'Well, you might remember that when the ranks reach the place where the Queen is standing, they give the order "Eyes right!" and the soldiers turn and salute Her Majesty.'

I nodded. 'I remember.'

'It falls to one man to keep looking straight ahead, not turning his head, and that was my job.'

'To stop them drifting off course!' interjected Kevin.

'Precisely,' continued Percy. 'It's a great honour – being the one who keeps his eyes fixed straight ahead. Otherwise the whole flaming lot of them would be blundering around in circles tripping over each other.'

We had a moderately successful meal, the only problem being the chicken, which seemed to have un-trussed itself in the oven and was lying recumbent, like a sunbather, in the roasting tray. The sherry trifle was a success too, although there was far too much for the three of us. When Percy had gone, I thought about what he had said. My life seems to consist of blundering around in circles tripping over other people. It reminded me of the verse in Hebrews, 'Let us fix our eyes on Jesus, the author and perfecter of our faith' ... even if we are saluting the Queen!

Sunday 4 February

Invited Mum and Dad round for tea to try to use up some of the leftover chicken and trifle. Dad was in good form. He has just invested some money in the stock market and sat there for most of the afternoon with his nose stuck in yesterday's *Financial Times*. We ate the chicken sandwiches, but no one except Dad wanted dessert. Even then, I'm not sure he was really hungry; he only wanted to say, 'Just a trifle,' when I offered it to him.

Mum and I played bezique while Kevin watched the football highlights. Dad didn't want to join in. He just sat with the newspaper in front of his face, making comments like, 'I see helium shares are up, but feathers are down. Paper is stationary.'

So we all ignored him.

Still half a trifle left. I couldn't persuade Mum and Dad to take it with them, and neither Kevin nor I could face any more of it, so I put it out in the garden, with some stale bread, for the birds.

Monday 5 February

Woke up and looked out of the window. There was next door's ginger tom, Oscar, having the time of his life as half a dozen inebriated sparrows flopped around the lawn. I squeaked at Kevin, and we both ran down to the garden to chase Oscar away. I scooped up the rest of the sherry trifle and put it in the dustbin while Kevin rounded up the sparrows and put them in a safe place until they sobered up. I didn't realize it was that strong. I don't think I'll be making sherry trifle again for a while. I'm not sure it was what Jesus had in mind when he said, 'Are not two sparrows sold for a penny? Yet not one of them will fall to the ground apart from the will of your Father.'

Wednesday 7 February

9:30 p.m.

Back to ante-natal class. We were doing breast-feeding today. Kevin was squirming in his seat.

'Sit still!' I snapped.

'This is one bit I really *can't* help with,' he muttered.

I think I shall do my best to breast-feed the baby, not really from any altruistic motives but more out of sheer laziness. What convinced me was the fact that my milk is free, available whenever it's needed and always at the right temperature, and the containers don't require sterilizing. Also, I'm very prone to losing things – umbrellas at the Post Office, my purse in shops, gloves on the bus. I'd probably leave a trail of baby bottles behind me. At least if I breast-feed, I'm very unlikely to misplace one of them!

Friday 9 February

Looking forward to the prospect of a day on the sofa curled up with a book (hey, I am nearly eight months pregnant!) when the phone rang. It was Chrissie.

'Oh good, you are there.' Her voice sounded tense.

'Where else would I be? Chrissie, is something wrong?'

'Mmm, you could say that.'

'What's the matter?'

'It's Jeremiah. There's been an accident.'

'Is he okay?'

'Not really.'

'What happened?'

'On Tuesday night he was driving along the by-pass when a lorry swerved and clipped his car. It spun round and hit another car. He's badly injured; broken bones, internal injuries. It was touch and go for a while.'

'This is terrible. Is there anything I can do?'

'I was hoping you would say that. He's in hospital, in a lot of pain and very scared, although he won't admit to either. I wondered if you could find the time to visit him. Jeremiah needs a friend right now.'

'I'd hardly call myself that!' I snorted. 'What about the people in his new church?'

'He's left St Umfridus'. It was Reverend Potter who contacted me. Jeremiah managed to upset so many people when he was there that no one from St Umfridus' is prepared to go and visit him.'

'That's a bit wretched. Why did he leave?'

'Reverend Potter said that they'd arranged a youth service at the church, some kind of outreach.'

'Yes, and ... ?'

'Well, the problem was that the youth came. They came in droves, with their coloured hair and offensive tee shirts and their disrespectful behaviour ...'

'And Jeremiah didn't like it and left.'

'Precisely. But not until after he'd had one of his little rants and told both the young people and the church members what he thought of them.'

'Oh dear!'

'So what with that and the general mayhem and upset he'd caused previously, Reverend Potter hasn't managed to get anyone to visit him. I just thought as you had some time on your hands and you seemed to get on with him ...'

'You are joking? The last conversation we had, he accused me of lax morals.'

'Coming from him, I'd take it as a compliment.'

'He really upset me. Anyway, what about you? Why can't you go and visit him?'

'I went last night and found a very lonely and distressed old man. I can't make you go, but the sight of a friendly face might help him – even if he doesn't think he needs to be helped.'

'I'll give it some thought.'

Chrissie gave me the name of the ward and the visiting times, and I put the phone down. Jeremiah has shown me nothing but contempt. I'd feel like a hypocrite if I pretended to like him just because he's in hospital. What is the alternative? Jeremiah sits there getting lonelier and even more bitter as the days go by. I do feel a sort of obligation. He came to see me when I had chickenpox. Perhaps the accident has changed him, softened him.

I put on my coat and drove to the hospital. If nothing else, it will help me to practise the route for when the time comes ...

I dropped into the visitors' shop and bought a card and some grapes, then I found Spearmint Ward – apparently, in a sponsorship deal, a toothpaste company has refurbished part of the hospital. Perhaps in addition to the names, the wards have been decorated in red and white stripes and make your breath smell minty fresh!

A nurse took me down a long row of beds to a bed by the window. A curtain was partially drawn around it. As the nurse and I went in, I saw an old man asleep on the bed. One of his legs was in plaster and attached to a contraption with strings and pulleys. He had drips in his arms, wires on his chest and a plastic tube across his face with outlets to send oxygen into his nose. He wore blue striped pyjamas, and his hair was long and unkempt. He had a growth of silver stubble on his chin, and as his lips moved I could see that his front teeth were missing. His left eye was blackened, and there were cuts to his forehead and hands.

The nurse invited me to sit in the high vinyl-upholstered armchair.

'I'm sure he will wake soon. He will be glad to see you – he doesn't get many visitors.'

Somehow I doubted that seeing me would make the sun shine brighter!

I put the grapes on the bedside cabinet. There were two get-well cards lying flat. One was from Chrissie, and the other was signed 'John'. I assumed John to be Reverend Potter. I stood the cards up. There were no other personal touches, no newspapers or magazines, no flowers, just a water jug and a plastic glass. I couldn't even see his large leather Bible. I supposed it must be inside the cabinet.

I sat in the chair and waited for what seemed like hours for Jeremiah to wake. As there was nothing to read, I sat and prayed. I prayed for healing for Jeremiah and for a softening of his heart. Then I prayed for just about everybody else I knew. I had just got around to Alfreda Polanski's mother's friend's rheumatism when Jeremiah gave a shudder and a yawn and opened his eyes.

'You!' he said. 'What are you doing here?'

'I came to visit. Chrissie rang me and told me you'd had an accident.'

'So you thought you'd do your duty. Or have you come to gloat?'

'Of course not!'

'Then why are you here?'

'Well ... when I heard about the accident, I was worried about you. I wanted to see how you were ...'

'Liar!'

'That's a bit harsh ... I just wanted to make sure that you are okay.'

'Well, you've seen that I'm not. Now you can go.'

'Jeremiah!'

'What do you expect? You and the other hypocrites from that place,' he shouted. '"For ye are like unto whited sepulchres, which indeed appear beautiful outward, but are within full of dead men's bones, and of all uncleanness."'

I snatched up my coat and handbag and ran out of the ward before the tears came. Jumping into the car, I rammed it into gear and reversed into an iron post. I didn't stop but drove home as quickly as I could, threw open the front door, ran upstairs, flung myself onto the bed and howled. How could he do it to me? I was trying to be nice, and he was being despicable! And to cap it all, I now had a large dent in my bumper. I know Jesus says we must love our enemies, but I'm finding it impossible even to tolerate Jeremiah.

I was making myself a cup of tea when Chrissie rang.

'How did it go?'

I gave her a blow-by-blow account.

'Will you go back tomorrow?'

'You are kidding?'

'No. I think you should visit him again tomorrow.'

'Why?'

'For all the reasons I gave you today. And because "whatever you did for one of the least of these brothers of mine, you did for me." That's what Jesus said. You can't get out of it. There in black and white, Matthew chapter twenty-five. Visiting the sick is on that list!'

'I can't imagine visiting anyone less like Jesus.'

'What are you, a sheep or a goat?'

'But the things he said!'

'Actually, he was quoting Jesus. Oh, I'm not saying he was right to say that. Quite the opposite. But you must remember, he's like a wounded animal, frightened and cornered. He's going to lash out.'

'They put down wounded animals.'

To my surprise, Chrissie laughed. 'I'm going tonight. Can you stop by for a while tomorrow afternoon? Just half an hour? Pretty please?'

She made me laugh. 'Oh, all right. But if he starts again ...'

⊙⊙⊙

I began telling Kevin about Jeremiah's accident. 'He was driving along the by-pass when a lorry swerved and clipped his car. He spun round and hit another car ...'

'That's terrible,' said Kevin, shaking his head.

'It certainly is,' I said.

'Poor Jeremiah,' he said, shaking his head. 'That beautiful car. Was it a write-off?'

Saturday 10 February

Spent all morning worrying about my visit to Jeremiah. I have to concede, though, that Chrissie is right. All that suffering is showing itself as anger. He has no power to hurt me. I'm the healthy one. I can get up and walk away. I can go into that hospital ward and be nice to him, and there's nothing he can do about it. Perhaps now he's in a position to listen to a few home truths. Buoyed up by these thoughts, I prayed then climbed into my car and drove back to the hospital. I took a little more time than yesterday in the hospital shop. I bought a bunch of flowers and the most respectable magazine I could find and set off for the ward. I met the same nurse.

'Your father's a little better today,' she said.

'Oh, he's not my father!' Perish the thought!

'I thought that, but why else would anyone keep coming to see the cantankerous old ...'

'He's just a friend,' I said. 'And he doesn't really have anyone else.'

'Then you're a saint,' she said. Then she added, 'Perhaps you could get through to him. He won't let the nurses wash him or even attend to his needs properly. He keeps shouting things like "harlot" and "Jezebel". I don't know what it means, but it doesn't sound very nice. Is he all right up there?' She pointed to her head.

'Jeremiah's rather ... set in his ways,' I explained.

'I see,' she said. 'But if you get the chance to talk to him ...'

I never expected my 'task for the day' to be to persuade Jeremiah Wedgwood to have a bed bath.

'Afternoon, Jeremiah,' I said, mustering as much cheeriness as I could.

'You again!'

'That's right. Me again. And I've brought you some flowers and a magazine.'

'Save your flowers for my funeral. And you can take your journalistic filth and leave.'

'It's a gardening magazine. The only filth in it is compost. Honestly, Jeremiah, I don't care what you do with it. Give it away, burn it if you like, but I'm leaving it here.'

'As you wish.' He shifted round in the bed, wincing with pain.

'Would you like me to plump your pillows?' I offered.

'Do not touch me, strumpet!'

'Don't flatter yourself,' I muttered.

'What did you say?'

'Jeremiah, we have something to sort out here, and with you lying horizontal on your back, now is a good time to do it. You keep making comments that question my morality, and I'm not putting up with it any more.'

He snorted. 'How you have the brazenness to say that with that bastard growing inside you ...'

'Stop!' I was aware that it had all gone quiet and everyone was staring at me. I had an audience. I could either say my piece and flounce out, or I could stay and try to be Christ in this place.

'Firstly, Jeremiah, even if this baby was conceived before the wedding, you'd have absolutely no right to speak to me, or anyone else, like that. Secondly, if you'd bothered to hear me out, and if you were really that concerned about the legitimacy of my baby, and if it was any of your business, I'd give you the dates so you could work it out, and then you'd know that I fell pregnant on honeymoon. Thirdly, the nurses said you've got to let them wash you because you're starting to stink!'

And I flounced out. Oh dear. I'm not very good at doing the 'being Christ' thing. It was as if God whispered in my ear, 'Keep trying; you need the practice.'

Sunday 11 February

Chrissie asked me how my visits to Jeremiah were going. I told her, and she threw back her head and laughed.

'Good for you!' she said. 'We'll make a Pastoral Visitor of you yet.'

Fat chance!

I have prayed, I have read the Bible, I have meditated, I have done my pre-natal exercises and I am now ready to face Jeremiah Wedgwood. This time, I am armed with a bottle of sparkling grape juice and a *Times* crossword puzzle book.

Jeremiah lay fast asleep wearing clean pyjamas. His hair had been combed, and he'd had a shave. My flowers were in a vase, and the cards were still standing upright. The gardening magazine lay open to a page that said, 'Carnations – A Carnival of Colour'.

I sat for fifteen minutes reading the gardening magazine, but he didn't wake. I placed the grape juice and puzzle book on his locker and left.

Monday 12 February

I had an appointment with the midwife, so I couldn't see Jeremiah this afternoon. It was reassuring to know the baby is doing everything expected of it, and it was a weight off my shoulders not to have to put up with Jeremiah's venom.

We decided to forgo the television tonight and take a sortie down to the Raj of Sidcup for a change. It may not be haute cuisine, but at least I don't have to wash up. Kevin walked out of the house leaving the lounge, kitchen and one bedroom light on.

'Hey – what about our electricity bill!' I said, jogging up the stairs as fast as my bump would let me. I went round flicking the light switches off, then joined Kevin outside the front door. The house was in darkness except for the hall light.

'You missed one,' said Kevin.

'No, you always leave the hall light on – for burglars.'

'What, so that they don't trip over on their way out with our stuff?'

'No! It's so they think someone's at home.'

'Well, naturally, everyone knows that British families spend entire winter evenings sitting in the hall!'

'Of course not. It's just a ... deterrent.'

'Let me get this straight.' He held out his gloved hand and counted off on his fingers. 'In this modern, high-tech age with burglar alarms and security cameras, not to mention Neighbourhood Watch, these particularly stupid burglars say to themselves, "Let's not rob Rose Cottage tonight; they're obviously at home waiting for us, because they've left a light on in the hall." If it was going to be a proper deterrent, we should leave all the lights on and the telly!'

I had to admit that he had a point. Perhaps we should install a security alarm, especially with a baby in the house. I mentioned it to Kevin.

'They're hardly going to steal the baby, are they?'

'No, it might just make me feel a bit safer.'

'Okay,' he conceded, 'I'll see what Vague Dave can do.'

Tuesday 13 February

Tomorrow's the start of Lent, and I've no vices left to give up. Chocolate makes me nauseous, and I haven't had anything stronger than orange squash since I found out I was pregnant.

Wednesday 14 February, Ash Wednesday, St Valentine's Day

Eek! My diary says it's Valentine's Day, and I forgot all about it. Kevin gave me a huge slushy card and a bunch of roses at breakfast, so I tried to make the lack of reciprocation seem mysterious, as if I had something special lined up.

'I've got something really phenomenal for you,' I said, winking seductively.

'Well, let's have it, then.'

'Oh, I can't possibly give it to you this morning. But when you get home tonight, it'll be waiting for you.'

'Brilliant.' Kevin rubbed his hands together. 'I can't wait.'

'Until tonight, *mon cheri*!'

'Tonight!'

And he left for work. Blast! That means I've got to think up something extra special. I suppose that means trekking round the shops. And I'm supposed to be putting my feet up.

Phoned Ariadne at work. She was even more impatient than usual as I'd caught her when she was just about to go to a board meeting.

'You have blundered, haven't you, dear sister! If it was me, I'd nip out at lunchtime and buy the ingredients for a terrific gourmet meal, which I would then prepare and cook lovingly with my own hands. In your case, I wouldn't recommend cooking unless you want Kevin to end up with a case of terminal indigestion.'

I nearly put the phone down at that point.

'Hang on a minute,' she said. 'What about giving him an evening of pampering? Have a hot bath ready when he comes home, offer him a massage and ... well, anything else you can think of ...'

Thursday 15 February

Too ... preoccupied to finish writing about yesterday in my diary. Bearing in mind Kevin's embargo on descriptions of anything that goes on in the bedroom, I'll just have to be content to say that my Valentine's Day gift to him did turn out to be phenomenal.

Friday 16 February

'You're here again.'

'Yes' I said, dumping a bag of bananas and a copy of *Horse and Hound* on the bed.

'Why?'

'You asked me that the first time I came, Jeremiah, and you were right: I didn't give you an honest answer. The reason I came was because Chrissie persuaded me to. She said that apart from her and Reverend Potter, you had no other visitors. So yes, I did come out of a sense of obligation. And you haven't made it easy.'

'Perhaps you should take the hint and leave.' He glared at me with his watery blue eyes.

'If you really find my company so unbearable, I'll go now.'

He opened his mouth to speak, then shut it again.

I stood up. 'The ball's in your court, Jeremiah. It's entirely up to you.'

'Well, as you're here now, you might as well stay.'

I sat down and handed him the fruit and magazine.

'I'm sorry, they didn't have much in the shop.'

'*Horse and Hound*, eh?'

'It was either that or *Woman's Weekly*.'

'Then you made the right choice.' He almost smiled.

The next ten minutes trying to make small talk with Jeremiah felt like pulling teeth. Eventually I did one of those 'stage' glances at my watch.

'Goodness! Is that the time? I must go. I'll come back tomorrow if you like.'

Jeremiah shrugged. 'Please yourself.'

'So if there's anything you want ...'

He hesitated. 'Would you do something for me?'

'Of course.'

Jeremiah leaned over and opened the top flap of his bed-side locker. He reached inside and pulled out a bunch of keys, flinching with the discomfort of moving.

'Would you go to my flat and fetch my Bible?'

He wrote down the address and handed it to me.

'Anything else?'

'No, that will be all.'

I thought for a moment he was going to say, 'Thank you,' but he didn't, so I tucked the keys and the piece of paper into my handbag and headed home.

Saturday 17 February

It took me nearly twenty minutes to find Jeremiah's flat yesterday afternoon. It turned out to be on a dismal low-rise development about three miles away in a labyrinth of cul-de-sacs. I parked my car and locked it carefully, wondering if there would still be tyres and wing mirrors when I returned. I went up a concrete stairway to the first floor and walked along an outside walkway to Flat 25. As I fumbled with the keys, a woman in a grubby velour tracksuit emerged from the next-door flat.

'Is he dead?'

'No! No, just in hospital. I'm getting a few bits to take in to him.'

'You his daughter?'

'No, I'm a friend.'

'Didn't think he had any of them.' She laughed a forty-a-day crackling laugh.

'Well, he has. Excuse me.'

I pushed open the door. Jeremiah's flat was as sparse as a monk's cell. There was no television, no pictures on the walls and no ornaments. There was an old stereo cassette player and a neat collection of tapes, mainly sermons, classical music and hymns. The walls were wage-packet beige and the curtains a muddy brown. I scooped up a pile of letters from the doormat. I sifted through, and as there seemed to be nothing urgent, I placed them on the dining table. I went into the tiny kitchenette and opened the fridge. I poured away the rancid milk. I also threw the out-of-date food and mouldy bread into a dustbin bag and put them outside.

Velour Tracksuit Woman was still standing in her doorway, puffing away. I nodded in acknowledgement. She nodded back. I returned to the flat and found Jeremiah's bedroom. I felt as if I was trespassing – I couldn't think of any other circumstance that would bring me here. His bed was neatly made with an old-fashioned candlewick bedspread. Here, among the theology tomes on his bookcase, were the only inklings of any personal belongings. One, two, three, four ... I counted five cups and trophies from his footballing days, a memento of his career as an international striker.

The rest of the bedroom was bare, as I'd imagined it to be, except for a cellophane-wrapped pink toy rabbit on his pillow. I was intrigued. Could it have been a present from a past girlfriend? It looked too new for it to have been a keepsake from his childhood. I longed to take it with me to the hospital and present it to Jeremiah, but that would be too cruel. I found his huge leather Bible on the bedside cabinet. As I picked it up, leaflets slid out and fluttered to the floor. Cartoon-strip stories with titles like *Repent or Perish*, *Judgement Day* and other equally encouraging sentiments, all followed by several exclamation marks. I picked them up and was about to tuck them back inside the Bible when I had the horrible thought he might give them out to people in the hospital. I slipped them down between the cabinet and the bed, hoping they might just disappear.

I let myself out. The woman was still hovering there.

'Let me know if he ... you know ... croaks. My sister-in-law's looking for a flat.'

Jeremiah actually looked quite cheerful when he saw me. I handed over the Bible, and he embraced it like a long-lost child.

'My Bible!' he exclaimed. He flipped through the pages, stopping to read a verse here and there. 'Were there any leaflets in it?' he asked.

'They must have slipped out.' I tried to sound innocent.

'Never mind, there's plenty of time.'

I waited again for him to thank me, but he didn't.

'I must be going now,' I said. 'I'll come back later in the week.' But he was too engrossed in his Bible to acknowledge me.

Monday 19 February

Less than one month to go! My appointments with the midwife are weekly now, and I'm starting to feel very pregnant.

My bump isn't enormous like some of the women I see at the maternity clinic. I still have no trouble fitting behind the steering wheel, and I don't do that waddling walk that some pregnant women seem to do. My ankles are still the normal size, and I don't seem to be anaemic any more. On the negative side, my back aches if I stand for too long, and it's difficult to find a comfortable position to sleep in. The baby is very active at night, and Kevin complains that it keeps kicking him in the back. Perhaps I'll just read a chapter or two of my baby book.

Tuesday 20 February

Argh! Less than one month to go, and the nursery is still full of junk. We haven't bought a pram yet, and I've no idea what nipple shields are.

Thursday 22 February

Jeremiah was almost chirpy this afternoon. I found a book about Smith Wigglesworth in the church library, and although I'm pretty sure he'd read it before, he took it graciously. The hospital chaplain visited him yesterday and was, according to Jeremiah, by the end of the visit very near to making a profession of faith.

'Miss Monroe was here this morning.' He still couldn't bring himself to use Chrissie's title, 'Reverend' Monroe. 'She told me that you might not be able to visit me for very much longer.'

'That's right,' I said. 'The baby's due in less than a month.'

'I understand.' He paused, and I noticed a flush of colour skim across his pallid cheeks. 'Thank you.'

I wanted to hug him, but I restrained myself.

'Any time,' I said.

Friday 23 February

Phoned Chrissie this evening.

'I'm worried about Jeremiah.'

'Why is that?'

'Well, he's actually being nice to me.'

'Jeremiah, nice. Not two words I'd expect to hear in the same sentence, but I'm delighted. Why is that a problem?'

'The baby's due pretty soon now, and I'm not sure how much longer I'll be able to go on visiting him. It's strange, but he almost sounded upset when I told him.'

'I know; I've been trying to break it to him gently.'

'Couldn't we get someone else to go?'

Chrissie made a whistling sound. 'Who?'

A thought struck me. 'He's got a nephew – Brian, the one who wrote that half-witted article about you in a bikini.'

'Don't remind me! Actually, I tried him before I asked you. Aside from the fact that there's no love lost between them, Brian wrote an article castigating the hospital for its record on cleanliness. "I'd rather be treated in a pigsty that had fallen into a sewer during an outbreak of dysentery than set foot inside that hospital." I think that was the sentiment.'

'Oh dear!'

'I don't think he'd be welcomed. In fact, I'd heard they've got the liquid nitrogen enema handy just in case.'

I giggled. 'I'll see if I can think of anyone else who can help out.'

Sunday 25 February

When we were drinking our post-Communion coffee today, I suggested to Charity that she might like to visit Jeremiah in hospital.

'Oh no!' she said. 'I couldn't possibly do that.'

'Why not?'

'He insulted Nigel dreadfully last month.' Her face began to colour.

'How?' My curiosity was aroused. I was beginning to enjoy this.

'He questioned Nigel's headship, and he implied that the authority in our home was unbiblical.'

'Surely not!'

'He said that Nigel was "under the thumb".' She gave a little gasp.

I tried to conceal a smirk. 'Never!'

'It's true.' She nodded vigorously.

'Charity, if ever there was anyone who knows exactly where their head is, that person is you.'

Monday 26 February

I seem to be coming down with a cold. One good thing about being a nearly natal mother is that you can spend the day stretched out on the sofa without feeling guilty. The bad thing about being a nearly natal mother is that you can't take any medicine to relieve the cold symptoms, you get crampy and fidgety on the sofa and you can't rest because you're up and down to the loo every half an hour.

Tuesday 27 February

Kevin has taken a day off work to look after me. Aaah! How sweet.

2 p.m.

I've had enough of this 'being looked after' malarkey. So far, I've made Kevin three cups of tea and one round of cheese and pickle sandwiches, I've done two loads of washing and I'm just about to do some weeding in the front garden – all on a box and a half of Kleenex. My Florence Nightingale, meanwhile, has been sprawled in a chair watching football videos all morning. I may just have a relapse around the time dinner needs to be prepared.

Wednesday 28 February

Cold a bit worse today, so I stayed in bed and sniffed. Kevin back at work – thank goodness.

MARCH

Thursday 1 March, St David's Day

Kevin didn't wake me up this morning, so I woke with a start at the sound of the dustcart. I glanced out of the bedroom window. As usual Kevin had forgotten to put out the rubbish. I hastily pulled on my dressing gown, which no longer meets around the bump, thrust my feet into a pair of Kevin's spare work boots and dashed out of the door with a bag of rubbish in each hand, my red nose dripping as I ran.

I rushed down the path, almost tripping over Kevin's gigantic footwear, and dumped the bags next to the gate. Then I heard a voice.

'Well, I must say, you're looking as gorgeous as ever.'

I wiped my nose on the back of my hand and tried to pull my dressing gown farther round the bump. I looked up into blue eyes sparkling under a floppy fringe of red hair.

'Declan!'

'Well, well, Theo; blooming, I see.' He glanced at my expansive midriff and plaster-covered steel-capped boots.

'What are you doing here?' I snapped.

'I live here. Well, just around the corner.'

'Since when?'

'About a month ago'

'How dare you!' I fought back tears of anger.

'There's no dare about it. I just went to the landlord and handed over me money and ...'

'I mean move *here*. You know I live here.'

'I know where you *used* to live. Last I'd heard you'd got married to Mr Universal Washer and were happily billing and cooing your life away in a little rose-covered cottage.'

'Yes, this rose-covered cottage.' I jabbed my finger towards our front door, which I noticed had slammed shut.

'Hand on heart, I did not know that.'

'What's Kevin going to say?'

'About what?'

'About you living practically next door. He'll never believe there's nothing going on.'

'Why should he think there's something going on?'

'Because of before, you idiot.'

'But there was nothing going on before. As I remember it, I declared my undying love to you, bared my soul, offered to give up my God-given vocation, and what did you do? Drove four hundred miles to see me, stayed five minutes, shouted abuse at me, then went home. What was I supposed to think?'

My mind raced. That wasn't how it happened. He wrecked my engagement; then, when I'd driven all the way to Manchester, I found him in the arms of another woman.

Declan was laughing. He was actually laughing. 'Theo, you are funny.'

'I'm not funny. I'm pregnant, freezing cold and furious. And,' I said, glancing back at the front door, 'now I'm locked out.'

'Well, there's a conundrum. How are we going to get you back inside?'

'I don't know!'

'Have you got a spare key under a flowerpot, or did you leave one with a neighbour?'

'No, Ariadne's got one, but she'll be at work, and Tom will have taken Phoebe to her playgroup.'

'What about an open window? I might be able to squeeze through.'

Declan took off his jacket and laid it round my shoulders to stop me shivering. We walked around the cottage. The only window that was open was the little one in the bathroom. Even in my pre-pregnancy state I would have had trouble squeezing through it. And I certainly didn't want Declan to try. All I wanted to do was to sit down and cry my eyes out, but a combination of pride and determination stopped me. I knocked on the neighbours' doors, to see if anyone could shelter me. Everyone was out.

'You're going to hate me, but I'll suggest it anyway. You could come round to my place, get warm, and if you must, you can call Kevin from there.'

'No!' I shouted. I don't know which idea seemed more loathsome: ringing Kevin and admitting to having locked myself out, or going to Declan's place.

'Suit yourself, but there's no sense in us both standing here freezing to death. If you'd be so kind as to return the jacket when you've finished with it ...'

'Hey, you can't leave me!'

'Well, if you won't come ...'

'Have you got a car? You could take me to Chrissie's.'

'You know I don't drive.'

'Ohhh!' I let out a howl of frustration and sat down on the garden wall, pulling the jacket tight around me.

'What's the matter? You're not having the baby now, are you?'

'No, I am not having the baby now, but I am coming very close to having a nervous breakdown.'

Declan sat down next to me. 'That's a very beautiful night-gown you're wearing, if I may say so.'

'No, you may not. Oh, Declan, what am I going to do? I can't wander round the streets like this until someone takes pity on me.'

'Would this help?' Excuse me ...' He pulled the edge of his jacket out of my grasp, stretched it away from my body and reached into an inside pocket, pulling out a mobile phone. He dangled it tantalizingly between his thumb and forefinger in front of my face. I snatched it from him and tried to dial. It was locked, so I thrust it back at him and he unlocked it. I dialled Chrissie's number, and when she'd stopped laughing she agreed to drive round and rescue me. I handed his phone back.

'Please go now, before Chrissie gets here.'

'What, are you ashamed of me?'

'It's not that ... Look, please just go. I'll get the jacket back to you later. And ... thank you.'

He stood up and gave me a wave as he headed off up the road.

'See you sometime.'

Chrissie arrived fifteen minutes later, still giggling at my predicament. I eased my frozen bottom off the garden wall.

'You'll get piles if you sit there!' she called out of the window.

I held up my hand to silence her. 'Just don't go there!'

She shovelled some papers off the front seat and helped me into her battered Mini.

'So this is what the well-dressed expectant mother is wearing these days, is it?'

'No, this is what the expectant mother who got locked out of her house at half past eight in the morning is wearing.'

'Lucky you had your jacket with you.'

I opened my mouth to tell her about Declan, then thought better of it. 'Yes, it is,' I said.

She drove me back to the vicarage. Upstairs, in her bedroom, I sat on the bed and watched as she burrowed through her wardrobe like a dog digging for a bone. Clothes flew out behind her, some of them nearly hitting me. A pile of garments – sparkly Lycra miniskirts and halter tops lay cheek-by-jowl with cassocks and surplices. Finally she produced an enormous gold-and-black-hooped rugby top and some jogging pants.

'Here, these should fit you.' She went to make a cup of tea while I got dressed. I had to roll the trouser legs up several times, and the rugby shirt made me look like a gigantic bumble bee. Nevertheless, I was grateful, and the vicarage was warmer than my garden.

Chrissie came back with the tea. 'I took the liberty and rang Kevin,' she said.

'Did he go mad?' I asked.

'Only a little bit. He says he'll come as soon as he can, but you're welcome to stay here as long as you want. I've got to get back to the finance committee meeting that you dragged me away from, kicking and screaming.' She made a face. 'With any luck they'll have got it all sorted out without me and I can get on with some proper work.'

Chrissie flitted off, and I sat in her kitchen, drinking tea, and thought about Declan. I was so stunned to see him again. Is it simply coincidence that he has moved just around the corner, or is he trying to make some kind of point? Perhaps he is stalking me. No, that's just silly. Whatever the situation, Kevin mustn't find out. He doesn't trust Declan an inch. He'd never believe it was a fluke.

Friday 2 March

Kevin turned up in time for elevenses. After initially falling about laughing over my outfit, he was surprisingly sympathetic, and when we got home we talked about a suitable place for concealing a spare key.

'It's a good job Vague Dave hasn't installed our alarm yet,' I commented.

'No, he hasn't had the time; he's up at the prison at the moment for counterfeiting.'

'Counterfeiting! You're thinking of taking on a convicted criminal to install a burglar alarm in our house? Great plan!'

'Not counterfeiting. Counter fitting. Putting new worktops in the prison kitchen!'

It was only after I'd got home and changed into my normalish clothes that I realized I'd left Declan's jacket at the vicarage. I toyed with the idea of breaking in to steal it back, but my train of thought was soon derailed when Chrissie, with the jacket in her hand, knocked on the door.

'You left this behind,' she said.

'Thanks,' I said, snatching it out of her hand.

'Is is yours?' she said.

'Yes ... I mean no. It's Kevin's.' I tried to shut the door.

'Theo, is everything all right?'

'Yes. Of course. Um ... thanks for bringing it back.' And I closed the door.

Now what do I do? What if Kevin finds it? I can't take it back to Declan, because I don't know where he lives. He told me it's around the corner, but I don't know exactly where. What if Kevin's here when he calls round for it?

I hid the coat in the back of the wardrobe and went to visit Jeremiah to take my mind off things.

He was looking almost perky. In my haste I hadn't brought him anything.

'Ta-ra!' He waved his fingers like a conjuror. 'No drips.'

'That's great!' I said. 'You're looking much better. How much longer are you on traction?'

'They said six weeks originally, but they are going to X-ray my leg tomorrow. I'm not used to this sitting still and ...' He beckoned me to come closer '... depending on others for my *needs.*'

'Yes, it must be difficult.' I shuddered at the thought of my impending sojourn in hospital in a fortnight.

'Of course, it has been a great source of comfort to have my Bible. It has meant I can read and worship, and when it gets hard to sleep, I can draw comfort from the Scriptures. It is a pity my leaflets are not here. There have been many occasions when I could have handed one out to a soul destined to perish in the eternal fires.'

'Oh dear, I guess you'll just have to engage them in conversation instead.'

Saturday 3 March

Kevin's team had a home match today, and Kevin insisted on ringing me every hour just to check that the baby wasn't on the way yet. It was very thoughtful of him, but what I really needed was an afternoon of unbroken dozing to make up for having to keep getting up in the middle of the night.

Sunday 4 March

Had my first twinges in the middle of the Kyrie Eleison today. At first I thought I was in labour, then I realized they were probably the 'Braxton-Hicks' contractions I'd read about in the baby book. It felt very peculiar; I had twinges in places I didn't even know I had places!

Monday 5 March

It's been a week and Declan still hasn't come to reclaim his jacket. I've tried looking him up in the phone directory, but as he only moved in a month ago, he's not listed yet. I've tried watching out of the window, but so far I haven't spotted him walking past.

By lunchtime I couldn't stand it any longer, so I rang Ariadne. She was trying to eat tuna sandwiches while checking out the lunchtime stock-market reports, but I soon had her full attention when I mentioned Declan.

'You don't mean your ex-boss, the one who used to play all those puerile practical jokes, who decided he'd been "called to the priesthood" then nearly wrecked your wedding by claiming that he was in love with you and when you went up there was having fun with some floozy?'

'That's the one.'

'And now he's stalking you?'

'Sort of ...'

'Slap a restraining order on him!' I heard her fist thud down on the desk.

'Good idea. How do I go about getting one of those?'

'Contact the police or a solicitor, I suppose, and make a list of what he's doing to persecute you.'

'Right ...' I must have sounded dubious, because Ariadne suggested that I run the list past her first.

'So,' she snapped, 'so far, he has walked past your house, lent you his coat, let you use his mobile phone and offered to help you when you were locked out ...' There was a long pause.

'Goodbye.'

And the phone went dead. I know it hardly constitutes harassment, but I still have the horrible feeling that he has come back for a reason, and I know that Kevin will feel that way too.

Tuesday 6 March

Bumped into Mr Wilberforce at the doctor's surgery today when I was having my weekly check-up. Fortunately, he had left Rex tied up outside. He hadn't heard about Jeremiah's accident, so I decided to stick my neck out and ask if he'd be prepared to visit him.

'Of course. I'll take a chessboard. Jeremiah always liked a game of chess. I could bring Rex with me, as a sort of "petting dog". They have those in hospitals now, you know. Supposed to be good for the patients. Lowers their blood pressure.'

I nodded cautiously. They may have lower blood pressure, but knowing Rex, they may end up with lacerated fingers and flea bites.

Wednesday 7 March

Ten

Found a note through the door from Declan. As well as including his address and phone number, his note read,

> I was surprised and delighted to bump into you again last week. Seeing you was like seeing a smile on the face of God … If you were able to return my jacket, I'd be grateful, as I've been freezing my globes off without it. All the best with the birth of the little one.
>
> Love,
> Declan

I scooped up his coat and set off for Shakespeare Avenue. The name, I discovered, was much nicer than the road itself. The trees were stunted or missing, and the houses were a mixture of terraces and semis, most of which had seen better days. I found the number and hesitated at the gate. What if he wasn't in ... what if he was in ... what if the latest of his 'women' answered the door? While I hesitated, the front door opened, and Declan stood there drying his hands on a tea towel.

'You brought it back. I was about to send round the bailiffs.'

I walked down the steps and handed him the coat.

'Thanks for the loan,' I said.

'My pleasure.' He gave a theatrical bow. ''Tis surely a delight to assist a fair damsel in distress.'

I tried to force a smile.

'Would you like to come in for a coffee ... or something?'

'No thanks,' I snapped.

'Okaay,' he said slowly. 'There's no need to bite my head off. I was trying to be civil.'

'Sorry, sorry ... I'm just a bit defensive.' I gazed at the man in the doorway, his smile that had brightened up my workdays for so many years, his friendship, then his betrayal. 'You really hurt me, you know.'

'Yes, I do know, and I regret it deeply.' He brushed his floppy hair back from his face, and my knees seemed to turn to jelly. I clutched the fence to regain my balance and to recapture my wandering thoughts.

'You've got your coat back,' I said. 'I appreciate your help when I was locked out, but I don't expect our paths to cross again.'

'You mean, "Keep away".'

'Yes. Yes, I do mean that. It's for the best.'

I turned my back on Declan and walked out of the garden, out of the street and back to Rose Cottage. I fumbled in my pocket for the keys, and a shiver of panic shot through me until I realized I'd put them in my handbag. I unlocked the door, went inside, sat on the sofa and cried my eyes out. I guess it must be a combination of relief and my pregnancy hormones.

Thursday 8 March

Nine

Mum phoned me a couple of days ago to warn me – I mean, tell me – that Ag and Cordelia will be down for a visit this evening. She wondered if I was getting bored waiting for the baby and if I would like to come for a meal and to see my brother and sister-in-law.

'I've covered the sofa in plastic sheets, just in case your waters go.'

As Kevin is going to a football match this evening, and she's right – I am bored – I decided to go.

Earlier, Charity had dropped some carob chip cookies in.

'As we haven't seen you at the MAMAL group for a while, I thought I'd bring you these.'

Too right she hadn't seen me. That bunch of middle-class, middle-aged women who think there's nothing more exciting in life than changing a vacuum cleaner bag are definitely not my mug of Darjeeling. Nevertheless, I was grateful for the sentiment ... and the cookies.

I got there at about half past seven and was relieved to find that Mum was only joking about the plastic sheets. Ag and Cordelia were already there, and I was astonished to find that Cordelia looks bigger than I do even though her baby isn't due for another four and a half months. She was wearing hipster trousers and a cropped top which exposed a draughty few inches of her bump. Despite her trendy clothes, Cordelia did not look well. Her skin was sallow, and she had dark circles under her eyes. My pangs of sympathy faded when she demanded that I get up and give her *my* armchair because it looked more comfortable and her 'back aches so much'.

For the rest of the afternoon, all the conversation revolved around Cordelia and her morning sickness, her scan photos, her refusal to push a trolley around the supermarket, and her insistence that Ag does all the housework when he gets home from work despite the fact that she gave up her job six weeks ago 'for the sake of the baby'. When they bought their house, she went to her parents' and left Ag to sort out the move on his own. By the end of it, I felt like going into labour just to spite her. Then I realized that it was me who was lucky to be feeling so well and to be able to do all the things I can do. Although I'm a bit apprehensive about the birth – I'm not allowed to say I've changed my mind and I'd like to send it back – I am so much looking forward to holding the baby and to us being a family. I wonder if Cordelia and Ag can say the same.

Friday 9 March

Eight

Kevin sent me flowers this morning. At least, I think it was Kevin. I hope it was Kevin.

1 p.m.

Kevin phoned me to ask if I'd received the flowers. I breathed a sigh of relief and thanked him. He muttered something like, 'Would it have killed you to have phoned me?'

Saturday 10 March

Seven

Last-minute trip to the shops to get the final few baby things. The nursery is ready, my bags are packed, Kevin has memorized the route to the hospital and I've spent hours learning to breathe properly. Funny, after breathing more or less continuously for the last thirty-one years, I would have thought that I'd got the hang of it.

Sunday 11 March

Six

If one more person had come up to me in church and said, 'Haven't you had that baby yet?' I swear I would have decked them. Do they think I like looking like this? Do they think I would have had the baby then stuck a cushion up my jumper just for fun?

Monday 12 March

Five

There is going to be a special Palm Sunday service at the cathedral on 25 March. Everyone from church is going, and I want to go too, but the baby will be so little that I'm not sure I'll manage it. It's not fair. It isn't even born yet, and already it's cramping my style ... as well as my bladder.

Tuesday 13 March

Four

Another check-up today. Although everything's fine, there are no signs of labour starting. Oh well, a lot can happen in four days.

Wednesday 14 March

Three

Wandered around the village looking at all the mums pushing prams and the toddlers, and the wait until Saturday seems interminable. Tried to doze a bit on the sofa after lunch, but I was uncomfortable and only managed about ten minutes. Decided to go and visit Jeremiah. Made a batch of sultana and cinnamon cookies from Tom's cookery book and chose the least burnt ones to take with me. I also found a stack of Kevin's old football magazines that he was intending to recycle. In view of Jeremiah's previous life as a top-notch footballer, I thought he may be interested.

Jeremiah was grateful for the biscuits, but his face darkened when he saw the football magazines.

'Why have you brought me this garbage?'

'Well, I just thought ... as you'd been a footballer ...'

'Then don't think! That life then, that person I used to be in my unredeemed state, stinking in my filth and corruption, what makes you think that I want to be reminded of that?'

'Jeremiah, it's only a game!'

'It's not only a game. To me, it was my life, my god, the thing that I worshipped and the thing that sustained me. It drew me in with its false adulation, its alcohol and its deceitful women. And it cost me my life to break free.'

'If you feel that strongly, why did you offer to help Kevin with the Saturday afternoon kids' team?'

'I thought it might be an opportunity to reach young minds, to snatch them back before that wicked indulgence that masquerades as sport could get its talons into their pliant young minds.'

'So you weren't going to help, just to spread your poisonous message that pretends to be Christianity? Well, you obviously won't be needing these.' I gathered up the magazines. 'I'll take them to the children's ward.'

❦

As I negotiated my way down the corridor with arms full of magazines, a familiar voice behind me called out, 'Maternity department's that way, love.'

I spun round to see Declan, in a shirt and tie, pushing a large trolley full of files.

'Declan?'

'We'll have to stop meeting like this.'

'What are you doing here?'

'I work here. What about you? It doesn't look as if you're in labour.'

'I'm not. I came to visit a friend.'

'Sports injury?' He nodded at the magazines.

'No, these were spare, so I was going to take them to the children's ward.'

'I'll take them for you if you like. I'm going down there later.' He helped me load the stack of magazines into the trolley.

'Thanks, bye.' I gave a casual wave and tried to scoot off down the corridor as quickly as my bump would let me.

'See you again sometime,' he called to my back.

I sincerely hoped not, but seeing as I'm likely to be spending time in the hospital soon, I don't see how I can avoid him. Oh well, the baby's due on Saturday, and I'll probably only stay in overnight. I just hope he doesn't work weekends.

Thursday 15 March

Two

Mum called round and gave me an 'Are you still here?' look. Nevertheless, she has brought me about a month's worth of frozen meals from her Aphrodite's Greek Delicacies range.

'They're unsaleable,' she explained. 'The labels have come off. Nothing wrong with them, though. Kevin can have them while you're in hospital, and it will save you cooking when the baby's tiny.'

It's very thoughtful of her, and I did manage to sound grateful, but I just know I'm going to end up pouring tomato sauce on my baklava and honey on my moussaka.

Friday 16 March

One

Ariadne has the day off work and wants to take Phoebe and me swimming.

'Oh, I don't know if I'm up to it,' I whined. 'The baby's due tomorrow ...'

'First babies never turn up on time. Everyone knows that.'

'This one better had. It's an away match. Kevin's got new batteries in his radio so that he can listen to the commentary in the delivery suite.'

'Then you'd better start doing some vigorous exercise. Swimming would be ideal.'

'What if I go into labour in the swimming pool?'

'What if you do? It would save you the cost of hiring a birthing pool.'

Saturday 17 March, St Patrick's Day

Zero!

We have lift-off – or rather, we don't. I'm certainly showing no signs of labour, even after all that energetic swimming yesterday. Not even a twinge. By lunchtime, Kevin was getting distinctly twitchy.

'Can't you hurry it along a bit?' Kevin glanced at his watch. 'Kick-off is in two and a half hours.'

'No, I can't,' I grumbled. 'Look, you might as well go off to your match.'

I rang Ariadne, who had gone shopping, but Tom was full of helpful advice.

'Um ... I've heard a bumpy car ride, a good hot curry and, um ... making love can help to bring on labour.'

When Kevin got back from football, I told him about Tom's suggestions. Kevin was delighted with the advice and was particularly enthusiastic about the last two. We could be in for an interesting evening.

Sunday 18 March

Still nothing happening. I did have a few twinges at about half past eight last night, but they dwindled away before the nine o'clock news had come on. I decided I couldn't face church this morning, so while Kevin and his five-a-side mates were out kicking a ball around, I took my coffee into the garden and sat on the rather rusty garden bench enjoying the spring sunshine. Although we mowed the lawn last autumn, it seems to have gone mad lately. The daffodils have rebelled too. Not content to stay in their flower beds, they've trespassed all over the lawn, thrusting their heads through the turf and covering the grass in patches of yellow.

I sat and prayed for the baby and handed all my fears, hopes and dreams to God. The baby is going to come late, and there is nothing I can do about it. Despite my impatience, I am determined to enjoy the days (weeks!) before the baby is born.

The phone rang: it was my mother checking that I was still in one piece. It rang again, and it was Chrissie to see if there was any news. Then it was Ariadne. I gave up on the 'tranquillity in the garden' idea and did some ironing until my back ached.

When Kevin came back we had lunch at the local carvery then took a stroll in the park. Some toddlers were pelting ducks with crusts of bread.

'That will be us soon,' remarked Kevin.

Not that soon. The way things are going, I feel as if I'll be pregnant for ever.

Monday 19 March

Wandered aimlessly around the house all day and had a long afternoon nap. This waiting is sooooo boring.

7:30 p.m.

Phone call from Gregory Pasternak. He'd heard that things were 'a bit quiet on the baby front' and wondered if I'd be interested in coming along to his planning meeting for the Dickensian Pageant. Normally I would run a mile at the thought of it, but today I'm grateful for anything that will take my mind off the baby.

The meeting was already in full flow by the time I arrived. They had sent letters to various local organizations who had agreed to dress up as characters from Dickens novels; the Scouts are taking on *Nicholas Nickleby*, the primary school *Oliver Twist* and the Woman's Institute *David Copperfield*. St Norbert's were supposed to be *A Tale of Two Cities*, but Chrissie has begged to change to *Great Expectations* so that she can play the ill-starred Miss Havisham. The committee agreed to the change, and now *A Tale of Two Cities* has been assigned to the Twinning Association. The only character I feel I could play at the moment with any authenticity is the rotund Mr Pickwick. They discussed the food stalls – I neatly escaped being volunteered for anything involving cooking – and the musicians to provide entertainment. I got out of that one too, on account of being famously tone-deaf. They also plan to run a craft tent with traditional Victorian handiwork and invite an old-fashioned funfair to set up on the village green. They have set a date – 2 June.

After my initial trepidation about the project, especially the locality's extremely tenuous links to Dickens, I'm now looking forward to the whole thing. I have offered to help as much as I can with the celebrations, but with a small baby, who knows what my contribution will be?

Tuesday 20 March

At my doctor's appointment today, even Dr Edison asked, 'Are you still here?' After examining me, she decided I was very much still here and the baby is showing every sign of staying there too.

'Still,' she said, 'we tend not to worry too much until the baby is a fortnight overdue.'

A fortnight!

She has booked me a hospital appointment for Thursday, when they will decide whether to induce labour yet or not.

Wednesday 21 March

Ariadne surprised me by arriving at my door at half past nine and whipping me off to have my hair and nails done.

'You sounded as if you needed cheering up,' she said. 'Besides, long acrylic nails are just the thing to dig into Kevin's hand during labour to ensure he shares in the full birth experience.'

(I declined the acrylic nails. I'm not sure I could manage to change nappies with them.)

Thursday 22 March

Kevin came to the hospital with me for my check-up. They agreed the baby was perfectly happy and healthy but fully intended to stay put for the time being. They have made me an appointment for next Thursday. If nothing has happened by then, they are going to induce labour.

'The only problem is, you do have rather small feet,' the midwife commented.

'Why? Do I have to give birth wearing special shoes?' I asked.

'No, but it can be an indication of a small pelvic opening – cephallo-pelvic disproportion. It makes it difficult for the baby's head to drop down properly.'

'What does that mean?' I had the vision of being pregnant for ever, or until the baby grew so much it exploded out of me.

'Well, the worst thing that would happen is that we would have to perform a caesarean section. But I wouldn't worry about it.'

Not worry about it! They've just warned me that they may have to slice me open, and I'm not to worry about it! Help me, God – I don't want an operation.

Friday 23 March

'There's not much you can do about it. It's in there and it's got to come out one way or another.'

'Ariadne! You're no help.'

'What do you want me to say? "There, there, everything will be all right"?'

'It would do for a start.'

'Thousands of women have a caesarean every day, and after a couple of weeks they're fine. What's more important: a so-called "natural" birth, or that you both end up alive and healthy?'

'I suppose.'

'Anyway, it's not definite. There's always a chance the baby will have a small head. Although with you as its mother, the chances are very slim ...'

At that point, I just had to pelt her with cushions.

Saturday 24 March

The baby's a whole week overdue, and I'm starting to get used to the idea that I'm going to be pregnant for ever. I can't concentrate on anything. I'm worried about going anywhere, and everyone I speak to asks the same old questions: 'How long is it now?' 'When is it due?' and my personal favourite, 'Haven't you had it yet?' If it's not the questions, it's statements such as 'Make the most of it; the baby's less trouble when it's in there' or 'I bet you can't wait.'

I can't face any more bumpy car rides, curries ... or the other suggestion. I'm just going to carry on as if nothing is happening, which of course it isn't.

Kevin was rubbing my feet and being generally nice to me when he got back from the match.

'Kevin, I really want to go to the cathedral service tomorrow. Would you drive me?'

'Are you sure it's a good idea?'

'Why not? I'm bored sitting here, waiting to hatch.'

'What if you go into labour? What if you give birth in the cathedral?'

'It's better than giving birth in Sainsbury's.'

'True. And you could organize the christening while you are there.'

Sunday 25 March, Palm Sunday

Woke up with a nagging backache, a huge pimple on my chin and Kevin in the spare room. Apparently I was fidgeting so much last night he couldn't stand it and went to find somewhere quieter to sleep. I was aware that the baby kept kicking me in the stomach, and that probably made me restless. Even so, I consider it 'unsupportive' of Kevin to disappear into the next room. I was surprised my grumpiness didn't put him into a bad mood. Instead he was attentive and eager to please, and nothing seemed too much trouble for him. I was starting to get extremely suspicious.

'Why are you being so nice to me?'

'You're my wife and I love you. Should there be any other reason?'

Hmm. Highly dubious. It was while he was rubbing my aching back, which lulled me into a false sense of security, that he finally came clean.

'You did what?'

'Said that we'd baby-sit Kayla today.'

'Kevin, you know how I feel about that little monster.'

'It's only one day – and not even a whole day, just while Mum and Moses are at the evening service. You'll be out anyway.'

'Exactly! And you promised to drive me to the cathedral. You promised.'

'There are loads of other people going. Can't one of them give you a lift? I'm sure Christina Monroe wouldn't mind.'

'But I want you to drive me.'

'Theo, don't do this …'

I stormed upstairs and threw pillows around until I felt better. Doesn't he understand I've got hormones?

I phoned Chrissie, who was, as Kevin predicted, quite happy to give me a lift.

I hope those pews are comfortable; my back is killing me.

Monday 26 March

Um ... Kevin here. Theo told me to write it in this, um ... diary. For the record, like.

Well, we've got a little girl. And she weighs ... can't remember. I think it was seven pounds ... or was it seven kilograms? And she was born at some unearthly hour this morning. Anyway, she's just beautiful. Oh, and Theo's fine, by the way.

Tuesday 27 March

Happy Birthday for tomorrow, Theo, love. I hope you like the present.

Thursday 29 March

Let me introduce someone who is going to change my life. Her first name is Estella, which means 'little star', in honour of Miss Chamberlain, and her middle name is Leah, which means weary. She is 48 centimetres or 19 inches long. She has soft brown hair, blue eyes and a cute little nose. She weighed in at 3.2 kilograms, just over 7 pounds. She was born on Monday 26 March at seventeen minutes past six by caesarean section. We're both doing well except that I'm still a bit sore from the operation. In addition, I have other injuries, which I will explain later.

I'd better go; she's due a feed and I can hear her waking up.

Friday 30 March

In the last 48 hours:

Feeds	13	
Nappy changes	17	
Hours of sleep	9	(me, not the baby)
Hours of sleep – Estella	27	
Rows with Kevin	4	
Visitors (family and friends)	19	
Birthday presents	6	(Nothing from Kevin yet, but we can't expect miracles.)
Baby presents	23	
Bars of chocolate consumed	5	
Sore breasts	2	

I'm just waiting for Kevin to come and collect me. We're going home today.

Saturday 31 March

Estella is asleep, Kevin has gone to the supermarket and I'm supposed to be resting, so I've got a chance to catch up with my diary.

Last Sunday, Chrissie drove to the cathedral with Miss Cranmer, Mrs McCarthy and Mrs Epstein, in their bizarre assorted millinery, lined up like the three wise monkeys in the back seat, and me in the front. As usual Chrissie was running late and arrived at my house dressed in her vestments. We must have looked a strange sight, squeezed into her Mini, as we hurtled and skidded down the back lanes as if we were competing in a rally.

We arrived safely, but my nagging backache was turning into unpleasant twinges. We sat in a pew right at the front as all the 'good' seats at the back had been taken by the early arrivals. The service started with a flourishing organ fanfare and a lively Palm Sunday hymn. The bishop looked splendid in his ecclesiastical robes, and as I sat there and drank in the atmosphere, I thought of all the Christians who had prayed and worshipped there over the last 1,400 years. Then the minister announced we would all process around the cathedral, led by the children who would be waving palm branches.

'Those on my left will process up the nave aisle and down the south aisle and back up the nave aisle to return to your seats. Those on my right will go up the nave aisle but will return to their seats via the north aisle and the nave aisle.'

Well, I was totally confused. The three old ladies and I shrugged. I resolved to stay in my seat and let everyone else conga their way around the cathedral. A rather imperious usher demanded that we stand up and join in the procession. Miss Cranmer, Mrs McCarthy and Mrs Epstein complied with his instruction, but I remained seated, another twinge gripping my back.

'Come on, up the nave aisle and down the south aisle and back up the nave aisle to return to your seat.'

'No, thank you, I'd rather stay here.' I smiled weakly.

'I'm sorry, you can't do that. You will be in the way when the worshippers return to their seats.'

'Then I'll move over and let them through.'

The cathedral worship band had struck up, and a blaring trumpet solo drowned out what the usher said next. He made a grab for my arm to help me up.

'I'm not moving!' I shouted as the children, waving palm leaves, and the rest of the congregation filed past. It was actually the persistent usher who was causing the obstruction, but he tugged at my elbow and tried to haul me up. The more he tried, the more determined I was not to move. I gave his hand a little slap. I felt like punching him in the eye, but the thought of the headline 'Pregnant Woman Floors Usher in Palm Sunday Pandemonium' made me stop.

'Leave me alone!' I shouted. 'I'm staying here.'

The line of worshippers was starting to back up. People were climbing over pews and scrambling over each other, trying to return to their seats. A panic-stricken Chrissie flapped over and took the usher to one side. He was threatening to have me thrown out of the cathedral. The band stopped playing, and the procession dwindled as people found new routes back to their seats. The whole thing was a shambles. My anger turned to tears, and the pain was getting really bad now, like spasms in my back and legs. I glared at the usher, who glared back. Chrissie and Charity helped me outside as the usher stood and looked on, smug in his victory. Finally I had moved.

We got into the cold air, and the pain gripped again. This time it went right round me like a belt. I stood, transfixed by the pain. Charity muttered something to Chrissie, who flew back inside the cathedral. She came out with a chair and a tall man in a suit. When the pain left, I sat down and looked at the man.

'Hello,' he said. 'I'm Doctor Ali. Can you tell me when the baby is due?'

'Just over a week ago.'

'Is it your first?'

I nodded.

'And you're getting pain?'

'Yes, on and off. In my back. It was a sort of an ache this morning, but it seems to be getting worse.'

'You say on and off. How often – every hour, every two minutes?'

'I don't know; I suppose about every five or ten minutes. It comes and goes. I seem to be all right in between.'

'Then I think, young lady, you'd better go to hospital.
You're almost certainly in labour.'

I looked at Chrissie.

'I'll ring Kevin,' she said.

'Do I need to call an ambulance?' Charity asked.

'First baby and fairly mild contractions. Does she have far
to go?'

'About ten miles. Her husband's on his way.'

'There should be time to take her to hospital safely. Someone should stay with her until he arrives. Call an ambulance if
she gets worse or if he isn't here within half an hour.'

'Of course,' Charity said.

'Do you need me to stay?' Dr Ali looked expectantly at us.
He clearly didn't want to crumple his smart suit and scuff his
shiny shoes.

We all shook our heads.

'Call me if there is a problem.' And he went back into the
cathedral.

'I'm, um ... supposed to be helping with the Eucharist,'
Chrissie said. 'Can I go too?'

Charity and I waved her away, and Charity held my hand
as another contraction started, peaked, then subsided. Sitting
on a chair on the grass outside a cathedral, holding hands with
a woman who, until recently, had been my sworn enemy, was
a strange experience. Was this really it? Was I in labour? This
was not how I'd planned to have my baby.

'How are you feeling?' Charity asked.

I wanted to scream. Instead it came out in a sort of a hiss.
'How do you think I'm feeling? I've just wrecked a beautiful
cathedral service!'

'It wasn't your fault. I saw that usher pulling you around.
I'm surprised someone with your temper managed to exercise
enough self-restraint not to jolly well belt him one.'

'Thank you, Charity.' I think!

I sat with my head in my hands.

'What are you doing to me, God?' I muttered.

'Teaching you,' came the reply in my head. Was it God or my wishful thinking? I was about to continue my conversation with the Almighty when a large white van screeched to a halt on the cobbled road.

'Is she okay?' Kevin jumped out of the driver's seat and knelt next to me.

'Yes, *she's* fine,' I said. 'She can still talk too! Why have you brought the van? Where's my car?'

'I'll explain later. Let's get you to hospital.'

He ran to open the back door of the van.

'Hey! Front seat!' I shouted.

He shrugged. 'Kayla.'

Kayla gave me a little wave from her booster seat.

Charity looked aghast. 'She's in labour. She can't possibly ride in the back of a plumber's van!'

'It'll be all right. I've laid down blankets and some carpet. She'll be quite comfortable. My niece has to have the passenger seat.'

Charity grabbed my coat and handbag.

'Stop!' I shouted. 'Why can't Charity take me?'

'I've got a minibus full,' she explained. 'How would they all get home?'

I resigned myself to my fate. Kevin scooped me up in his arms, Rhett Butler style. Another contraction started, and I cried out. This had the effect of panicking Kevin, who bolted towards the van. In his haste, he forgot to turn me round and slammed my head into the van door. The pain and shock certainly took my mind off the contraction. I yelled, and he tried to turn me, catching my foot on the other door. Eventually I managed to half climb, half crawl into the back of the van and wedge myself into a relatively comfortable position. I hung on grimly, my head still spinning and my foot throbbing as he took off like a rocket, the van bouncing down the cobbled road.

Fortunately, the streets were clear and I only had one more contraction on the fifteen-minute journey to the hospital. I clung to the pedestal of a washbasin that was strapped to the side of Kevin's van and prayed.

He parked outside the hospital, and I declined his offer to help me out of the van. Instead I sent him inside to fetch a wheelchair.

Riding in a wheelchair with Kayla perched on my lap, I arrived in the maternity unit at a quarter past eight. Kevin went to call Eloise again so she could collect Kayla, but her church service still hadn't finished.

A midwife called Jo booked me in and examined me. In his panic, Kevin had left behind the bag I'd packed with my nightdress, wash bag, favourite CDs and nourishing snacks, so I ended up wearing a hideous hospital nightdress and had no hairbrush and no sustenance. I realized I'd also left my diary at home, so in true Oscar Wilde style, I'd have nothing 'sensational to read'.

A nurse examined the lump on my head, checking me for concussion, then cleaned up the scrape on my foot. I could see the midwife biting her lip and trying not to laugh when I explained it.

'Should we let him hold the baby when it arrives, or will he drop that too?' she asked with a grin.

Jo examined me again and declared me to be three centimetres dilated. Roughly translated, that meant we were in for a long wait!

Kevin returned with a very excited Kayla.

'Do you want a little brother or a sister?' Jo asked.

'My mummy says they don't want any more children. She says that I'm quite enough.'

Kevin and I laughed.

'Oh!' said Jo.

'But I'd like a little cousin,' Kayla explained.

Kevin's mum arrived at just after nine and fussed around me. I was quite glad when she had gone. By ten thirty, my contractions were diminishing rather than getting stronger, and I was worried they were going to send me home. A doctor examined me again and put up a drip to help the labour along. The contractions returned, but I still wasn't making much progress. Around midnight, after yet more prodding and poking, they decided the baby's head wasn't down in the pelvis properly.

With this startling news they all went off and left me for an hour. By now Kevin wasn't much company either, as he had dozed off in the chair. I sat there with only the gas-and-air and prayed for it all to end. At just after three, the doctor and midwife came back and had another look. They decided that I could have an epidural, which happened when the anaesthetist arrived at a quarter to four. When the pain had gone, I slept fitfully into the early hours. Around five, I woke to find I was surrounded by a committee. They all discussed my case and, finally, talked directly to me. They were concerned about the failure to progress and the baby's heartbeat; they were worried that its head wasn't in the right position and that if I did ever get into the 'pushing' stage of labour, I'd be too tired to do anything.

They handed me a consent form and gave me half an hour to consider a caesarean section. Who needed half an hour? I kicked Kevin until he woke up, and he got dressed in a green overall and shower cap and I was wheeled down to an operating theatre. Fifteen minutes later we were holding our baby. It was the most amazing moment. I've never been one for spontaneous praise, but I just wanted to shout and laugh and sing hymns and thank God for this beautiful little person. And, looking at the grin on Kevin's face, I could tell he felt the same way.

APRIL

Sunday 1 April, Easter Sunday

Gorged myself on Easter eggs this morning. Estella had been given three of her own, so I had to eat those as well. I'm making up for lost time as I've hardly had a morsel of chocolate throughout my pregnancy.

Watched the Easter Day service on the television and got a bit weepy that I couldn't be with my church family to celebrate Jesus' resurrection.

Eloise dropped in to bring us our lunch – roast lamb and all the trimmings, all ready to be reheated in the microwave. She ended up staying for half an hour to admire Estella.

Ariadne, Tom and Phoebe called in at teatime with sandwiches and a simnel cake. All this food! I'll have to have babies more often. If I time it right, I may never have to cook again.

Friday 6 April

I haven't had much time to write in my diary this week. Any spare moments seem to have been taken up with washing, cooking (unfortunately, the flood of helpful relatives with food parcels seems to have dried up), cleaning and resting to try to recover from the night feeds. Kevin has been really good with her in the daytime, every inch the doting father, but at night he seems to have developed a sort of deafness. I pointed this fact out to him. He said, 'What's the point? Even if I did wake up, I couldn't feed her. I don't have the right equipment.'

I suppose he's right, and as I said he's very good with her in other ways. Sometimes we just sit and hold her, gazing at this little person, marvelling at each movement, sound and expression. I'm just overwhelmed with love for her and gratitude to God for entrusting her to us. She has completely changed our lives and will continue to do so for ever.

Better stop. I'm getting all weepy again.

Sunday 8 April

Still haven't managed to get to church, but church has brought itself to me. Mrs McCarthy called in on Tuesday and asked how I was feeling. As soon as I mentioned the caesarean, I knew I'd made a mistake. There's nothing Mrs McCarthy enjoys more than a good operation, unless, of course, it's a good war. Before I could stop her, she'd launched into a tale of when her son Derek was born.

'Of course, in them days, they didn't have none of them fancy Caucasian sections. You just had to push harder!'

I gave up on the idea of explaining the history of the Roman Empire and just nodded attentively as she apprised me of the gory details of her confinement.

'You young things have it easy with your epidermis and your general aesthetics. We knew what pain was ...'

'Yes, the contractions were quite painful.'

'Contraptions, don't tell me about contraptions. My contraptions bent me double. Jolly near broke me in 'alf, they did.'

'How awful for you. At least the whole thing's over fairly quickly ...'

'Three weeks I was in labour, *three weeks*. And haemorrhage, the doctors had never seen anything like it! "Mrs McCarthy," they said, "we've never seen haemorrhaging like it." Sixteen pints of blood I lost. Of course we never had none of them fancy blood transgressions ...'

Tuesday 10 April

Have spent the morning sorting out Estella's baby presents. She has more clothes than I do, and she has the distinct advantage that none of her outfits make her tummy look like a bag full of oranges. I set out her cuddly toys in her bedroom. She has seven teddy bears, two lambs, a dog, a clown, a large singing purple dinosaur and a pink rabbit from Jeremiah Wedgwood.

It was three days after I'd had Estella. She'd fed four times in the night and the 'baby blues' had just kicked in. If things were going badly, I cried; if they were going well, I cried; if anyone was nice to me, I cried. I tried watching television and I cried at quiz shows, for the winners and the losers; the daytime chat shows made me weep as Mavis from Scunthorpe managed to lose ten pounds for her daughter's wedding, and I couldn't even watch the opening credits of *Animal Hospital*! One of the nurses had taken Estella down to the nursery to give me a break so I could have a shower and wash my hair. I felt so overwhelmingly tired that I decided to lie down and close my eyes for a few minutes. I must have dozed off, as the next thing I was aware of was a squeaking noise, followed by heavy breathing in my ear. I opened my eyes, and a pair of water-blue eyes stared straight back from a few inches away. I gave a little scream and hauled myself into a sitting position.

'Jeremiah! You frightened the life out of me! What are you doing here?'

'I brought this for the baby.' The rubber tyres squeaked on the floor as he manoeuvred his wheelchair parallel to my bed. He placed a card and a brown paper bag on the blanket.

'Thank you. I'm sorry I shouted at you. You just took me by surprise.'

'I imagined you'd be awake by now. It is nearly eleven.'

'I ... I had rather a bad night, you see ...'

'Spare me the details. I need to go now. I wish you well.'

And he wheeled himself back to his ward. I opened the envelope first and pulled out a card with a sea scene which would have been more appropriate for a great-uncle's birthday than a new baby card. Inside, Jeremiah had written,

I will greatly increase your pains in childbearing; with pain you will give birth to children. Your desire will be for your husband, and he will rule over you.

Cheerful stuff! He had also written,

I will not visit again – Leviticus 12.

I looked it up in my Bible. Leviticus 12 is all about ceremonial uncleanness following childbirth. The good news is I should be free of visits from Mr Wedgwood for at least sixty-six days; the bad news is that at the end of it, I have to find a couple of pigeons to sacrifice in the temple.

I opened the brown paper bag and found the pink rabbit I'd seen on Jeremiah's bed, and even if I hadn't had the 'baby blues', I still would have cried.

Wednesday 11 April

Kevin looked rather shifty ever since he got back from work today. He has been working short hours since Estella's birth to give me a chance to rest and to drive me around, as I'm not allowed behind the wheel for another couple of weeks. He's just been doing short jobs and urgent work, but today he was working in London and was evasive when I asked him what he had been doing.

He had just bathed Estella while I was cooking dinner. If we had done it the other way round, the dinner would have been less black and there wouldn't have been water dripping through the ceiling.

'Theo, there's something I need to talk to you about,' he said during the crème brûlée (I have found it safer to cook food that is supposed to be burnt).

'Oh yes,' I said with just a hint of scepticism.

'Do you remember Zippy?'

'Yes, and George and Bungle too!'

'No, Zippy who had the flat in London and the holiday cottage in Portsmouth.'

'I remember. That was the time that Charity's budgie ran away to sea.'

'Well, Zippy has bought another place that he wants to renovate. It will be a holiday home again, on the beach, and he wants us, Jez, Kev 2, Paul and me to do it.'

'Okay ...'

'It will mean me working away again.'

'Where?'

'New South Wales.'

'Land of my fathers.' I laughed.

'No, *New* South Wales – Western Australia. Actually, it's the land of my father.'

'Australia!' I dropped my spoon.

'Yes, and he's offering me and the lads free accommodation over there in payment for renovating the place. The employment laws are a bit dodgy, so he can't pay us as such.'

'Of course you turned him down.'

Kevin shifted in his chair and coughed.

'You accepted? Tell me you're not going to work in Australia, leaving me and Estella here.'

'I can't tell you that because it wouldn't be true.'

'I can't believe you accepted without even discussing it.'

'We're discussing it now.'

'No, we're not! You're presenting it to me as a fait accompli and I'm shouting at you for being so inconsiderate. That's not what I'd call a discussion!'

Estella started crying, so I stomped off and fed her upstairs.

Thursday 12 April

Kevin has been sulking all day. Exchanges between us have been curt and polite. Last night we slept back to back.

Friday 13 April

Charity called round and dropped in some shopping for me. The triplets crawled all over my lounge like a swarm of baby hamsters. Charity whisked Estella out of my arms and cradled her.

'I miss this,' she sighed, as Martha (or was it Mary?) bull-dozed her way across to the fireplace and started eating the ash. I retrieved her and cleaned her up with a wipe.

'You've got the triplets. They're still babies,' I said.

'But when they're like this, so little, so dependent ...'

I thought Charity was going to burst into tears. Perhaps she could give me some advice on how to handle Kevin's attempt at 'The Great Escape'.

'Charity, would you let Nigel go off to work away from home and leave you and the children behind?'

'Goodness, no! Nigel would never do that. It's only men whose wives don't know how to keep them content at home who feel the need to "work away" all over the place. I know Nigel's trustworthy, but men have wandering eyes and are easily led. I would never trust other women around my husband!'

Thank you, Charity. You've just given shape to my nightmares for the next twenty years!

Saturday 14 April

Kevin and I orbited around each other again until it was time for him to go to football.

'Bye.' He gave me a perfunctory peck on the cheek.

'Bye.' I gave him a half-hearted wave. As soon as he had gone, I grabbed the phone and rang Ariadne. I blurted the whole thing out.

'Calm down, dear sister; calm down. He wants to go to Australia for a fortnight to do this work and benefit from the facilities, and frankly, who can blame him? You don't want to be left, quite literally, holding the baby. Solution's simple: go with him.'

'But I couldn't do that!'

'Why not? You're not tied down to a job, Estella's small enough to be portable and you'd get a cheap fare for her.'

'I got the impression we weren't wanted. I think it's a sort of glorified "boys' night out". The last time I tried to crash one of his lads' fishing trips, it was a disaster.'

'Up to you, but I know what I'd do.'

I know what she would do too, but she's not me.

Sunday 15 April

Got the buggy out; strapped Estella in; loaded up a bag with nappies, wipes, changes of clothes and spare blankets;

and pushed it up the hill to St Norbert's. Was immediately mobbed. Estella is now officially the most beautiful baby in the world; it isn't just Kevin and me that think so. She managed to gaze around attentively during the prayers, wail through the hymns and fall asleep during Nigel's sermon – and she wasn't the only one.

I found Chrissie after the service. She was in the vestry getting changed. I managed to nudge the buggy through the vestry door with my knee and handed Chrissie a coffee.

'Hello, stranger. Have you been avoiding me?' I smiled as she pulled her surplice over her head.

'No ... sorry. Meant to come ... just been busy.'

Estella started to stir.

'She's waking up. Would you like to hold her?'

'I ... not at the moment. If you don't mind. I promised I'd see Mr Wilberforce straight after church. Excuse me.'

And she left. I stood there for a few moments wondering what I'd done to upset her. If it was having a baby, there wasn't much I could do about that. I pushed the buggy back into church and got pounced on immediately. Estella was passed around again like a parcel until I decided it was time for lunch and headed off back down the hill. When I got home, Kevin had cooked a roast chicken dinner. He hasn't mentioned Australia again, and neither have I.

Tuesday 17 April

I was hanging out some washing while Estella slept when I heard a van pull up in the drive. Although Kevin hadn't been working full hours, I was surprised to see him this early and even more surprised when he handed me a bunch of roses.

'What are they for?' I said.

'To say sorry for being so selfish,' he replied. 'I don't know how I could even have thought about leaving you two for a whole fortnight.'

'Have you told Zippy this?'

'Not yet. He's ringing me this afternoon.'

'A fortnight, you say?'

'That's right. In May. It's a pity because Zippy said we could go over any time we liked and stay in the house ...'

'Hang on. You say that in exchange for a fortnight's work, he'd put *us* up in his beach house in New South Wales ...'

'Jervis Bay. It's supposed to be beautiful. Clear blue waters, white sand.'

'Oh, Kevin!'

'He wants the lads and me because he's happy with our work and knows he can trust us, and although he won't be paying us, it could be the opportunity of a lifetime. I guess there's a sort of link for me too. My dad was born in Darwin.'

'I didn't know that.'

'Yeah, his family travelled around a lot. He grew up in England and the Caribbean, where he met Mum, then they settled here. It would have been a chance to go back to my roots.'

'Why didn't you tell me this before?'

'Don't know. It never really came up.'

I looked at him for a long time.

'Forget it. It would be difficult for you looking after Estella on your own.'

'It would be awful. We'd both miss you so much.'

'I know.' He kicked a stone along the ground. He looked so disappointed. It would be difficult ... but the benefits ...

'And we could have unlimited stays, whenever we liked?' I asked.

'I guess the stays wouldn't be unlimited, but all we'd have to do is find a date when it's not booked out and we can have it. And escape from cold grey English winters.'

'What an opportunity. It would be a pity if you miss it. You might not get another chance.'

'What do you think, then? Can I go?' His face brightened.

'When?'

'Fourth of May.'

'Just over two weeks' time.'

I looked at Kevin's earnest face and thought of Estella.

'Hmmm …' I scratched my chin.

'Come on, Theo, put me out of my misery!'

'Over the years, I've got used to being on my own … I just didn't think I would still be doing it when I was married.'

'You won't be on your own.'

No, I thought, I won't be. I'll have a six-week-old baby to care for.

Kevin's mobile phone started ringing.

'This will be him,' he said, pressing the button. 'What shall I tell him?'

I chewed my bottom lip for a moment. 'Tell him: yes.'

Wednesday 18 April

I sorted out the last carrier bag I brought back from hospital. Under a spare nightie, an old newspaper and a bottle of squash, I found a card from Declan. A nurse had brought it over to me. I was extremely grateful Declan didn't try to make a personal visit, even if he does work in the hospital. I was expecting the card to be a funny one, even to contain a whoopee cushion or a fake puddle of baby puke, but it didn't. It was just a nice pink card with a picture of a baby and the word 'Congratulations'. I looked at the card, thought about it, then tore it up and put it in the bin. I just don't want to be reminded of Declan.

Thursday 19 April

Mrs Thomas called in at half past four this afternoon. She brought a huge card the children had made and a Mothercare voucher and a card from the staff. Estella obligingly woke up right on cue, and Mrs Thomas cuddled her until the need for food and a clean nappy got too much for Estella and she started yelling. Mrs Thomas asked if I'd consider bringing her into school one day so the children could meet her.

'They keep asking about you,' she said. 'I know it's early days, but they all want to know if you are coming back.'

Friday 20 April

Kevin found Declan's card in the bin and confronted me about it.

'Why have you thrown this away?'

'It was from Declan. He's in the past. I didn't want to be reminded of him.'

'If he was in the past, how come he knows that you've had a baby? Has he been here?'

'Of course not!' Even though I knew I had nothing to hide, I could feel my face reddening.

'Then how do you explain this?' He held out a library card. It had Declan's name on it.

'Where did you get that?'

'I found it,' he paused, 'in the wardrobe. Can you enlighten me?'

'Yes, yes, it must have fallen out of his pocket.'

'So he was here!' Kevin's eyes became bright, and the muscles in his jaw started to clench.

'No. He wasn't; his jacket was. Remember the day I got locked out? He lent me his jacket. I was standing in the garden in my nightdress, freezing to death, and he happened to be passing and lent me his jacket.'

'"Happened to be passing"?'

'It's true!'

His voice became very quiet. 'Theodora, what are you not telling me?'

'Nothing!' I protested. 'I got locked out, Declan walked past, he offered me his coat and lent me his phone so I could ring Chrissie ...'

'Quite the knight in shining armour.'

'She took me to the vicarage and lent me some clothes. I accidentally left Declan's jacket there, and she returned it to me. I put it into the wardrobe; the library card must have fallen out of his pocket. Then I dropped the jacket round to his house ...'

'So you've been to his house?'

'Only to drop his jacket back. That's all.'

'And where does he live?'

'A couple of streets away.'

'Great! And you didn't think to tell me any of this.'

'I knew you'd be upset.'

'Too right I'm upset! Is there anything else you need to tell me about Declan?'

'He ... works at the hospital.'

'Next you'll be telling me that he delivered the baby!' He ran his hands over his face. 'Look, I need to think about all this. I'm going out.'

Saturday 21 April

'The course of true love never did run smooth,' Shakespeare said, and he was right. It feels as if our marriage is like the English Channel in a force eight gale. I have no feelings for Declan. It went from friendship at work, to stupefaction when he asked me to marry him, to abhorrence when I found that he'd deceived me, to indifference, which is the current state. I wouldn't wish him any ill. But I wouldn't be concerned if I never saw him again. I'd never thought of Kevin as a jealous man. I can understand him not trusting Declan because of what he's done. But me? He must trust me. If not, it makes me wonder about the basis of our marriage. I chose to marry Kevin because I love him, and I couldn't face life without him. No other reason. Why does he think I'm interested in a rootless, spineless loser like Declan? Doesn't he credit me with more sense?

Sunday 22 April

Skipped church and Kevin and I went for a walk in the park. The daffodils were still blooming, and the April sun warmed our backs as Estella slept contentedly in her buggy. We found a bench and sat side by side.

'I need to know, Theo, why did you marry me?'

What a question! 'Because I love you, of course. What is this, some kind of test?' The tears started welling up in my eyes.

'No, Theo, I'm not trying to make you feel bad. I was just wondering if you could be sure that marrying me was the right decision.'

A year ago I'd wondered the same thing, but not now.

'Some of your mates – they think you married the wrong bloke.' Kevin looked at the ground.

'Well ...' I hesitated, not wanting the words to come out ambiguously. 'To be honest, I did wonder. Declan was funny, clever, he could always cheer me up, he's not bad looking ...'

Kevin appeared to deflate.

'Oh, I didn't mean ...' But I knew instantly I had said the wrong thing.

'Kevin ...' I took his hands. 'Those things were not enough. Nowhere near. While I was in Greece, I had all that time to think, and there was only one person I missed, one person I wanted to be with, and that was you. I didn't want Declan. At first I hated him for what he did, but now ... now I'm grateful.'

Kevin glared at me.

'Yes, grateful for showing me that I couldn't live without you. You only know how much you love something when it is taken away ...' I looked down. My eyes filled with tears, which dripped onto the grass. Kevin put his hand under my chin and raised it.

'Theo,' he said, 'have you ever thought of writing the verses in greeting cards?'

Tuesday 24 April

I still can't drive for a week or so, but I got the urge to sit in the driver's seat of my car today. I found the key, unlocked the garage doors, hauled them open and found that the garage was completely empty. I rang Kevin.

'Kevin, something dreadful has happened. My car has been stolen.'

'Um, actually, I can explain that.'

'Explain away,' I demanded.

'I sold it.'

'You did what!'

'It was meant to be a surprise.'

'It certainly is a surprise. Although I can think of some other words too.'

'For your birthday. I've bought you a new car, from Vague Dave, only it's not quite ready yet.'

'The police are still dusting it for fingerprints?'

'No, nothing like that. Safety checks, valeting, that sort of thing. I just wanted it to be perfect for you.'

'But my birthday was nearly a month ago!'

'I realized you wouldn't be driving for a while. I would have told you sooner, but I wanted to have everything ready for when you could drive again.'

'How could you sell my car without my permission?'

'I part-exchanged it with Dave. Anyway, I didn't think you were attached to the old banger. You were always complaining about it.'

'Kevin, that's not the point. It was *my* car, and you had no right, legal or moral, to do anything with it without my permission.'

'I didn't sign the document.'

'Of course you didn't. I have to sign that.'

'Don't worry. Dave forged your signature. I'm picking up the new one in a couple of days. I promise you, you'll love it.'

Wednesday 25 April

Took Estella to the baby clinic that takes place in St Norbert's Church Hall. She is 'performing' exactly as she should be, putting on weight and doing all the things babies are supposed to do. Met Alyson (with a *y*) Hughes-Churchill there, with her new baby called Adam, who looks disturbingly like Jimmy Greaves.

'Hello, Alyson. I didn't expect to see you here. It is NHS, you know.'

'Oh, I know that! Gosh, we only go private for the delivery. All this routine stuff is a waste of money.'

Her brashness seemed a little forced today.

'Oh, from what you were saying, I didn't think money was a problem.'

'Not a problem exactly ...' She started to look a little uncomfortable. 'Look,' she whispered confidentially, 'don't tell anyone, but we're having a little cash-flow situation at the moment. Quentin had to leave his city job rather ... suddenly. Some kind of financial mix-up, and he may have to go abroad for a while until it is sorted. Our bank account has been frozen, and ... it looks as if I may have to go to work. There's a danger we might lose the house too. I'm investigating the possibility of selling part of the grounds to a developer.'

'Alyson, that's terrible. Why don't you tell your MAMAL group? I'm sure they'll all be glad to help out.'

'I've had to resign from MAMAL, of course. A single parent in the workplace doesn't belong in that group.'

'But aren't they your friends?'

'Not really – "useful social contacts", more like. No, I could never let any of my friends know what has happened. It's all too, too dreadful.'

'But you've told me.'

She laughed. 'You? But you don't count.'

And to think I was about to be nice to her.

Thursday 26 April

Dad had a day off work, so he and Mum picked Estella and me up and whisked us off for a day in the country. They have decided to visit Tadhurst Place, a stately home with a moat and drawbridge. In the car, between answering questions on Estella's well-being, feeding habits and weight gain, I regaled

Mum and Dad with the story of the car. They agreed that what Kevin has done is a bit beyond the pale.

'I used to call my first car "Baby",' said Dad.

'Why was that?' I asked, knowing instantly I was going to regret the question.

'Because it wouldn't go anywhere without a rattle.'

I just had to ask!

When we arrived, Mum and Dad wanted to walk around the house, but I couldn't face either trying to struggle around with the buggy or depositing Estella in the baby sling. Nine and a half months of carrying her inside me had put me off carrying her around attached to my front. I waved goodbye to my parents as they set off across the drawbridge over the moat. I negotiated the buggy through an archway and into a walled garden. The air was warm and the garden full of tulips, magnolias and cherry blossom. The birds were singing and darting back and forth with beaks full of nesting material.

I found a bench and freed Estella from the straps of her buggy. She blinked and sneezed in the sharp spring sunshine. I fed her and checked that she didn't need changing, then I carried her around the garden naming all the flowers and describing them to her. I know she won't remember anything, but it makes me feel close to her, and she seems to like me nuzzling her soft hair and whispering in her ear. Her breathing became heavier, and I realized she had gone to sleep. I laid her back in the buggy and glanced at my watch. It was lunchtime, so I trundled the buggy over the drawbridge and into the little courtyard at the centre of the house. A school party in red jumpers scurried through, their flustered teacher trying to rein in the children who seemed determined to race ahead to be 'first', and at the same time chivvying the dawdlers.

Mum appeared from a doorway, followed by Dad, who was only just visible behind a multitude of carrier bags. Mum had been to the shop. She pulled out armfuls of cookery books: perhaps she is going to supplement her Greek range with mediaeval dishes. From another bag she fished out a sweet little sweatshirt with a picture of a sheep for Estella.

We found the café and sat down to gammon ham and mustard sandwiches followed by gooseberry syllabub. Our appetites satisfied, we went for a stroll along the woodland path. Dad marched on ahead, lecturing nobody in particular on the description, habitat, natural distribution, propagation and growth of common British woodland species. Mum took my arm and whispered conspiratorially, 'Do you mind if I ask you something?'

'No, of course not. Fire away.'

'Who was that man I saw at the hospital?'

'What man?'

'He always seemed to be hanging around. I saw him watching you.'

'I don't know. Probably a cleaner. Certainly not a doctor. You never saw them from one day to the next.' I gave a little laugh, but Mum still looked worried.

'I think he worked there; he was wearing a badge. It just seemed odd. I saw him several times. He seemed to be there every time we visited. He just stood watching you. Of course he soon disappeared when he realized we'd seen him.'

'Weird. What did he look like?'

'I don't know. Pretty ordinary. Medium height, your age, a bit thin, floppy reddish hair.'

I tried not to show any emotion.

'Probably some kind of perv who gets his kicks hanging round hospitals. Oh well, I haven't seen him,' I said, trying to sound dismissive, 'so I'm sure there's nothing to worry about.'

'Yes, you're right. Just thought I'd mention it. Theodora' – she laid a hand on my arm – 'be careful.'

I will, I thought. Very careful.

Kevin had got back before me and had started cooking a chicken stew. The house was filled with the delicious scent of vegetables and herbs. I fed Estella, then I took over the cooking while Kevin whisked Estella upstairs for a bath.

'A package arrived for you,' he called down the stairs. My hands trembled slightly. I hunted through a heap of junk mail and found a padded envelope. My heart was thudding. I turned it over. To my relief, there was a Northampton postmark and the 'Return to' address had Percival Burns' name on it. I opened the package to find a little photo album and a hat and pair of knitted booties with pink ribbon. I opened the letter.

I heard you'd had a baby girl. Many congratulations to you both. I found these little things my Joanie had knitted when I was clearing out some of her belongings. I hope you can make use of them. She loved knitting, and I'm sure she would have loved you to have them.

I wiped away the tears and went to find a thank-you card.

Friday 27 April

Gregory Pasternak had another Dickens Festival meeting in the church hall tonight. I bundled Estella into the buggy and wheeled her up the hill. I arrived a little late, and the meeting was already in full swing. It felt as if I'd slipped into a time warp.

'Well, in my 'umble opinion ...' began Gregory Pasternak.

A woman I recognized as Mrs Beckett the librarian said, 'We need to investigate the situation with the council lest we become skewered through and through with office pens and bound hand and foot with red tape.'

'It was as true ... as turnips is. It was as true ... as taxes is. And nothing's truer than them,' put in the mayor.

'What is happening?' I asked. 'Why is everyone being so strange?'

'We're just getting into character,' explained a portly gentleman in a waistcoat. 'And you are ...'

'I'm Theodora. I'm a friend of Gregory's.'

'Pleased to meet you. I'm Mr Pickwick.'

I couldn't help smirking.

'No, really,' he explained. 'After a lifetime of people taking the rise, I decided to go along with it. You could say I grew into the part.' He patted his broad middle. I stayed another half an hour while this strange selection of friends discussed costumes, travel arrangements and their passion for Dickens' novels. I was quite sorry when Estella woke up damp and fractious and I had to leave. After my initial misgivings, I think it will be a fantastic day.

Saturday 28 April

I woke late to the sound of the garage doors crashing closed. I dived back under the duvet but couldn't doze off again. Estella had woken me twice in the night, so I wasn't surprised to find her still fast asleep. I pulled on some clothes and ventured downstairs to find Kevin in the front garden waving to someone who was driving off down the road.

'Thanks, mate! Bye.' He turned around, practically knocking me over. 'Theo! What are you doing here?'

'I live here, or had you forgotten? What's the time?' I yawned.

'Twenty to eight.'

'That's too early!' I groaned. 'What was all that crashing for?'

'Come here, I've got something to show you. Vague Dave just brought it round. It's a pity you missed him.'

He was practically dancing with excitement. He unlocked the garage doors and pushed them open.

'There! What do you think? Happy birthday, love.'

I peered into the dark interior. There was a car, bright silver as a spaceship. A convertible. A sports car.

'What is it?'

'It's a car!'

'I can see that. What kind of a car?'

'A Peugeot 206 CC. Isn't she beautiful?'

It always worries me when men refer to cars as 'she'.

'Very nice.'

'It's got rear seats, so you can strap Estella in the back.'

'It's got no roof. What happens when it rains?'

'Watch.'

Kevin climbed inside and switched on the ignition. He pressed a button, and a motor whirred gently to close the roof.

'What do you think?'

'It's lovely. Another week and I should be able to drive it.'

'I think I'll take it for a little spin. Just to test it. Then I can make sure it's safe and let you know about anything you need to be aware of. Coming?'

'Estella's asleep ...'

'Okay. See you later.'

And with that he was gone. I stood at the front door and watched as the little silver car disappeared down the road and turned the corner. It certainly is a beautiful car, and it must have cost him a fortune, but I can't help wondering if he bought it for me or for him.

Sunday 29 April

I went to church while Kevin stayed at home and cleaned my car. Chrissie was covering at another church this morning, so we had to endure one of Nigel's seemingly endless sermons. I longed to poke Estella so I could have an excuse to go outside, but she refused to wake up and howl. I suppose Nigel's preaching must be a real gift, a kind of verbal anaesthetic. If any of the little Hubbles couldn't sleep, I wonder if Charity played Nigel's sermon tapes to them.

Charity bounded up to me after the service.

'I just wondered ...' She squirmed. 'I just wondered if you'd decided ... I mean if you'd got around to ...'

'Spit it out, Charity!'

'Have you selected Estella's godparents yet? Only, I'm available, should you wish to enlist someone with a high moral and spiritual standing, rather than the token "best friend" who never darkens the doors of the church but is good for a hefty cheque every birthday.'

'Thank you for the offer, Charity, but to tell you the truth, I haven't even thought about the christening yet.'

'Oh! But she must be six weeks old.'

'Yes, but I've had a lot of other things to think about.'

'It's never too early to plant spiritual seeds. "Train a child in the way he should go, and when he is old he will not turn from it."'

I suppose she is right. We need to start planning for it.

I phoned Ariadne when I got home. She's good at organizing things.

'What are your plans for Phoebe?'

'We're Baptists, dear. None of that sprinkling stuff for us ... But if you're looking for a godmother ...'

Monday 30 April

Raised the subject of Estella's baptism with Kevin over breakfast this morning, or I tried to. Kevin was in a tearing hurry as he was supposed to be at a job at Blackwall by half past eight and it was already a quarter to nine. He swigged down half a mug of coffee and through a mouthful of toast muttered something that sounded like, 'Over my dead body.'

MAY

Tuesday 1 May

When he got back from work, Kevin took us all for a spin in *my* new car. I secured Estella's seat in the back. He put the roof down so it felt like we were sitting in a wind tunnel, and I ended up with hair that looked as if I'd spent the afternoon playing hairdressers with an orang-utan. I clung on as we rounded corners and closed my eyes as we sped down winding lanes. One thing is for certain: when I can drive again, I will not be driving like this. We ended up at a secluded little pub, but as I was feeding Estella and Kevin was driving, we both sat with a glass of cola until it started to drizzle. Even though it was raining, Kevin still refused to put the roof up.

'It's only a shower,' he maintained as the rain lashed his face.

Eventually, when I had threatened to get out and walk, he pressed the button and the roof purred its way into position.

When we got home, I took Estella upstairs and changed her into dry clothes while Kevin swabbed down the Peugeot's upholstery.

Wednesday 2 May

Two days until Kevin disappears off to the other side of the world. While we were packing his suitcase, I asked him again about Estella's christening.

'I don't see why it's so important,' he grumbled. 'Why can't you do what my parents did and let her make up her own mind? Then when she is older she can decide for herself if she wants to be baptized.'

'Because she might end up like you and decide she never wants to be baptized.'

'In my mum's church they don't "do" babies, anyway.'

'Some churches don't, but ours does. It's a way of welcoming her into the Christian family. Apparently, in the early church, whole families were baptized – presumably that included any children and babies. Anyway, it's us that make the promises, on her behalf, and when she grows up she can still make them for herself. You do want her to be brought up as a Christian, don't you?'

'Of course!'

'Well, while you're away, let me arrange the service ...'

'I don't want to go.'

'Don't be ridiculous. You're her father.'

'You're not getting me inside that place, and I'm certainly not standing up in front of that lot.'

I sighed. I was just too weary to battle that one. Kevin may have an aversion to churches – I can understand that – but he *has* to be there for his daughter's baptism.

'We'll talk later.'

Thursday 3 May

I decided to blitz the supermarket this afternoon to stock up on food, nappies and other essential items while Kevin is away. We got a bus into town, and Kevin agreed to collect us in the van when I had finished. I stood outside the supermarket, surrounded by shopping bags, with a screaming baby, for fifteen minutes, waiting. Eventually I rang his mobile number. He'd been delayed at a job. What should have been a simple task of repairing a tap had turned into a major leak, and Kevin had to renew a whole lot of old piping. He'd get back as soon as he could. Quite frankly, I didn't care. I just needed to get home. I waved at a sullen-looking cab driver, who didn't even bother getting out of the cab to help me load the shopping into the boot.

'Does she have to make that noise?' he grumbled as Estella made known the fact that she was tired, cold and hungry by screaming hysterically. I felt like joining in.

The cab drew up outside Rose Cottage, and the driver sat glued to his seat as I unloaded the shopping and the caterwauling Estella. I fumbled in my purse for the correct change so that I didn't have to give him a tip. He scowled at me and drove off. I hesitated for a moment on the kerb, unsure whether to sort out Estella and leave the shopping or to put her indoors and leave her to scream a bit longer while I ferried twenty or more bags inside. I thought all sorts of nasty things about Kevin. He promised he would help me, but he wasn't here when I needed him. How would I cope for a whole fortnight? Could things get any worse?

'Now if I didn't know you better, I'd think that you were a tiny bit peeved. It wasn't naughty words you were thinking just then, was it?' Declan said, smiling.

Yes, things could get worse, and they just had.

'Left holding the baby? Can't leave you alone for a minute, can I? If you're not locking yourself out of your house, you're spreading your messages all over the road.'

'Look, Kevin will be here to help me in a minute.'

'Shame he's not here to help you now.'

I thought of Mum's warning.

'Please go away, Declan.'

'What have I done?'

'Nothing … I don't have time for this. Just go. Now. Please.'

'Not before I've helped you get your purchases off the pavement. Now you go and sort out the little one, and I'll fetch these to your front door.'

I grabbed the red-faced little bundle that used to be my daughter and put her in the lounge. Declan started ferrying my bags up the garden path and deposited them in the hall. I took Estella out of her car seat and laid her on the changing mat when I heard a screech of brakes, a door slamming and raised voices. Clutching her to me, I ran outside.

'What do you think you're doing?' Kevin yelled.

'Helping your wife with the shopping. What you should be doing, you eejit,' Declan screamed back.

I stopped, transfixed by the scene unfolding in front of me.

Declan stood there with a shopping bag in each hand. Kevin tried to snatch the bags, but Declan took a swing at him with a bag full of vegetables. It hit Kevin mid-thigh, but he managed to grab hold of it. The handle gave way, and the contents, including the frighteningly expensive cherry tomatoes and frilly lettuce I had so carefully selected, spilled out over the grass verge. Kevin picked up a cucumber, studied it briefly and then took a swing at Declan.

He attacked Declan with the cucumber as if it was a baseball bat. Declan snatched a French loaf and parried the blows. The loaf broke first. There was a horrible moment when I thought Kevin was going to do Declan a serious injury with the cucumber as the blows rained down on his head, shoulders and back. Finally the cucumber snapped.

Declan took a step backwards and tripped over the bags of shopping. He lay on his back with his legs in the air, winded and momentarily helpless.

Kevin rushed at him brandishing a parsnip. Declan grabbed a can of aerosol cream and let Kevin have it in the face. Kevin yelled and wiped the cream from his eyes. That gave Declan time to get to his feet.

There was a brief lull as Kevin looked around for his next weapon. Declan stood, finger on the button, ready to blast Kevin with more whipped cream. Kevin glanced down and seized a plastic bottle of ketchup. He squeezed it in Declan's direction, but nothing happened. The foil seal, the one you have to stab with a sharp knife before the ketchup will come out, was holding up admirably.

Kevin changed tack, grasped the bottle by its neck and swung it like a club. Declan let off a round of cream, but Kevin walked straight through it, wiping the cloying white foam from his face. He took aim with the bottle of ketchup and struck Declan hard on the shoulder. Declan yelled and picked up a bag of apples. He ran into the road, hurling apples in Kevin's direction.

'Stop!' I shouted.

Both men paused. Kevin, his ketchup bottle still raised, ketchup dripping like blood from a split in the side; Declan, apple in hand.

'You're like a couple of kids. No, you're worse than kids. Look at all this mess!'

They glanced around. The road, pavement and verge were littered with spilled food, broken packaging and trampled vegetables. Neighbours had emerged from their houses to watch the debacle.

'You' – I pointed at Declan – 'go home now.'

'And you ...' I gave Kevin a look of utter disgust. 'You can get washed, you can clear up this mess, then you can go to the supermarket and replace the shopping.'

Kevin and Declan stood eyeing each other for a moment. I thought the fight was going to break out again, but Declan let the apple fall from his fingers and held his hands out in a gesture of surrender. He laughed as he looked around at the debris. He felt his sore shoulder. When he took his hand away and examined it, it was smeared with red. He sniffed it, grinned and licked the ketchup from his fingers.

'You look after her,' he called behind him as he sauntered up the road. Kevin picked up a tin of baked beans and threw it in the direction of the receding figure. It fell short by a good three metres. Declan raised one hand and gave Kevin a final defiant gesture, then disappeared round the corner.

I looked down. Estella had fallen asleep in my arms. The neighbours drifted back indoors, and Kevin began to clear up. I put Estella in her Moses basket and took a dustbin bag out to Kevin.

'Why was he here?' Kevin asked.

'I don't know. I imagine he was just walking past.'

'Very convenient.'

'Yes, it was!'

'Did you plan it?'

How could he even think that? 'Of course not!'

'I can't go to Australia now, can I?'

'Why ever not?'

'With him sniffing around you.'

'He wasn't sniffing around. He was just helping me with the shopping because ...'

'Because I wasn't here.' Kevin resumed the clearing up.

I went indoors to make a cup of tea. I poured it out, then I started unpacking the shopping that had escaped unscathed.

What had I done wrong? I never encouraged Declan. I don't even like him. If things had been different, perhaps we could have been friends, but under the circumstances ...

The front door slammed shut. Kevin, his face covered in a sickly mix of whipped cream and ketchup, came into the kitchen with the bin bag. I took it from him and handed him a cup of tea.

'I'll just go and get cleaned up, then I'll get some more shopping. Do you mind if I take your car? I'll take Estella too, if you like.'

'She's asleep.'

'I'm sorry, love.' He moved to hug me, but I pushed him away. Apart from not wanting to get sticky, I didn't want him near me at the moment.

'Why are you so jealous of Declan?'

'I don't know how you feel about him.'

I snorted with laughter. 'I've told you enough times!'

'Oh, I know what you've said, but I don't know what you're thinking. You never tell me what you're thinking. It's like I always have to guess. You write it all down in that flaming diary, though, don't you?'

The diary! 'Yes, yes, you're right. I *do* write it all down in the diary. If you want to know what I really think about Declan, read my diary! It's all there. I haven't changed anything.'

I rushed into the bedroom and grabbed my diary. I threw it at Kevin.

'There you are! Read it.'

I sat down as Kevin half-heartedly flicked through the pages.

'Well, don't watch me.'

I could hear Estella starting to grizzle and went to sort her out. When I came back, Kevin was sitting with the diary closed.

'I'm sorry,' he said and tried to hug me again. Again I pushed him away.

'Go and get cleaned up first,' I said.

᷈◦᷈

Kevin showered, went to the supermarket to replace the damaged food and came home with a Chinese takeaway. Although I was extraordinarily cross with them for being so childish and causing so much damage, I have to admit it felt quite nice having two men fighting over me. Even if it was with groceries. Poor Declan, covered in ketchup. I couldn't help smiling at the image. I hope that's the last I see of him. Kevin and I cuddled up close on the sofa.

'Have you decided, are you still going tomorrow?'

'If you're sure you will be all right.'

'I'll be fine.'

'I love you, Theodora.'

Friday 4 May

Kevin's taxi to the airport arrived at half past six. Estella was already awake. Kevin kissed me, then he handed me a list of emergency numbers in case anything went wrong.

'What do I need this for? Don't forget, I've lived on my own for ten years. I think I know exactly what to do if something goes wrong!'

'Yes, you ring me.'

'True.'

'Anyway, take it. Just in case. I'll miss you. Bye.'

And he was gone. I went indoors, played with Estella for a while, blowing raspberries on her tummy to make her smile, then I had breakfast and my quiet time, then I sat down and made a list.

I made a list of all the things I could do now that Kevin had gone.

Have the whole of the bed
Watch what I want on TV (no football)
Eat (or not eat) what I fancy without worrying about
    having to cook
Play my Justin Timberlake CD without having to
    apologize
Drive my own car

I can't wait for the last item on the list. I have my six-week check-up on Monday; I hope everything will be back to normal and I can get behind the wheel again.

Saturday 5 May

Estella woke early then went back to sleep, so it was gone eleven before I surfaced properly. I've just wandered round the quiet, empty house. It's only eleven thirty, and I'm bored already.

12:30 p.m.

Kevin has just phoned to say he has arrived safely. He was reacquainted with his luggage eventually and said he hopes Jez will turn up at some point. They left him in the toilet on the plane and haven't seen him since landing.

It is autumn out there, but the temperature is still around sixteen degrees, so it will be quite pleasant to work. Zippy is due to pick them up shortly. Kevin said he will ring again this evening.

2:30 p.m.

Saturday afternoon would have been clothes shopping in my single days. Even though it was less than a year ago, I feel as if a lifetime has passed. Now, even if I could fit into the clothes, I can't drive, and I would have a constant little companion. I'm sure it will seem like no time before we are sharing clothes and she is borrowing my mascara.

7 p.m.

Back to microwave meals for one for dinner. Whoopee!

9:30 p.m.

Kevin has just phoned back. They grabbed some sleep at the beach house. It is now the morning, and he has just described the place to me. The house is a two-bedroom bungalow right on the beach. The sand is white and the sea is clear. They are hoping to arrange a fishing trip, a day's sailing and a dolphin-watching excursion. There are bars and clubs nearby as well as restaurants and shops. Goodness knows when they are going to get time to do any work! He said I had gone very quiet and was I all right. I told him I was fine and was planning a thrill-packed shopping jaunt to Sidcup High Street myself. He just laughed. We said our goodbyes, and I put the phone down.

Jealous? Not me!

Sunday 6 May

Took Estella to church again this morning. Tried to speak to Chrissie about the baptism, but she had to rush off to help count the collection money. Funny, I thought Mr Wilberforce usually did that.

Monday 7 May

Tried to ring Diana while Kevin wasn't here to complain about the phone bill. Diana's grandmother answered.

'*Kalispera*, Yaya.'

I tried to carry on a conversation with the old lady the best I could in my now-rusty Greek. I told her about Estella, and she seemed to understand. She invited us back over to Evia, and I had to admit, I felt like jumping on a plane there and then. I asked to speak to Diana, but it transpired that she was out with her 'boyfriend'. I do hope she is being more careful now. Her grandmother agreed to pass on the message.

Tuesday 8 May

Went to the doctor for my six-week check-up today. Everything has healed nicely, and I only have a little scar.

'Beautiful scar – it hardly shows. You'll still be able to wear a bikini,' she reassured me.

Okay, I thought, the scar is fine, but what about the cellulite-ridden thighs, the excess poundage and the stretch marks?

Sat in my car when I got home. Haven't plucked up the courage to drive it yet. Checked with my insurance company, and that is one of the little details Kevin has overlooked. Sorted it out and I should be able to drive whenever I want. Found the document of ownership today and was astounded to find that Kevin has registered the car in Estella's name. I corrected the details to send off the form to the DVLA when I realized that he probably did it on the same day that he registered her birth. Rushed off to find her birth certificate, horrified that our poor baby might be condemned to being a Theodora. I let out a sigh of relief to discover it had Estella's name on it too.

Wednesday 9 May

Kevin rang. It's a hard life, between fishing trips and relaxing by the pool! Apparently the work is going well and they are keeping to time and, more surprisingly, to budget.

'Oh, Theo, you should see it here; it's just breathtaking.'
All right, don't rub it in!

Friday 11 May

Phone call from Chrissie apologizing for avoiding me.
'Look, can I come round and talk to you?'
'About the christening?'
'Yes, that too.'
'When?'
'Now.'
'Fine, I'll put the kettle on.'
I made a pot of tea, and Chrissie turned up half an hour later.
'Theo, I'm sorry ...'
'That's okay, I can always make another pot.'
'Not about the tea. About the way I've been ignoring you.'
I didn't know what to say. I had been a bit upset that she
hadn't even visited me in the last few weeks, but I know she
gets overwhelmed with work sometimes. I wondered again
about her reaction when I told her about Diana's abortion, and
I wondered again if I had touched a raw nerve.
'Have you been busy?'
'No more than usual.'
'Is it me, then? Have I done something wrong?'
'You've had a baby.'
'And ...' I was really puzzled now.
'It's just that all sorts of things get ... stirred up.'
I tried to make light of it.
'Tick-tock!'
'Pardon?'
'You know, the old biological clock, ticking away in there?'
'No, it's not really that. I think I've accepted that I'm called
to a single life. I'm one of that rare breed of "happy celibates".'

'You will be a rare breed; you'll all die out eventually if you don't have children. At least lifelong celibacy cannot be genetic.'

'Are you being serious?' Chrissie looked puzzled.

'Sorry, just rambling. Ignore me.'

I poured out the tea and handed round the chocolate biscuits. I could hear Estella starting to make snuffling noises upstairs. I looked at my watch.

'She'll need feeding soon. Do you mind if I ...'

'You go ahead.'

I trotted upstairs, changed Estella and dressed her in one of her prettiest outfits – a little white tee shirt and pink-and-white-striped dungarees. I brushed her hair and wiped her face. I gave her a big kiss and brought her down. I handed Chrissie a shawl and then the baby. She took her and immediately started the baby talk that I seem to be so poor at. Estella smiled and gurgled back. Chrissie looked as if she wanted to hold on to her for ever. I took her and started to give her a feed. As she guzzled away, Chrissie started to talk.

'I know you think I'm quite unorthodox in some of what I do, the way I live out my faith ...'

'You can say that again!' She ignored me.

'... but one issue I just can't come to terms with is deliberately ending a human life. Oh, I'm not afraid of death – I've sat by the bedside of elderly parishioners and prayed for them in their final minutes; I've comforted grieving families; I've worked in orphanages in several parts of Africa, where families have been devastated with HIV and AIDS; but ... that.' She shuddered. 'I can see all the reasons why women do it – some feel they have no choice, some are pressurized into it, sometimes there are medical reasons – but for some it doesn't just end one life.'

'What do you mean?'

'When I was at college, training for the priesthood, I shared a room with a girl called Grace. Grace came from a very strict Christian family, and her father insisted on coming up with her and checking out her accommodation to make sure the arrangements were "suitable". My dad, as I remember, drove me to the station, gave me fifty quid and made plans to rent out my bedroom. Her father was one of those scary sort of ministers that always make you feel as if you're doing something sinful even when you're not. I don't know what he made of me!' She gave a little laugh.

'Grace was a sweet girl, but not really equipped to cope with what university life threw at her. She was doing a different course than me, so I didn't see much of her in lectures and we didn't really socialize – she was into embroidery, and I hung around with the rugby club. Anyway, Grace found a boyfriend, David, who was about as naive as she was. David was also going for ordination, so I took him to one side and gave him a kind of "man to man" talk, which was rather difficult under the circumstances. I told him about Grace's father and warned them to be, you know, careful. Turns out I was too late. Grace was already pregnant, and both of them were in a flat spin. I sat her down and talked to her. I promised to help her and support her whatever she chose to do. She was petrified of her father finding out, so she and David decided to terminate the pregnancy. I went with her to the clinic and held her hand before she went in.'

Chrissie's eyes filled with tears. Estella had gone to sleep, so I put her in the Moses basket and went to sit next to Chrissie.

'Something happened to Grace in there.'

'You mean the operation went wrong?'

'No, the operation in itself was textbook. But when Grace came round, I knew that something had changed. She recovered physically, but emotionally she was a wreck. I tried to get her to talk to a doctor, a counsellor, the chaplain, even David, but she wouldn't talk to anyone. I tried to involve her in social activities, but she preferred to stay in our room reading.

'After one particularly raucous night with the rugby club, I got home to find her in bed. It wasn't until the morning when I tried to wake her ...'

I fetched a box of tissues from the kitchen.

'I have no idea where she got the sleeping pills. I called for help, rang for an ambulance, tried mouth-to-mouth, but it was far too late. She didn't leave a note. I spent the rest of the term wondering if I could have done anything differently, how I could have helped her. The looks her father gave me when he came to collect her stuff ... I know God was capable of forgiving what she did, but her father clearly wasn't. It was also clear that he blamed me for what had happened to his daughter. I felt like giving it all up, the priesthood, God, everything. There were nights when I could cheerfully have taken pills myself ...'

She blew her nose and tried to smile.

'I knew that wasn't the way. I had to carry on. I just about got through that semester. I spent a lot of time talking to all the people Grace should have talked to – doctors, counsellors, my parents, the chaplain and, most of all, to God. The following year, I shared digs with some of my rugby mates and some girls who were training to be teachers. I was determined to do it, for Grace and for me. I suppose it got easier after that. It's just that sometimes, when I hear things like this, it all comes flooding back. Grace's baby, if she had gone on to have it, would be nearly ten now. Seeing a little one, I can't help thinking how different it could have been for Grace and for David.

'I'm very happy for you and Kevin. You know that, don't you?'

'Of course I do.' I gave Chrissie a hug, and she wiped her eyes.

'Right. Back to business. I understand you wanted to organize a baptism,' she said.

'Sure do.'

'Okey-dokey. Now if you'd like to fill in these forms …'

Saturday 12 May

Today is Kevin's birthday. I've just checked in my diary, and this is the third year running we've been apart on this day. I rang him to wish him many happy returns, but I'd got the time-zone thing all wrong and woke him up in the early hours.

'Happy birthday!'

'Arrrgh! Theo, do you know what time it is?'

'Time to get a watch,' I quipped.

'It's half past four in the morning!'

'Sorry. I just wanted to talk to you and say I hope you have a great day.'

'It was yesterday.'

'No, it wasn't.' I squinted at the calendar. 'It is Saturday 12 May – your birthday.'

'Today's Sunday 13 May. It's the time difference.'

'So I missed it.'

'Afraid so.'

'Oh!' I slapped my hand to my forehead. I can't believe I missed Kevin's birthday yet again.

'Never mind,' he said with forced cheerfulness, 'it's the thought that counts.'

'Kevin … I miss you.'

'I miss you too. I wish you and Estella could be here.'

'So do I.'

'Bye, love. See you on Friday.'

Sunday 13 May

Going with Mum and Dad to visit Ag and Cordelia in their new house. They moved to North Finchingham shortly after Christmas, and I'm dying to see if Cordelia's taste in home furnishings matches her taste in clothes, which can best be described as retro-Goth-euro-chic.

8:40 p.m.

I am totally exhausted! If they made talking an Olympic event, Cordelia would be sure to win gold. From the moment we arrived to the second we dragged ourselves back into the car, she bombarded me with questions about my pregnancy, the birth, the first few weeks of caring for a new baby and even what brand of washing powder I used. I thought she was going to ask me where I bought my underwear next!

As soon as we got there, she took us on a tour of their house. It is a newly built detached house on an executive estate on the outskirts of the village, bold, bland and almost devoid of personality. Four bedrooms, one en-suite, conservatory, family bathroom and downstairs cloak, three receptions, double garage and utility. To my surprise, it was decorated almost exclusively in white. White walls, white carpets, white curtains and chairs, a whiteness relieved only by a thoughtfully placed modern art print, photograph or souvenir from their many travels, making the whole place look like an art gallery or a show home. That's going to change when you have children, I thought. Even Ariadne's cream carpets and sofas were now covered with throws and rugs, and her designer kitchen is bedecked with blobby finger-paintings.

Cordelia looked slightly healthier than when I saw her at Christmas, but, always a well-built girl, the pregnancy had made her balloon, and at six months pregnant she seemed barely mobile. She told me that the doctors are concerned about her blood pressure, and they are testing her weekly for diabetes. I handed her Estella, who blinked up at Cordelia, watching her auntie with a knowing look on her little face. Then she yawned and went back to sleep. I settled her in the car seat, and Cordelia handed me a mug of coffee. Mum, Dad and Ag had gone for a walk around the village. Cordelia and I sat at their bistro-style kitchen table, and she started firing questions at me.

'Right, tell me about the birth. I want to know *everything*.'

So I did. And Cordelia hung on every word, oohing and aahing as if she was at a fireworks display. I was tempted to embellish the details, but I decided to tell it straight. When I got to the bit about the caesarean, Cordelia winced and laid her hand on my arm.

'You poor thing. I don't suppose you'll ever recover.'

'Well, it's all healed very nicely, thank you. The doctor said so.'

'What about the emotional scars?'

'What emotional scars?'

'You know, from not being able to give birth "properly".'

Whatever did she mean? I was here and healthy, and so was my baby. What was improper about that?

'Pardon?'

'From never having propelled the child out from your loins. From not connecting with the primitive maternal travail. From not reaching back through the aeons the pain that binds us to our mother, Eve. All these, the things that make us truly women.'

I toyed with the idea of giving her a lesson in basic biology to educate her in 'the things that make us truly women'.

'Are you saying that because my baby was delivered by an operation, I'm somehow not a real woman?'

I could feel my face reddening. My maternal hormones seemed to be pounding through my bloodstream. If anyone attacked my baby, physically or verbally, or even looked at her funny, I'd be ready to flatten them. I felt as if I would explode with umbrage; then something gentler inside me, a little voice, whispered that here was a very frightened lady and that getting angry with her wouldn't help at all.

'What are you really worried about?' I asked Cordelia.

Then it all flooded out. Although she has always wanted children, now that it has finally happened, she is terrified. She is worried about how it will affect her and Ag's relationship, how she will cope with the demands of a baby, about work and whether she should stay at home or resume her career, and mostly about the birth. She's afraid of the pain, of being out of control and for the health of the baby. The doctor has told her to watch out for the signs of pre-eclampsia, and now every little twinge or flutter has the poor woman in a panic. She's been warned that she might need an emergency caesarean section and that the baby might be born prematurely. In short, Cordelia is almost afraid to breathe.

'Would you like me to pray with you?' I asked. Hang on! That was something Ariadne or Chrissie would say, not me. I didn't even know what to say in these sorts of circumstances.

'Oh yes, please. Would you?'

Cordelia sounded relieved. I didn't know what to pray, so I just held her hands, closed my eyes and poured out all she had told me. I asked for safety for the baby and peace for Cordelia. When I opened my eyes again, Cordelia was smiling.

'Thank you,' she said.

Tuesday 15 May

Jeremiah is back at home now. He can walk short distances on crutches but can't do much for himself. I decided to take Estella with me and pay a visit. Goodness knows what we are going to talk about.

I will have to get used to driving the Peugeot. Nervously, I strapped Estella in securely and climbed into the driver's seat. I sat there until I had stopped shaking. I was so terrified of scratching the paintwork or scraping the wing mirrors, it took almost ten minutes to reverse it out of the garage. I pulled out onto the main road and drove cautiously around the block to get used to the controls. Then I made my way carefully through the maze of lanes that lead to Jeremiah's flat. I sounded the horn at every corner and paused at every passing place. I sat happily for three miles behind a tractor. It was going at a comfortable speed, and if anything was coming too fast in the opposite direction, it would have a head-on with the tractor first. Pedestrians overtook me, and old gentlemen in flat caps and driving gloves fumed impatiently behind me, cursing my lack of velocity. I reached the big crossroads and edged gingerly forward to turn right.

The road was clear, the lights were just about to change, this was my one chance ... and I stalled the engine. By the time I started it again, the oncoming traffic had started moving, and I was stuck. Horns were blaring. I could see other drivers mouthing things at me. I had effectively managed to bring the whole junction to a standstill. The car to my right managed to edge back, and she gestured for me to pull round to the right. Cars on her outside tried to push past us, so I still couldn't move.

I was terrified someone would phone the police and I'd end up being prosecuted for 'causing an obstruction' or 'dangerous driving'. Eventually the woman got out of her car and stood in the middle of the road and stopped the cars to let me through. I wanted to jump out and thank her, but that would have blocked the traffic even more, so I just gave her a wave. She

gave me such a kind smile that I felt like crying. As I pulled
away, I saw the road clear. I don't know if there are such
things as 'traffic angels' or if there are just some kind motor-
ists, but I felt some sort of divine intervention was at work on
that road.

I pulled up in the courtyard outside Jeremiah's flat and
sat in the car until I had calmed down. It had been a horrible
experience. How come it had never happened in my old car?
Actually, it probably had. I just wasn't aware of it. I wasn't so
obsessively vigilant about the paintwork – a few more knocks
and scrapes would have made little difference. I was also
aware that now I was responsible not just for myself, but for
another little life. I unfastened Estella's car seat, carried her
up the stairs and knocked on Jeremiah's front door. The door
opened more quickly than I'd expected. Jeremiah must have
been standing right next to it.

'I saw you arrive,' he said. 'New car?'

'Yes, it was a birthday present from Kevin. First time I've
driven it. How are you feeling now?'

'I'm sound. A little wearied.' He looked past me, down to
the courtyard. 'What make is it?'

'Peugeot 206 CC.'

'Lovely! What kind of mpg are you getting? Around
twenty-five?'

'I don't really know; it's the first time I've driven it.'

'She certainly is a beauty!'

I thought back to how Jeremiah had got his car – dead
man's wheels – and was concerned that he was thinking of
ways to polish me off. Then it occurred to me that the kindest
thing I could do for Jeremiah wasn't to sit indoors and talk
babies for half an hour.

'Can I take you for a spin?'

'Would you? There's nothing I'd like better.'

He eased his way slowly and painfully down the stone steps. I adjusted the passenger seat and helped him in. I strapped Estella back in her place on the back seat, pulled her hood over her head and tucked her blanket round her. I started the engine and pressed the button. The roof slid back. Jeremiah was rapturous.

I pulled out onto the main road.

'Go left at the lights,' said Jeremiah. I looked at him. That was the coast road. He nodded, and I signalled left. Soon we were on a dual carriageway.

'Ease it down to third, get past this van ... now into fourth. Hold it ... and up to fifth.'

I obeyed his directions, and soon the wind was whipping my hair. We were only doing sixty-five, but it felt as if we were flying. I never wanted to stop.

Jeremiah looked at me and grinned. 'Marvellous,' he said.

The road was clear, and I nudged it up to just under seventy. It felt as if it could do double that. Jeremiah leaned down and turned on the radio. He selected a station that was blaring out classic rock tracks, and with Van Halen blasting in our ears, we headed for the coast. I felt invincible. This is what having a sports car is all about. This was fun!

'Stop!' Jeremiah yelled.

'What's the matter?' I yelled back as I applied the brakes and pulled over to the inside lane.

'We can't do this.'

'Do what?' I reached out and killed the Van Halen.

'I can't go alone in a car with a married woman. People might talk.'

'Who might talk?' I said, indicating the nearly empty road.

'People,' he said in a hushed whisper.

There was a sign for a Little Chef, so I pulled over and stopped in the car park. I climbed out and gathered up Estella and her belongings.

'I'll stay here,' said Jeremiah, pulling up his collar.

'Oh, come inside, you daft thing. I'll buy you a tea while I sort out the baby.'

'How dare you!'

I sighed and shook my head. If he wanted to sit in the car, I certainly didn't. I changed Estella and sat at a table with a pot of tea and a chicken sandwich as I fed her. I glanced out of the window a few times, but Jeremiah had slid down in the seat so he was barely visible. What did he think I was going to do? Throw myself at him?

I finished my lunch, felt guilty and ordered a takeaway tea and sandwich. The waiter helped me carry it to the car while I brought Estella.

'I don't want them,' Jeremiah said.

'Suits me. I'll eat them later.' I started the engine and put up the roof. I thought Jeremiah might feel a bit less conspicuous like that. In contrast to our wild rock 'n' roll road trip on the way down, we drove home in silence. A few streets away from his flat, he ordered me to stop the car again.

'You can't walk all that way on crutches!' I protested. But Jeremiah was insistent and wouldn't even let me help him get the crutches out of the car.

'What have I done wrong, Jeremiah! Tell me.'

' "O God, thou knowest my foolishness; and my sins are not hid from thee." '

'Jeremiah!'

But he was gone. His coat flapped on his scarecrow-like figure as he hobbled up the road. I drove home thinking about his strange reaction. Perhaps I have known Jeremiah Wedgwood long enough to consider nothing he does as strange any more.

Wednesday 16 May

Went shopping to buy food for Kevin's special birthday meal on Friday. I'm cooking his favourite, onion bajis followed by chicken tikka, mushroom rice and sag aloo. Only two days and he will be back. I can hardly wait.

Thursday 17 May

Cleaned the house, picked fresh flowers from the garden and had my hair cut so that everything will be perfect for tomorrow. Kevin's plane is due to land at five thirty in the evening. He's going to get a taxi home, so he should be here around seven.

Friday 18 May

6:30 a.m.

Estella woke up half an hour ago, and I'm too excited to get back to sleep. I played with her for a little while, then she dozed off again. I have been walking round the garden. Everything smells so new and fresh. The lilac is blooming, and soon the roses will be out. The clouds have cleared, and it is going to be a wonderful day.

Kevin will be back in twelve and a half hours.

10 a.m.

Have started marinating the chicken tikka that I am cooking for Kevin's 'welcome home' meal. Just realized I forgot to get onions for the onion bajis and we have none of his favourite brand of lager. Oh well, just nip to the shops.

❦

Kevin will be back in nine hours.

11:30 a.m.

My quick trip to the local shop ended up as a bit of a marathon. I managed to get the onions and the lager. I was just putting them on the buggy when Mrs Epstein beckoned me from across the road. She was still wearing her nightdress, and it turns out she is suffering from a nasty bout of bronchitis. She needed some shopping, so I wheeled the buggy back to the shops, bought her groceries, put them away, made her a cup of tea and settled her back in bed.

❦

Kevin will be back in seven and a half hours.

1:30 p.m.

Sat in the garden to feed Estella and to try to hear my first cuckoo of the season. Unfortunately got stung by the first wasp of the season.

Back to the kitchen. My chapatis won't rise. Must ring Tom.

❦

Kevin will be back in five and a half hours.

2:30 p.m.

Tom informs me that chapatis are not supposed to rise and that you don't need to peel mangoes to make mango chutney; you just buy a jar from the shop. It will be nice to eat outside. It's such a lovely day. I think I'll just mow the lawn.

❦

Kevin will be back in four and a half hours.

5 p.m.

I've just managed to cut through the cord of the lawn mower. It's a wonder I didn't electrocute myself! Must hide it before Kevin finds it. The damage has caused a circuit-breaker to trip, so we have no electricity. Rummaged around in the cupboard under the stairs and in the loft looking for the circuit-breaker box. Couldn't find it anywhere. Why don't they just put it in the middle of the hall where anyone can find it?

Kevin will be back in two hours.

6:30 p.m.

Had to phone Dad to come round to find the circuit-breaker. Said he just couldn't 're-fuse'. Much to my chagrin, it actually *was* in the middle of the hall, boxed in to look like a cupboard, just behind the front door. Restored the power and started cooking Kevin's food. It has started to rain, so we can't eat outside.

Kevin will be back in half an hour.

6:50 p.m.

Kevin will be back in ten minutes. Hang on, the phone's ringing ...

Kevin has just called from Vienna. There was a technical problem with the plane, and it couldn't take off and they are now trying to find them alternative flights or, more likely, overnight accommodation.

Kevin won't be back in ten minutes.

∽◯∾

It looks as if Kevin won't be back at all tonight. I'm going to switch the cooker off, then I'm going to bed.

Saturday 19 May

Estella cried all night. Kevin still isn't back, and the food is in the bin.

Sunday 20 May

Kevin eventually arrived home just after midnight. The house had got untidy, there was no sumptuous feast on the table, and instead of a glowing, radiant wife to meet him, he got a Marmite sandwich served to him by a dishevelled, snivelling wreck.

Still, it was fantastic to see him again, and he didn't mind that all the special treats I'd planned had gone down the pan. Estella started screaming again, and Kevin went to see to her while I went to bed.

Monday 21 May

Kevin asked me if I'd driven the car yet. The implication was, did I love it? The truth is, I'm still rather scared of it. I didn't say that in so many words. I told him it was beautiful and I was enjoying having it, which is true, but in some ways I'd rather it was a slightly battered ten-year-old Nissan Micra. Then I told him of my strange outing with Jeremiah.

Kevin laughed. 'Alone in a fabulous car with an even more fabulous woman – no wonder the poor old chap couldn't cope.'

'No way!' I screeched. 'Jeremiah's not like that!'

'Believe me' – Kevin looked at me over a pair of imaginary glasses – 'he's like that.'

My thoughts flitted to Declan. Perhaps that is the root of Kevin's insecurity. Perhaps he cannot believe that a man and a woman can just be friends. Kevin's thoughts had obviously headed in the same direction.

'Has Declan been round?'

'No,' I answered, looking Kevin straight in the eye. 'I haven't seen him.'

Kevin looked doubtful.

'And if you don't believe me, you can read the diary.'

I got up to make some tea. It was as if an icy draught had just blown through our marriage.

Tuesday 22 May

Kevin brought home a takeaway curry to replace the meal I almost cooked him on Friday. Estella is still crying most of the time, although she is feeding well and I can't find anything else wrong. We took turns eating our food and carrying Estella around, jiggling her to try to stop her yelling. I felt her forehead to see if she had a high temperature, but she just seemed hot and bothered from all the crying, so I couldn't tell. I'll see how she is tomorrow.

Wednesday 23 May

Took her to the doctor. Dr Edison told me Estella has colic. They don't know what causes it, a lot of babies get it and it will pass eventually. Fat lot of help that is to me here and now.

Thursday 24 May

Two more days and nights of crying. I'm trying to sleep when I can. Haven't been out or seen anyone. Every time I try to do anything, even have a bath or put the milk bottles out, she seems to scream. Kevin is grumpy too, from a combination of lingering jet lag and being woken in the night.

Friday 25 May

I've had enough! I left her to cry indoors while I sat in the garden with a cup of tea and the radio blaring so I couldn't hear her. I was out there for less than ten minutes, but when I went back inside, it had all gone quiet. I rushed upstairs, thinking I'd somehow killed her, but she had just fallen asleep. I sat down and cried with relief and tiredness. I feel like the worst mother in the world.

Saturday 26 May

Estella finally settled down and slept through the night. I hope it isn't just a one-off. I'd heard babies can suffer from colic, but I didn't appreciate how much the parents suffer too. Just realized Estella's christening is booked for a week tomorrow and I've done nothing to organize it.

Both Ariadne and Charity have offered to be godmothers, so I shall check that they are free. Perhaps Kevin can choose a godfather. I need to book somewhere for the buffet and buy gifts. I'll need a new outfit. Kevin can wear his wedding suit, but I could hardly wear my dress – apart from anything else, it won't fit with my mega-boobs and flabby belly. What about a christening robe? Do babies still wear them? Perhaps I could get a little dress instead – at least she could wear that again. I have phoned Mum and Dad and Ag and Cordelia. Mum said that Dad's Auntie Marjory will be up from Porthcawl then, so I'll have to invite her. Mum says she is extremely deaf and fiercely 'chapel', nonconformist, teetotal and opposed to female ministers, so that should add to the fun.

Monday 28 May, Bank Holiday

Estella has started screaming again, so I decided to go shopping. She can cry just as well there as she can at home.

Bought Kevin a new tie. I hope he likes it. Estella actually slept as I pushed her around. The only problem was that the instant we got home, she started howling again.

Tuesday 29 May

Showed Kevin the tie. I'd just launched into my update on the catering arrangements and who would he choose as a godfather when he nearly bit my head off.

'How? How could you do it? How could you arrange this all behind my back?'

I was stunned.

'But we talked about it. Before you went away,' I explained.

'And I told you that I didn't want her christened.'

'But I didn't think you meant it!'

'What did you think I meant?'

'I don't know. Perhaps that you weren't too keen on the idea but that you'd come round to it.'

'Look, I've been to our wedding and Mum and Moses' wedding. Isn't that enough for one year?'

'This is different. This is a christening.'

'But I've still got to put a suit on. I've still got to sit in that church.'

'Don't you think this is all rather childish? This is our daughter's future, and you are willing to sabotage it all because you don't want to wear a suit?'

'You're accusing me of being childish! When I tell you I'm not happy with something and you go ahead and arrange it behind my back!'

'Okay, I was wrong to do that, but think of Estella, not yourself.'

'I am thinking of Estella. What say has she got in all this? We're making promises on her behalf! We're taking away her freedom!'

'No, we're giving her freedom. We're giving her the opportunity to be part of the church family. Don't you want her to be brought up a Christian?'

'Of course I do. I just don't want something like baptism forced on her. Getting baptized is something she can decide to do, for herself, when she's older.'

'But why not do it now?'

'You just don't see it, do you?' He shook his head in dismay.

'No, I don't see it. Explain it to me.'

'Not now.'

'When?'

'I … I don't know.'

'All right.' I could see this arguing was getting us nowhere. 'I'll ring Chrissie and postpone it.'

'No,' he shouted. 'Don't postpone it; cancel it!'

He walked out into the garden. I was afraid that the shouting had woken Estella. I went upstairs and took some deep breaths. Estella was still fast asleep. I really don't understand Kevin's objection. It's not as if he doesn't believe. He just refuses to follow the party line. He won't go to church, doesn't associate with Christian people, has no time for any of the trappings of Christianity at all. I used to call him 'spiritually

degenerate', but I've always known that he has a deep faith. He
just has a different way of living it out. I can cope with that.
He prefers to pray quietly, on his own, rather than joining a
church liturgy. When I've found him reading the Bible, he
looks almost guilty, as if he's been discovered in some repre-
hensible clandestine activity.

Even the people he spends time with – his dodgy mates –
are a mystery to me. But I do know that he had a long talk with
Kev 2 which led to Kev 2 renouncing the beer. Kevin's service
isn't in handing out hymnbooks or teaching a Sunday school
class, but I know he gives his time and skills to help out the old
people in the village, and the way he befriended that gang of
teenagers that used to hang around vandalizing the phone box
… I heard he'd got one of them started in an apprenticeship.
I know he's a good man; it's just that sometimes he seems so
violently against everything that is so important to me.

I went downstairs and found Kevin in the garden, taking
out his feelings on the privet hedge with a pair of shears. I
put my hand on his shoulder. He turned round and started to
speak. I put my finger on his lips.

'I'm not going to say any more about it. I just wish you
would talk to someone, talk properly.'

'I'm not letting any of that St Norbert's lot get their hands
on me.'

'I'm not suggesting that, just someone.' I searched my brain.
'Tom, perhaps.'

Kevin snorted. Apart from his mates, the Three Musketeers with the emphasis on the 'musk', I'd not known him to
talk in depth with anyone … except, of course, Digger. 'Digger' Graves was our vicar before Chrissie, but he returned to
his native Australia, and right now he was probably wearing

a dog-collar with his boardshorts somewhere on Bondi Beach. Kevin would often go off for a pint of something amber with Digger, and I know they talked about God. Perhaps if he could talk to Digger ...

There was no time to waste. I charged upstairs and dug out a postcard with a surfer doing something impossible on a wave. Sure enough, there was a contact address and an e-mail. How frustrating! Kevin would have been a relatively short distance from Bondi just a couple of weeks ago. I booted up the computer and sent off a quick e-mail asking Digger to get in contact.

Wednesday 30 May

Everything has calmed down as long as I don't mention the christening. I've decided not to cancel it. I am convinced Digger is going to come through for me and he will help to sort Kevin out. The only thing that worries me is that time is short and he hasn't replied to the e-mail yet.

Thursday 31 May

Still no e-mail. I don't have his phone number, only his address, and it's too late to write. I'll try international directory enquiries.

Got a number and tried it. No reply. Then it occurred to me it was the early hours of the morning over there. I will try again later.

8:30 p.m.

Still no reply; perhaps he is at work. I have phoned round members of the church to try to get a mobile number, but no one has it. I give up. I'll just have to cancel everything.

10:30 p.m.

Unbelievable! Kevin asked me why I was moping around the house like a wet Wednesday. I decided to come clean and told him about Digger.

'I know exactly where Digger is,' said Kevin.

'Where?'

'Maidenhead.'

'What? Maidenhead in Oxfordshire?'

'Berkshire, actually.'

'How do you know?'

'Oh, we met at Sydney Airport. He's over here visiting for a few weeks.'

'Why didn't you tell me?'

'Sorry. I forgot. He said he'd ring me. We talked about meeting up. I thought you'd like that.'

'Like it? I'd love it! When?'

'Don't know.'

'Have you got a number?'

'No. I just gave him mine.'

I managed to refrain myself from strangling him.

'Where's your phone?'

Kevin held his hands up in front of him. 'Whoa, wait a minute. You can call him, and I'd enjoy seeing him, but you're not going to try to get him to "sort me out", as you put it. There's nothing wrong with me, and I won't be pressured into doing something I don't believe in. Okay?'

'Okay,' I agreed.

He fished it out of his back pocket and handed it to me. I pressed the buttons and listened to his voice messages. There, among the plumbing trade suppliers and customers with leaky immersion tanks, was Digger's familiar twang. I called out the number, and Kevin wrote it down. My fingers shook as I pressed the buttons. The number rang, and I heard Digger answer. My heart was beating so loudly I was afraid that he would hear it. We made small talk and chatted about the 'amazing coincidence'. Then it turns out that Digger usually visits England three or four times a year. As the organization he works with is based near Reading, and he runs training courses and seminars over here, the amazing thing is that our paths haven't crossed before.

'I'd been meaning to get in touch …' he said.

We have fixed up to meet tomorrow night at a little place overlooking the Thames.

JUNE

Friday 1 June

Gregory Pasternak has just phoned me about the Dickens Festival tomorrow. I tried to sound as if I hadn't forgotten all about it.

'As part of St Norbert's, you are supposed to be *Great Expectations*, but I won't hold you to it.'

When I told Kevin, he suggested that I stick a football up my jumper, so I hit him. I don't think that's what Gregory had in mind. Chrissie has already claimed Miss Havisham, and Charity is being Mrs Joe, and Nine-stone Nigel Hubble will make a rather weedy Joe Gargery. Estella is a bit young to be Estella, so perhaps I should do it for her. I'll have to sort out the costume in the morning. I need to gather Estella's bits and pack the car for the trip to Maidenhead to see Digger.

11:30 p.m.

Well! What an eventful evening.

When Kevin got home from work, we packed up my car with Estella and her belongings and set off for Maidenhead. The M25 on a Friday evening was not much fun, and we arrived hot and bothered. We found the place relatively easily

and ordered some iced colas. We found a table by the riverbank and settled Estella in her buggy.

'G'day!'

A familiar voice rang out from the car park. Digger vaulted
over the low wall and jogged over to meet us. He looked
tanned and relaxed and more like a surfer than ever. He gave
me a hug and shook hands with Kevin. He went gooey over
Estella, who smiled obligingly. We talked church and Jeremiah, Australia and beaches. I told Digger the respectable
version of Estella's birth and about the good and bad aspects
of parenthood.

'We're having her christened on Sunday. I wondered if
you'd like to come.'

Kevin tutted and let out a sigh. Digger picked up on it as I
hoped he would.

'Come on, mate, what's bothering you? Spill the beans.'

'It's her.' He nodded towards me. 'She keeps organizing
things without telling me, then expecting me to go along with
them.'

I folded my arms crossly. Perhaps I shouldn't be present at
this 'man to man' talk.

'That's marriage, I'm afraid, mate. The easiest thing is to go
with the flow. Anything for a quiet life.'

At this point I decided to go in and buy another round of
drinks. So much for Digger's marriage guidance!

When I returned, I sensed a change in atmosphere. I don't
know what Digger had said to him, but whatever it was, it had
got Kevin talking. I hesitated, unsure that I was wanted, but
Digger beckoned me over. I sat down. Digger spoke gently to
Kevin.

'So you didn't mind going to church with your mum?'

'No, I didn't mind it. They were nice, and the old people
made a bit of a fuss of me. They'd buy me sweets and ask me
how I was getting on at school. All things like that.'

'So what changed?'

Kevin rubbed the palms of his hands together. 'It started after Dad died. I was going through a pretty bad time ... Well, we all were. Mum wasn't coping well; Deyanna had started getting into trouble at school. Mum used to send me off to Auntie Betty's when things got a bit hot at home.'

'Did you like Auntie Betty?'

'Oh yes. She was really good to me. She cooked me these huge dinners, fish and chips, shepherd's pie, roast beef and Yorkshire. Man, I tell you, I was the only one of us who was putting on any weight at that time. I had a belly like a little round football.'

'And how did you cope with your dad's death? You say your mum and your sister took it badly. How old were you?'

'I was only eight. It felt like my world ended. Yet it was funny, at the same time it was as if nothing had changed. At the times my dad wasn't usually there, like when I was at school or when I was out playing with my mates, it was like everything was normal. Then when I got home, when I went to bed or on a Saturday, match days, that's when I'd suddenly realize he wasn't there, and it was as if he'd just died all over again.'

I tried to speak, but Digger held up his hand to silence me.

'And I ... well ... I started having these bad dreams. Nightmares, I suppose you'd call them. I'd dream that I could see my dad in the distance, or across a road or up a hill, and I'd be trying to run towards him, but there was always something blocking my way, or he'd disappear before I could reach him. I'd wake up the house with my shouting and thrashing about. I felt guilty because I knew I was making Mum more upset.'

'So what did your mum do to help her cope? Did she find the church a comfort to her?'

'Not really. She sort of stopped going for a while. I still wanted to go, though. I guess I missed all the attention more than anything. When I told Auntie Betty, she said she'd take me to her church the next Sunday. I got all dressed up like a dog's dinner, and Auntie Betty came and collected me. Well, as soon as I got in that place, I knew it was a mistake. Instead of all the friendly people who would ask me how I was getting on, they all looked like they'd escaped from a funeral parlour.

'Man, they scared me. They were singing, and some of the women were dancing, but it wasn't the happy-clappy stuff like in our usual church; some were screaming and wailing and throwing themselves about like they were on fire or something.

'And when the sermon started, instead of telling us how we could be good, like our pastor used to, this bloke told us all how bad we were and how we were all going to hell.

'Well, I whispered to Auntie Betty that I wanted to go home. She said not until they had "laid hands" on me. I didn't even know what this "laying hands on" thing was. I know Mum sometimes threatened to lay her hand on my behind if I was giving her lip, so that made it sound even worse. I just wanted to run ... but I couldn't.'

Kevin paused, so I handed round the colas and we all took a swig.

'So what did you do?' Digger asked.

'I just sat there and prayed for it to finish. It seemed to go on for years. At the end, I tried to make a break for the door, but Auntie Betty kind of rounded me up and took me to the front of the church.

'There must have been five or six people there, men and women. She told them about how my father had died, which I was quite pleased about because people usually told me how sorry they were and gave me some money for sweets. She also told them about the bad dreams, which I wasn't so pleased about. That was private, and I didn't want them to know. Anyway, next thing I knew, they grabbed hold of me, not gently but gripping on to my arms and shoulders.

'One of the men put his hands tight on my head. I tried to wiggle free, but they held on tighter. It felt like they were trying to squeeze the life out of me. The man with his hands on my head started praying – at least I think that is what he was doing, but it wasn't in English or Patois or French, or in what my mum used to call "Angel Language", the special words they sometimes used for praising in her church. This was like growling and spitting, and then his eyes kind of rolled back in his head so I could only see the whites. The others around me started to join in with the noise. I was struggling and fighting and swearing, and I think I started to cry. I was only a little boy.'

'I'm not surprised,' I said.

'What happened next?' Digger asked.

'I was still struggling to get free. It felt like I was fighting with them now. Then one of them shouts out, "He must have a demon in him." I tried to tell them I didn't, but one woman put her hand over my mouth and started to shout at me. "Come out! Come out!" she shouted. I'm ashamed to say I bit her hand, quite hard too, but I just wanted to get away. She let go of my mouth, so at least I could breathe properly.

'Next thing, I heard this scream. Not like the low moaning and wailing they were doing, but high and clear, like a siren. It took quite a while to realize that it was me, screaming.

'One of the women released her grip to put her hands over her ears. I gave an almighty twist and managed to get free. I pushed past them and, I tell you, I ran. Out of the church, down the road, across the park to a piece of derelict land where we used to play football before they built the houses. I stayed there for three hours. I didn't want to go home. But eventually I got hungry. Goodness knows what Auntie Betty told Mum, but she never sent me to her house again.'

'That's awful!' I said.

'The next Sunday I announced to Mum that I was never going back to church. She couldn't get Deyanna to go anyway, so she just left me at home with her. I know our church wasn't like that but I just felt I couldn't risk it. Even now, every time I go into a church, I feel ... sort of ... trapped. I'm always looking for the door and making sure I can get out. Daft, really, because I know it wouldn't happen again.'

I felt guilty: I had no idea that Kevin felt so strongly about being in a church. If I had, I wouldn't have put so much pressure on him to come with me.

'Why didn't you tell me all this?'

'I don't know. I suppose I just felt a bit daft.'

'You still went to youth group, though,' I said.

'That was different,' he said. 'It was just in a room and no one wanted to tell you that you were going to hell, or shouted, or gripped your head. You didn't sit in rows ... and they usually left the door open. I learnt about Jesus there. And,' he said with a wink, 'there were girls. It's funny, I didn't blame God for what happened. Even then, I knew it was people, people who thought they were doing the right thing but were really doing the wrong thing.'

'I'm sorry.' I clutched Kevin's hand. 'I'm sorry about all the times I tried to pressure you into going to church, and I'm sorry about bulldozing you into this christening. Of course I'll cancel it. I'll ring round tomorrow.'

'Well,' he said slowly, 'I've been thinking about it, and perhaps it's not such a bad thing. She can still get confirmed or renew her vows when she's older. We would have brought her up in the Christian faith anyway, and you could take her to church, and I wouldn't have to go ... unless I wanted to. It's all booked. It would be a pity to change it all now.'

'But you'd have to wear a suit and sit there, and feel trapped ...'

He thought for a moment. 'Perhaps they'd leave the door open.'

I hugged him. I could see that it would take a lot of courage to stand up there and make promises on our daughter's behalf. It would take a long time and probably several more drinks with Digger before he felt comfortable in church, but at least he'd made a start.

'One problem, though,' I said. 'We are still one godfather short.'

Kevin turned to Digger. 'Would you?' he said.

'Sure thing!' replied Digger in his best Marlon Brando accent.

Saturday 2 June

Today might or might not be the day that Dickens might or might not have once passed through our village, if indeed he did. The sun has chosen to shine, as it has on so many village events.

I found a long skirt and a shawl, put my hair up and tried to look disdainful and haughty. Try as I might, Kevin could not be persuaded to come as Pip.

'Not likely!' he sneered.

Although it looked rather incongruous with my Victorian costume, I strapped Estella into her buggy and set off for the village green.

It was as if I'd stepped into another era. The lampposts, signs and benches on the green had always had a slightly Victorian feel but were probably 1980, not 1880. The gaudy fairground organ piped out a stirring march which was not quite drowned out by the accordion and bells of a troupe of Morris dancers. The funfair added its own tune to the clamour. There were stalls selling candy floss and bric-a-brac, the WI (*David*

Copperfield) had a stall selling home-made produce and the village school (*Oliver Twist*) had a hoopla and bottle tombola.

It's a pity Jeremiah Wedgwood wasn't in attendance. He would have made the perfect Ebenezer Scrooge. It seemed that everyone in the village had turned out in long skirts and bonnets or cravats and top hats. I kept my eyes open for Kevin, who said he'd come over as soon as he'd seen to Mary Walpole's leaking lavatory. Gregory Pasternak in a tailcoat and Mr Pickwick in the role he was born to play were swanning around like a fine pair of Victorian gentlemen. I shook hands with the half-dozen American tourists Gregory and Mr Pickwick were ushering round. They seemed to be having a fantastic time and didn't appear to care one jot that the historical Dickensian connection was tenuous, to say the least.

I browsed round the stalls and bought some jam and a very un-Dickensian copy of *Bridget Jones's Diary* from the bookstall. I've always intended to read that book. I bought a cup of tea and a scone with jam and clotted cream. Then I noticed a lace stall with some pretty bookmarks and doilies. Hanging at the back of the stall was the most gorgeous thing I had ever seen. It was a fine cotton muslin christening gown, trimmed with delicate lacework and pink rosebuds embroidered on the bodice. I gasped in delight. The woman behind the stall started to give me a funny look.

'That christening gown is beautiful,' I said. 'Is it for sale?'

'That one's a sample, me dear, but I'm taking orders.'

'Oh!' I whined. 'It's too late for that; the christening's tomorrow. I don't suppose there's any way you could sell me that one?'

'I would have, me dear,' she said, 'but someone's already bought it. They agreed to let me keep it hanging up till the end of the afternoon in case anyone wanted to order one.'

A pang of disappointment shot through me. It would have been perfect. Oh well, I had already bought her a little dress with yellow and white daisies. That would have to do.

Sunday 3 June

Another beautiful summer's day. The scent of the roses on the trellis under the window climbed into the bedroom and filled it with sweet perfume. I turned over in bed and looked at Kevin. It would take a lot of guts for him to get through today. I made a mental note to hide the brandy.

I showered and dressed and saw to Estella. It was too early to put her clothes on in case she puked her milk down her dress. I checked that the gifts were ready for the godparents and made tea and toast for Kevin and me.

The church clock struck eight, and I took Kevin's tea upstairs and tucked Estella into bed next to him. He woke up and smiled. Estella waved her arms and gurgled.

'Come on, get up. We've got loads to do.' I flung open the curtains and pulled back the duvet.

'Early!' he groaned.

'It won't be early for long,' I said, realizing that was the sort of thing my mother would say.

'Oh, I got something for you,' said Kevin. 'Well, for Estella, actually. I meant to show you yesterday. I thought you'd like it.'

He reached under the bed and pulled out a box. He took off the lid, and under the layers of tissue paper was the christening robe with the lace and the pink rosebuds. I squealed and threw myself at Kevin. Poor Estella almost got squashed on the bed.

∽◯∾

We arrived at St Norbert's just before half past nine. Chrissie greeted us, wearing her robes and a white stole. She hugged me and kissed Estella on the cheek, leaving behind a trace of her trademark red lipstick.

Mum and Dad and Auntie Marjorie were the next to arrive, followed by Digger, Floyd, Deyanna and Kayla, who stomped in sulking because she wasn't the centre of attention.

'Why can't I be a bridesmaid again?' she demanded.

Eloise and Moses entered, and Eloise whisked Kayla off for a quick jaunt around the graveyard. I greeted them and Kevin showed them to their seats. Charity, like a mother hen, ushered her brood into three pews near the front. I was rather disturbed to see that Charity appeared to have bought a whole bolt of chintz fabric and turned it into dresses for herself and all the girls and ties and waistcoats for the boys. Nigel was the only one who escaped this treatment, and he looked highly relieved to be wearing his black suit and dog-collar. Neb looked a complete twit in his flowery waistcoat, and judging by the expression on his face, he felt like one too. His appearance these days is veering towards Goth. I could see that he was wearing a black leather wrist band with studs, and Charity had obviously failed to persuade him to remove his black nail varnish. The St Norbert's regulars started streaming in, and they almost formed a queue to hand me cards and gifts and to cuddle Estella. Percy Burns waved at me. I'm so glad he could come. Finally at twenty-five past ten, Ariadne, Tom and Phoebe burst in. They apologized, thrust a gift at me and found a seat. Mr Wilberforce went to close the huge oak door. I dashed up to him and asked him to leave it wide open.

'It is a glorious day,' he said. 'Pity to shut all the sunshine out.'

That's one reason, I thought.

Gregory Pasternak struck up the first hymn, and we all stood up. I squeezed Kevin's hand, and he smiled at me. We followed the liturgy and confessed our sins. We said the words of the creed that bound us together in our family of faith. I looked around. Although we were all so different, we were one in Christ. I wanted to cry.

Chrissie stood up.

'Theodora was the first person who greeted me when I came here just over a year and a half ago. There were times when, apart from my faith, her friendship was the only thing that kept me going. She supported me when the newspapers printed rubbish about me, she stood in as my secretary to ensure that you had something to read during, as she put it, "the boring bits of the sermon".'

Everyone laughed. I felt as if I was listening to my own funeral address.

'I was delighted, after a couple of false starts, to join Theodora and Kevin in marriage last year. And now,' she continued, 'it is a particular pleasure to baptize their beautiful baby daughter, Estella.'

It was no good; I was blubbering uncontrollably. Mum handed me a tissue, and Ariadne poked me in the back.

'Stop it!' she hissed. 'You'll make your mascara run.'

Chrissie beckoned us and our godparents to the font. I smoothed out Estella's robe. Kevin held her as we stood and made our promises. She only cried a little when Chrissie poured the water on her forehead and baptized her 'in the name of the Father, and the Son and the Holy Spirit'. I'm pleased to report I only cried a little too.

After the service, we all filed across the road to the Red Lion. Kevin went around taking drink orders, I changed Estella and the Hubbles headed for the buffet table. I chatted to as many people as I could, which was difficult as everyone had spilled out of the room we had booked and into the garden. I discovered Kevin sitting at a table under a blue and white umbrella, chatting with Digger. They had taken off their ties and removed their jackets. Kevin beckoned me over.

'Theo, I've got something to show you.'

He pulled out a wallet of photographs of Jervis Bay. I looked at the blue sea and white sand. Even as a five-by-seven photograph, it was breathtaking. Digger extolled the virtues of Jervis Bay and the Sydney area in general.

It was then that Kevin dropped his bombshell.

'While I was in Australia, I looked into the possibility of spending more time out there.'

'Yes, Digger,' I chipped in. 'We've got use of the beach house whenever – well, almost whenever – we want it.'

'Too right, and you'll have to call in to see me when you come over.'

'Of course we will.' I smiled, Digger smiled, even Estella smiled. Only Kevin looked serious.

'No, I mean more time than that. I mean permanently.'

'What, emigrating?'

'Yes. With my trade qualifications and my dad's nationality, we stand a good chance of having enough points to fit the criteria.'

'You mean leaving Rose Cottage, and the village, and my family, and St Norbert's and ... Sidcup?'

'And the cold British winters, and the graffiti and the crowded little towns,' finished Kevin.

'The lifestyle certainly is bonzer!' agreed Digger.

'I know ... but ... it's such a big change. I belong here. I've never belonged anywhere else.'

'I could get work on the holiday complexes. They're practically crying out for good plumbers. We could invite our families over to stay. Estella could grow up near the beach ...'

'Stop!' I shouted. 'There's no way you can expect me
to make a decision on this sort of thing on the spur of the
moment.'

'No, of course not, love. Think about it, though. We could
make a new start, as a family. After all, there's nothing and
no one to keep us here. You have a think, and we'll talk it over
later. It's just such a brilliant opportunity. Now I need a drink.'

He performed a 'raising a glass' mime, and Digger nodded.
I excused myself and found a bench in a quiet corner. Estella
had fallen asleep in my arms, and I held her close to me. I
looked around. Almost everyone I knew had come to celebrate
the baptism. Dad in his suit, Mum laughing with Ag and
Cordelia, little Phoebe toddling over the grass towards Ariadne and Tom, Chrissie in her cassock laughing with Auntie
Marjory, Eloise and Moses, still gazing at one another.

Across the road, St Norbert's spire sprouted up out of the
horse chestnut trees. Could I really leave all this? 'Nothing
and no one to keep us here'? I knew he meant Declan. Was it
really worth going to live on the other side of the world just to
get away from him?

As I sat, deep in thought, the voices of my family and
friends carried on the soft summer breeze. Out of the corner of
my eye, I caught a glimpse of a man with floppy red hair and
his hands in his pockets. He looked across, smiled and waved.
At least I think I saw him. Or it might have been a trick of the
light.

faith,
love &
chocolate

THEODORA'S
WEDDING

Penny Culliford

Author of Theodora's Diary

Enjoy this sample chapter from

THEODORA'S WEDDING

Monday 5 July

Well, I've done it.

I've actually done it!

Nobody thought I'd persevere, least of all me. But I
have done it. I've kept up my diary for over a year. Ariadne
sneered when I started. She actually sneered. 'I'll give it a
fortnight,' she said. My sister, my own flesh and blood,
doubting my resolve. And now I've really shown her. I shall
go and wave it under her nose and say, 'See, I'm not a flash
in the pan, a five-minute wonder, a here today, gone tomorrow sort of person. I have written something lasting, something that will endure. Future generations will benefit from
my incisive, yet entertaining, commentary on life.'

Actually, I think I won't. I can hear the derisive snort
already and, having flicked back through last year's diary, I
can see that a lot of it could come under the category 'neu-
rotic ramblings'. Besides, poor Ariadne looks so exhausted,
what with baby Phoebe and getting ready to go back to
work, I don't think her eyes would stay open long enough

to focus. I'm sorry to say she's also letting herself go. She looks kind of tired and crumpled somehow. And she's rather plump. Perhaps she doesn't realize. Perhaps I ought to tell her.

However, I think the diary has achieved its aim. I may not have grown very much spiritually, nor am I any nearer finding my ministry, nor have I been hailed as the next British supermodel, but it has been an eventful year. I have seen friends come and go, I have a new baby niece and I have gained a fiancé, even if at times I think he is spiritually degenerate. And to cap it all, I weigh half a stone less than I did this time last year.

Tuesday 6 July

Cooking! Why on earth did Charity Hubble volunteer me to do cooking? And baking cakes, at that. She knows I hate cooking. She knows I would rather bungee-jump naked from the bell tower or enter a Michael Jackson look-alike competition than bake a cake. Just because she's the curate's wife, is responsible for a one-woman population explosion and dresses like Laura Ashley's furniture department, just because she was born knowing how to make six different kinds of preserves from fresh fruit, does not give Charity Hubble the right to conscript me into baking for the produce stall at the flaming summer fete.

Wednesday 7 July

Confessed to Kevin about my cake problem. As my future husband, I would expect a little support. Instead, he

laughed like a drain as usual (and being a plumber, I suppose he should know how a drain laughs).

'How do you get yourself into these situations in the
first place?' he guffawed. 'If you didn't want to make a
cake, why did you volunteer?'

'I didn't . . . it just sort of happened.'

'What's it for, anyway?'

'Oh, a good cause. The village fete. The church has got
some stalls there, including a home-made produce stall.
Just doing my bit,' I declared proudly.

'Village fete? Bit twee isn't it? I thought your church
was into preaching the gospel, fighting for justice and setting the captives free. Where do village fetes come into it?'

I couldn't answer that one.

Thursday 8 July

I have been reading an excellent book. It's called *I'm
Going to be Assertive Now, If That's OK with You*. It's written by
Hiram B. Jefferson III who's got just loads and loads of
degrees and diplomas from all sorts of universities, so he
should jolly well know what he's talking about.

'Are you a human doormat?' Hiram demands.

'Yes, I am,' I answer.

'Do you say yes when you mean no?' he inquires.

'Yes I do – I mean no I don't, I mean yes but I want to
say no!'

'Then take control. You have a right to your feelings and
a right to express those feelings. Use positive statements
such as "I am . . .", "I will . . .", to show those who would
wipe their feet on you that here's one doormat who's gonna
stand up and say "No more!"'

I decided, for once, to have it out with Charity. I'm not really a coward who shies away from confrontation; it's just that she is impossible to argue with. An encounter with Charity Hubble always seems to end with her making me say the opposite to what I really think. How does she do it? How will she stand up to Hiram B. Jefferson III?

Friday 9 July

Found a box of stink bombs, knife-through-the-head headbands and synthetic dog poop in the bottom drawer of Declan's old filing cabinet today. His practical jokes used to drive me up the wall when he worked here. I wondered how he had managed to become a section supervisor when he seemed to spend so little time working and so much time playing practical jokes. But since he left, work seems a lot duller. Safer, yes: there is no danger of finding the toilet covered with cling film or discovering your coat pockets are full of cold spaghetti or standing up to find that your shoelaces have been tied together – but for some perverse reason I actually miss all that. Even the extra pay and status (ha! It's all very well being made a section supervisor but I was the only person on the section so now I'm just supervising myself) doesn't make up for it. I wonder how Declan is getting on in Manchester. I wonder what kind of priest he will make.

Saturday 10 July

I finally tracked Charity down outside the post office, with baby Methuselah in a pram and three other hamster-faced offspring in tow as she stuffed Nigel's mail into the post box.

I pounced.

'Charity, why did you put my name down for baking a cake when you know I hate cooking?'

She paused for a moment to wipe a dribbly trail of slime away from baby Methuselah's mouth and to restrain Ahimelech, who was trying to climb the pillar box, then turned to me, beaming.

'I thought it would be a wonderful opportunity to practise. After all, you'll have to cook for Kevin after you're married, unless of course you're hiring help. One never knows with you "career women".'

Her eyes twinkled mischievously, and I suddenly saw a side to Charity I hadn't believed existed. If she hadn't been so unbearably holy I would have called it 'devilment'. She was really enjoying this.

'Of course not,' I retorted, much too quickly. Once again my mouth was moving faster than my brain and I realized that unless we planned to live on takeaways for our entire married life, cooking something at some point was inevitable. And Charity knew it. She just wanted to make me suffer. I panicked.

'Kevin can cook,' I blurted. This was a lie. Kevin can *eat*. In fact Kevin could eat for England. I have yet to find something Kevin won't eat; even Kippers in Garlic Mayonnaise somehow found their way down his gullet without complaint.

But Kevin can't cook. His mum has seen to that.

'Super! Then I can put him down for a cake too.'

'No! No, he'll be far too busy, what with work and everything. B . . . besides, have you thought about the places plumbers have to put their hands? Yuck, even I wouldn't eat a cake he had touched.'

'So you can make two, one for you and one on his behalf.'

'Charity! I know you're doing this on purpose. I don't *do* cooking. When I put my name on that list to help out, you know and I know that I didn't put it under anything to do with baking, boiling, fricasseeing or any other kind of food preparation.'

'Do you know where you *did* write it?'

My brain searched the archives. No record found.

Charity reached into her enormous handbag and pulled out a neatly folded piece of paper. She opened it and waved it under my nose. True, my name was not on the list of people volunteering to bake cakes. Nor was anyone else's. My name appeared at the bottom under 'anything', a section created for people who were either so versatile that they could turn their hand to any task or so ineffectual that they had no particular talents. I definitely fell into the latter category. My indecisiveness had once again become my downfall. Charity had spotted my weakness and gone in for the kill. I bet Hiram B. Jefferson III himself would be no match for Charity Hubble.

'Well, you *did* say you'd do anything,' she said, fluttering her eyelids coyly. At that point Ahimelech made a dash for the road and Charity had to scurry off to apprehend him. Otherwise I would have told her . . .

Sunday 11 July

There was a correction in today's *Church Organ*.

It was reported in last week's publication that the Street Evangelism Team would be offensive in spreading the gospel around the village in the next few weeks. This item should have read that the Street Evangelism Team would be <u>on the offensive</u>, spreading the gospel. The editor apologizes sincerely for this error.

I have the uneasy feeling that the editor was right in the first place.

Monday 12 July

Kevin's five-a-side team is taking part in an exchange with a French club this summer. First they're coming over here, staying with English supporters, then the English are going to stay in France for a fortnight. Kevin has *asked* me (a breakthrough in itself – in our relationship so far, I've been lucky if he's even *informed* me he's going) if he can go with them.

He has also decided to better himself and learn the language. He has an ambition to be able to order a beer in twenty different languages.

I hope he has more luck learning French than my mother has had learning Greek. Despite having a love for the country that borders on obsession, her attempts to speak Greek have been little short of disastrous. My mother is enough to make the Linguaphone lady resign. The other day she informed us that Archimedes jumped in the bath and shouted, 'Euthanasia!'

Theodora's Diary
Faith, Hope and Chocolate

Penny Culliford

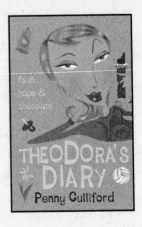

Saturday 8th May. Emergency!

It is 11:30 p.m. and I am suffering from an incredibly intense chocolate craving that will not leave me in spite of prayer, distraction activities and half a loaf of bread and butter. Got out of bed and searched the flat. No luck. Not even a bourbon biscuit. Not even a cream egg left from Easter. All the shops are closed so no nipping out to replenish supplies. Nothing else for it. I'm reduced to the chocoholic's equivalent of meths—cooking chocolate.

It's been one of those days for Theodora. Her mother has become the Greek equivalent of Delia Smith, her boyfriend would rather watch twenty-two men kick a ball around a field than go shopping with her, and chintzy Charity Hubble wants to pray for her. And of course, the crowning insult is her utter lack of chocolate. Join in her daily life with all of its challenges and joys, tears and laughter.

'Theodora's Diary is a hilarious and realistic peek into the life of a sprightly Christian sister living "across the pond." I found myself laughing out loud and thinking, "Yes, life is just like this!" Penny Culliford is a welcome new voice in inspirational fiction.'
— Angela Hunt, author of *The Debt*

Softcover: 0007110014

Pick up a copy today at your favourite bookstore!

ZONDERVAN™

GRAND RAPIDS, MICHIGAN 49530 USA

WWW.ZONDERVAN.COM

Theodora's Wedding
Faith, Love and Chocolate
Penny Culliford

Monday 5 July

I've actually done it! I've kept up my diary for over a year.

I may not have grown very much spiritually, nor have I been hailed as the next British supermodel, but I have gained a fiancé, even if he is football mad. And to cap it all, I weigh half a stone less than I did this time last year.

Welcome back to Theodora's world. Now a bit older but not much wiser, thirty-something Theodora Llewellyn begins her second year as a diarist. And as usual, the results are endearing, hilarious and delightfully human.

In her search for life, love and a plentiful supply of chocolate, Theodora discovers that the course of true love never runs smoothly, especially when a voice from the past precipitates a crisis. But fear not – Theodora's humour and wit are up to the challenge. In the end, just one question remains unanswered: Exactly how much vitamin C is there in a chocolate orange?

Softcover: 0310250390

Pick up a copy today at your favourite bookstore!

ZONDERVAN™

GRAND RAPIDS, MICHIGAN 49530 USA

WWW.ZONDERVAN.COM

We want to hear from you. Please send your comments about this book to us in care of zreview@zondervan.com. Thank you.

ZONDERVAN™

GRAND RAPIDS, MICHIGAN 49530 USA

ZONDERVAN.COM/
AUTHORTRACKER